CRY OF THE INNOCENT

CRY OF THE INNOCENT

A Faith Clarke Mystery

Julie Bates

To Bill & Chris who are at the heart of everything I do

Chapter One

1774

Muffled pounding jolted Faith awake. A few coals glowed from the fire but offered little illumination to the pitch-blackness surrounding the bed. Nearby her son, Andrew slept soundly in a trundle bed undisturbed by the excited barks of dogs outside in the streets of Williamsburg. Her heart jumped as she looked over to the door separating her bedroom from the main hall of the tavern and saw light coming in from the cracks between the door and its frame. A voice hissed outside.

"Mistress, you need to wake up."

Olivia's voice held the rich cadence of someone who had been born far from the English colonies. Faith suspected she had come from somewhere in the West Indies, but she had never asked. Given how long it had taken to build trust, she trod carefully.

There was no reason for Olivia to be outside the door. Given the hour, she and her husband, Titus, should be stirring the fires and fixing breakfast before their guests rose with the dawn. Faith's feet hit the floor, and she gasped at the cold. Grabbing a coverlet for decency, she stumbled to the door, where her head hit the top of the doorframe. Pain struck like a hammer.

Opening the door, a little, Faith stared at the other woman. "What's wrong?"

"There's a dead man in the private room." Olivia's breath came out in silvery puffs that peppered the air. Flour lightly dusted her hands and apron which indicated a sudden interruption from work.

"Are you sure?" Together they had dealt with a number of drunks in the year since the tavern had opened. Seven months since her husband Jon had died, leaving Faith in charge.

"I'm sure. Titus found him when he went to start fires before breakfast."

Cold sweat broke out on Faith's face as her stomach tied itself in knots. Titus was not one to panic. If he was correct, they had to act fast. Such an incident would only cause trouble.

Outside a rooster crowed warning that dawn paused for no one. Soon her guests would come downstairs for breakfast, and the streets would fill with merchants, slaves, and others needing to do business in the capitol. Taking a breath, Faith forced an illusion of calm into her voice.

"Our guests will still expect breakfast. Take care of them. Make use of the boys if you need to. Tell Titus not to let anyone near the private room. I am on my way." She turned back into her room, stopping by Andrew's bed when she heard him move restlessly.

"What is it?" He began to stir out of his nest of blankets.

"Go back to sleep. It's early yet."

Hurriedly, she threw a skirt and bodice over her shift and stuffed her hair into a mob cap. Grabbing a heavy, woolen shawl, she slipped out and down the steps to the backyard. The private room was separated from the main tavern by a narrow alley. It had its own front and back entrance, which made it perfect for meetings and extra work to provide meals and drinks. Side doors opened into the alley, which made delivering food and drink convenient, although the walls of both buildings kept the narrow aperture cast in shadows.

Olivia watched her from the doorway of the kitchen, which stood apart from the tavern to lessen the risk of fire. Her son, Joshua, slept upstairs. Faith's gaze circled the long backyard from where it ended at the path that separated it from the tenement next door to the small barn where animals were just beginning to stir. Something about the quiet made her feel jumpy, as if strange and unfriendly eyes watched. Mist rising from the dew added a ghostly air to the scene. Unnerved, she hurried to the door of the private room. She pulled her shawl closer to combat shivers induced by more than the cold.

The breath left Faith's body as she took in the scene. However, running from trouble was a luxury no worker could afford. A weak fire from the hearth illuminated a man lying on the floor. The fine pewter of an upended tankard nearby glimmered faintly through the shadows. The room reeked of liquor. Perhaps he had simply passed out. In her few months as mistress of Clarke Tavern, she had handled men worse for drink.

Drunk was preferable to dead. Faith cleared her throat, which was suddenly too dry.

"Please be drunk," she prayed. Moving closer, she hoped for some indication of life. Reflected light gleamed off the brass buttons of his coat and made threads from his silk stockings gleam like ice. Fine lace covered his belly as the drift of his shirt hung out and onto the floor.

"My lord?" Faith inched forward, frowning. She now remembered who had demanded the use of her private room last night. Phineas Bullard acted like an odious bully sober. God only knew how he would behave drunk.

"Master Bullard!" she yelled, not bothering to be gentle.

The reek of wine made her queasy. She glanced about in disgust. It would take hours to make the room decent again. A bottle of port lay on its side, dripping off the table while a nearly empty wine bottle lay on the floor. The tavern had very little of that in stock, too little to marinate the floor in it. Finally, fury at the man's sloth overtook her.

Before reason returned, she grabbed his shoulder and shook it "Get up!"

As she aimed her toe to kick him, Faith stepped into something sticky.

Bending over to examine him more closely, her nostrils filled with the sickly scent of blood and other foul bodily substances. She gagged and backed away. The rising sun streaked in the door, allowing her to see what had not been clear before.

Blood soaked his breeches and collar down to the floorboards; his fine linen shirt savagely sliced into rags, revealing the damage beneath. Drying blood caked his throat and belly. Bullard's wide open eyes and slack jaw implied the spectacle of his demise shocked him as well. Shaking him had rucked up his shirt exposing what she would have given anything not to see.

As the sun's rays lit the room fully for the first time, horror overwhelmed her. Life had left him long ago.

"God have mercy." Faith ran out the door, unable to view the nightmare any longer. Stomach revolting, she retched behind the branches of a bush. Her eyes watered as her stomach clenched into knots and set off another round.

"Miss Faith? Miss Faith!"

She shrieked and whirled around. Titus stood a few steps away. She drew in a relieved breath although she could not stop shaking.

Never had she been so glad to see a familiar face.

Wood chips were scattered in his clothes from where he had been chopping wood for the fires. The fresh scent of pine comforted her assaulted nose. His solid presence as well as the axe he carried, comforted her shattered nerves. Titus would be a formidable detriment to any physical threat.

"Are you ill?"

Faith swallowed nausea and pushed tendrils of hair back up into her cap. She gestured at the open doorway. The thought of what lay inside caused her gorge to rise again. Her nose and throat burned as she struggled to speak. "I will be alright. We need a physician, quickly."

Titus shook his head. "He's dead ma'am. No doctor can help him now. Let me get you back to the kitchen. The boys can get the sheriff. Best I stay here until I have had time to look around." His voice roughened, "He has not been dead long, Miss Faith. Body is not all that cold. We had best not to take any chances. I will feed the chickens for the boys today, and they can go on to school. They should be safe enough in the street."

Titus walked quietly beside her as they passed the smokehouse. A breeze stirred the dead leaves from the nearby street. The big man said nothing as they walked past the barn where the horses shifted about in their stalls. Faith jumped but settled when the big man said, "They're just waiting for breakfast." His glance seemed to stop briefly at the small barn where the cow and a few horses resided then continued on their circuit.

Her head whirled as she considered the consequences of what she had seen. Bullard could be an insufferable bully, but she did not want him dead in her tavern. Once the sheriff came, news would spread. The authorities would want answers, and she had none. Given the current strife in the colonies, it was all too easy to find oneself unintentionally wearing a noose.

Taking a deep breath, she tried to put that idea out of her head.

The sun ascended the horizon, lighting the sky, as her feet crossed the threshold of the kitchen. Titus left her there and returned outside. Busy with breakfast preparations, Faith was grateful that Olivia did not mention that her mistress looked terrible and smelled worse. She poured herself a small amount of short beer and rinsed out her mouth. Stepping outside, she spat into the grass away from the walkway before returning to speak.

"Someone killed Phineas Bullard last night. The boys need to get the sheriff. Faith paused to gather her spinning thoughts grateful that Olivia was too busy to turn about and see her.

Her breath came too fast and shallow making her dizzy. She needed to gain control of her wits. Sitting at a nearby bench, she leaned over putting her head in her hands.

This was no time to panic. Too much was at stake. She forced herself to inhale and exhale. Gradually, her head cleared. There was no time to panic. Regardless of how she felt, life continued and with it, the work that survival entailed.

From her seat Faith could see inside the open door of the outdoor kitchen, She watched Olivia stirring the huge stewpot hanging over the fire. Nearby lay a stack of knives with rusty stains waiting for scrubbing. Some looked as if they had been used to separate a carcass. The idea made her gorge rise again. Faith frowned. If she did not know better, she would swear Olivia was keeping her back to her. It made little sense but then nothing this morning did. Shrugging, she walked out the door back to the tavern.

Outside the door, Titus lingered carrying a plate covered with a napkin. At her glance, he looked nervous.

Faith smiled. "No worries, Titus. I'm sure you worked up quite an appetite this morning."

"What? Oh sure, mistress. Quite an appetite."

He was sweating despite the chill of the predawn air. Faith wondered how much wood he had chopped. She felt guilty for sitting when he and his wife had been working. Faith touched his sleeve. "It is of no concern to me Titus."

"Yes, ma'am."

Faith shook her head as she moved past him. Why would he think her worried about a little food? Surely, he knew her better than that. Normally Titus ate in the kitchen with Olivia. Pushing the distracting thought from her mind, she moved onward, determined to ignore the soft whispers behind her.

She managed to catch the door behind her before it slammed. She hurried down the tavern's hall to the one private space she possessed. Creaking upstairs warned Faith to hurry. Other sounds told her that there would be chamber pots to empty and clean. Pouring water from the pitcher she had filled last night she washed her face and combed her hair. This time, she took time to coil her hair and pin it in a respectable manner. Her hands shook as she tidied herself. The steel mirror showed a face pale and frightened.

"God help me," she whispered before turning to where her son slept. "Andrew, it's time to rise. I need you and Joshua to go get the sheriff."

A moan emitted from the cocoon of coverlets. His hair, golden-red like his Grandfather Payne, lay tangled around his head. He struggled to sit up and open both eyes at the same time. Andrew looked older than nine. The past few months had been rough on both of them.

"What?"

"Someone died in the private room. No one you know," she added quickly. Not that they were strangers to death. Whenever she looked at Andrew, Faith saw bits of Jon: the tapering freckled fingers and the long legs that would one day enable him to tower over his mother. However, Faith saw bits of herself too in the dreaminess of the eyes and the set of the mouth. He, too, would one day struggle with the weight of reality, as opposed to the richness of one's dreams.

Not pausing for any further questions her son might have, Faith returned to the kitchen to help feed the men already heading down to her common room. The iron stewpot dominated the interior of the kitchen fireplace bubbling with a hearty stew for later.

Out on the table, Olivia's muscled arms kneaded dough into bread. Despite the coolness of the morning, her skin was already dewy from proximity to the cooking fire. In the summer, the kitchen's heat became hellish. However, this early in the year, the kitchen was comfortable, full of the scent of yeast and roasting meat.

"Titus blocked the door to the private room." Olivia's focus remained on the hot fire she manipulated into doing her bidding.

Faith nodded and then, realizing the cook had not seen, said, "Good."

The flames shot up as a piece of fat dripped onto the logs. Olivia backed away with a shudder, despite having her skirt tucked into her waistband to prevent it from catching fire.

A small halo of dark curls escaped from where Olivia had tied up her hair with a blue kerchief. She would have been beautiful but for the burn scars that snaked up one side of her neck. Jon had once told Faith that his mother had gotten the girl cheaply after a fire. The previous owner had not believed she would survive.

With the sun up she had to hurry. Faith carried a platter of warm corn cakes into the tavern, pasted a smile on her face, and hoped it hid the nerves underneath. If she acted as if nothing were amiss, no one would be the wiser.

On her return trip, she helped Olivia fill platters with rabbit and applesauce. Olivia had prepared a large pot of mush as well. Faith ladled it into bowls before lifting a tray to carry into the tavern. She avoided looking at anyone and hoped no one saw the panic rising within.

Titus refilled tankards, his deep voice reverberating through the walls. For all she knew, the killer was eating inside. The idea made Faith queasy. She stopped to take a quick swallow of ale, and the spirit burned down her throat and made her eyes water. Being a tavern keeper meant she often dealt with unfamiliar people, but it had never bothered her before.

She returned to the security of the kitchen. Andrew and Joshua were eating at the large wooden table when she entered. Andrew stuffed down a large bite of corn cake smothered in molasses.

She raised an eyebrow at the lapse in manners. "Aren't you supposed to be getting the sheriff?"

"We'll be heading out in a moment, Ma. Olivia promised us rabbit and gravy."

"Very well, but leave by the front entrance to go out to the street."

"Why? We are already here, and we still have chores to do when we get back." His eyes met hers in a mild challenge. A stray lock crept loose from his clubbed hair as if it, too, wanted to rebel.

"Titus will tend the stock this morning for you and Joshua. It will be safer."

Joshua watched her as well. Olivia and Titus' son was older than Andrew by three years, not far from being a man. His eyes were serious when they met hers. "Ma says someone got killed."

Faith nodded. "That is why I need you to go together to get the sheriff."

"Why both of us?" Andrew asked. "I know the way."

"It's safer that way."

"Let's just go." Joshua nudged him. "It's more fun than dealing with Solomon."

Andrew said, "That rooster hates everybody."

"Not his hens," Joshua observed.

Not to be distracted, Andrew turned to his mother. "Who died? What happened?"

Faith could not think of what to say. The image of the mutilated body remained burned in her brain. They did not need to know how terrible it was.

"He had an accident," Olivia said briskly as she handed him a second plate, this one steaming with rabbit and other choice bits. She handed the next plate to Joshua. "Finish breakfast before you go."

Faith frowned at her; The sooner this situation was resolved, the better for everyone.

The cook shrugged. "Bullard's not going to get any more dead."

Both boys looked up.

"Phineas Bullard," Faith answered . "I don't want you two out back until this has been handled. Titus is far more capable of dealing with trouble than you two boys."

"What about the woman who was with him?" Andrew asked. "Is she dead too?"

Her breath hitched. She had forgotten the girl. "Olivia, have you seen her?"

"Stella," Joshua corrected. "Ma knows her."

The girl could not have been more than fifteen, although her eyes had looked older, as if her life had not been that of a child for some time. The horrifying thought of two dead bodies caused her to gasp evoking stares from the boys. Surely, she would have noticed another body. "Tell Titus to keep his eyes open for her."

Olivia nodded and turned back to the fire.

"Do you think Stella did it?" Joshua asked his mother.

"That child didn't kill nobody. No one would have blamed her if she had," Olivia said with quiet ferocity so low Faith almost did not hear.

Pretending not to hear, she watched the other woman from the corner of her eyes, troubled. The cook's body was stiff as she turned away and stirred the pot savagely, slopping some juices into the fire where they hissed. Why was Olivia so angry?

"Hopefully, the authorities will discover what happened." She needed to talk to her and discover what was wrong but not until the crisis had passed.

"Somebody cut him to pieces," Titus said from the doorway. He shook his head. "Nothing good will come of this."

Faith's jaw clenched. Truer words had never been spoken. She despised Bullard. Jon had foolishly borrowed money from him, and every month she scraped together the coin to pay him because he would take nothing else. Every time she saw Bullard enter her tavern she gritted her teeth.

What was maddening was his obvious enjoyment of her discomfort. That he could call in his loan due at any time cost her sleep many a night. Giving him use of the room on demand had been an aggravation, particularly when she could have used the money from renting it. The lout had claimed his unpaid use of it a privilege that came with their use of his coin.

Was it unchristian to feel relieved at his passing?

The boys were watching her. Faith turned before they read too much in her expression. "You need to go now."

Joshua gasped as his mother poked him.

"Go with him to find the sheriff, and then you both need to go to school."
Olivia was proud that her son attended the Bray school for Blacks.

Faith was thankful to get them out and away.

Two men came to her door a few hours later. The sheriff was an older man; she had seen him in town but could not recall his name. The other one looked quite young. Faith was relieved that they had come after breakfast. Only three men remained in the room. Two energetically debated the merits of a horse advertised in the newspaper, while the other slowly sipped his ale, his bloodshot eyes indicating he had overindulged the previous evening.

"Mistress Clarke, your boys reported a death in your tavern." While the sheriff's tone was polite, almost courtly, his eyes darted about, looking for what, she could not imagine.

"Come with me." Faith led them out back, past where Titus was digging the ground for spring planting. Although he continued working the soil, she knew he watched them. She stopped outside the door and turned. "He's in there."

The men looked at each other, then the younger one moved the log propping the door shut before they entered. She stayed by the open door. They stayed inside only a few minutes before the younger man ran outside toward the necessary. The sound of his gut-wrenching reaction carried across the yard.

The sheriff looked pale as he too walked out. He drew in a breath. "Do you know him?"

"Phineas Bullard." Faith twined her hair with a nervous finger.

He nodded, "Bullard. You mean the one who owns the store on Duke of Gloucester Street?"

She nodded, mildly dazed to be discussing a man who lay dead inside.

"Do you have any idea who would want to kill him?" Despite the easy tone, he watched her intently.

Faith looked at him, startled. "No, I don't."

The younger man returned, still looking green. The sheriff eyed him with disgust. "Go get the captain, Graves. He'll want to tend to this himself."

"Sheriff Jones?"

"Sheriff Johnson, Mistress."

"Sheriff Johnson," she amended. "Who is this captain?"

"Captain Grant of his majesty's army located here in town. Bullard was a man of some substance in Williamsburg known for his support of the king. The Captain will want to talk to you."

Taking a breath, she decided not to waste an opportunity for information, "Do you have any thoughts about what may have happened?"

Johnson stared at her for a moment, "Likely killed with that fancy side piece he liked to carry. It would take something substantial to cut a man to pieces like that."

Faith vaguely remembered the saber when he had come to the inn that afternoon. It had looked ridiculous. No one would mistake Bullard for a man of military background. She would have liked to know more, but the sheriff turned away. Anxiety knotted her stomach. Johnson was an easy man to read, he wondered if either she or her slaves had killed Bullard. She bit her lip as the man turned to go before grabbing his arm. "Surely you don't believe anyone here was responsible for this?"

The sheriff gently removed her hand before saying, "I must go inform the family. Captain Grant will likely be along shortly."

A vision of Bullard's body appeared in her mind. Her stomach roiled. Nauseated, she paused to take a deep breath.

"I can do this," Faith whispered. It was a plea to the almighty. She hoped that he was listening.

After seeing Johnson and his men out the gate, she returned to the inn. Rare quiet filled the downstairs. Guests had either checked out or gone into town providing her some time to go over the accounts. Faith pulled a slim ledger from the desk near the front of the tavern. Turning the page, she read the columns to determine who owed her money. She spent the next little while resolving accounts, adding in the coins given to her by men as they left. A few burgesses still owed her for meals, but there were no overwhelming debts.

Yet a few pages over, her own debts stood out. The inn made a decent profit, but there were still many of Jon's debts left to pay. The largest had been a loan from the dead man.

Dead, he was a greater burden than alive. Bullard's family would soon come for his body and ask questions she could not answer. Just thinking about it made her feel shaky.

Stepping out onto her front porch to clear her head, she saw an equestrian headed toward the capitol. A few wagons rattled up the street. Life continued in its normal cycle except where she lived. A slight man with a rucksack on his back stopped to ask directions to the apothecary. Faith frowned as she studied his pale hair. He had been in her tavern earlier but so had a dozen or so other men. A familiar face should not spook her. In her work, there were many.

Glancing into the common room, she saw a familiar face. Martin Staunton was more than a family physician; he was a dear friend. Jon had known Martin from when he had lived in rooms let by Jon's stepfather while studying medicine when Jon had been a boy. In better times, Faith had enjoyed visiting his wife.

Catching his eye, she beckoned with a finger. When his lean frame paused against the doorway of her office, she felt a sense of relief.

"I need your help," she began. "A man has died in my private meeting room."

"Would you like me to take a look?" Staunton looked thinner and older than she remembered, as if time was wearing away at the threads of his life. At her nod, he leaned down and picked up the black, leather bag he kept with him.

"This way," Faith said.

As they walked, she tried to fill in the details, but he held up his hand. "Let me look and see for myself."

Out in the yard, the chickens clucked and chattered as Olivia fed them. The scent of freshly turned earth and manure filled the air. Titus' strong baritone resonated in song as he chopped more wood for the fire.

As the door swung open, the sweet, metallic, and sickening smell permeated the air. Her gorge rose as memories of what she had witnessed earlier sharpened in her mind's eye.

"There's no need for you to come in." Staunton gauged her expression. "If you need a draught, I can prepare one before I go." He brushed past her into the dimness of the empty room. Death held no fear for him; he had seen it many times.

Faith felt shame. He had come at her request. Quailing at the doorway was not an option. Death led to a far better place. She was acting spineless… Sheer stubbornness made her meet his gaze. "I'll be fine, Martin. If you need anything…"

"I'll call Titus." Staunton entered the room.

The darkened pool of blood was obvious, even in the shadows of the room. The midmorning sun provided a pool of light in the center of the room's interior. The man's body looked no less horrible than it had earlier. A fly buzzed by on its way to the carnage.

"Leave the door open. I need light."

Faith propped the door with a rock and left, trying to remove the image of death from her mind. Out in the streets, horses snorted as their hooves struck the ground. Williamsburg was the heartbeat of colonial Virginia, the center of trade, news, and government. Not far away, noise traveled from Waller Street as horses and tradesmen entered the capitol. Men required drink as they conducted their business. Her livelihood counted on it.

As she passed the doorway to her main room, a faint whiff of toilet water told her someone was taking exceptional care with his appearance, unless it was to mask how long it had been since his last bath. No matter where she went, images of the nightmare scene out back intruded. Frantic to dispel the dark thoughts from her head Faith grabbed a broom and began sweeping dirt tracked in by scores of patrons as if by cleaning this she could cleanse her memory as well. It felt like a futile task. Looking up she could see Titus checking for late sleepers and emptying chamber pots.

No task kept her mind from the murdered man for long. Bolstered by shame, Faith returned to Dr. Staunton to see how she could help.

He squatted by the body, his medical case to the side, out of the way. His rolled-up sleeves exposed his sinewy arms. Dark hair ran down each arm to strong, square hands stained from his examination of the dead man. He wore no wig, the salt and pepper of his short, cropped hair was evident. His eyes remained intent on his task.

Faith handed him a cloth to wipe his hands. He nodded his thanks, and his spectacles reflected light from the open doorway.

Daylight highlighted the horror of the scene. The blood had dried into a dark, sticky substance. Bullard's skin had taken on a grayish, waxy hue, as he lay sprawled on the floor where he had died. Staunton had closed the man's eyes, but it did nothing to change the grotesqueness of the scene.

To distract herself, she walked around the room. It was not as elegant as at larger taverns such as the Raleigh or Christiana Campbell could provide, but it was clean, with a sturdy mantel over a modest fireplace. Firewood was stacked to one side. The table was a wooden square, much like those in the public rooms, surrounded by four chairs with turned legs and no arms. The remains of a meal were visible in a place setting in front of one of the chairs.

Staunton rose carefully and backed away to avoid stepping into the pool of blood. "A nasty business, this, but then Bullard was a prominent man. I daresay someone attempted to rob him and killed him when he fought them off. Either that or he angered the wrong party."

She still could not look at Bullard. As it was, the only way she could stay was by breathing through her mouth. With her foot, she turned over the wine bottle on the floor. It was none of hers. Fancy French wine was not something she could afford, although she had a few less expensive varieties. Bullard must have brought it in. Whom was he hoping to impress?

As she righted the bottle, something fluttered from the nearest chair. She grasped a rectangle of sewn strips of red-and-white cloth.

Faith frowned. She had never seen anything like it.

Staunton looked at her hand. "That's a Sons of Liberty banner. Given what I have heard happening in Boston, it would be dangerous to anger them. He died swiftly from the cut to the throat. The belly wound was unnecessary; he was already mortally wounded. Whoever killed him did so for personal reasons."

"God have mercy on his soul."

"Was it God's mercy or God's judgment? Bullard was a prominent man, with trade interests. He was ruthless and wealthy, not the sort to accrue a great number of friends. His support of King George was well known. It made many in this town unhappy. He may well have angered the wrong man either over his business or political dealings."

Faith winced. The last thing she needed was the attention of the British Crown. The British military had been a growing presence in the colonies for some months. Red-coated officers and enlisted men patrolled most streets in town, some billeted in homes. She made a point of being neutral. Involvement would be costly on a personal as well as financial level.

She had far more pressing concerns. Faith had been relieved of having to face Bullard and his rapacious greed, but his heirs would come for their pound of flesh soon enough.

"I know nothing about the Sons of Liberty being here." She had heard of them, men who despised the machinations of the British government and met secretly to plan how to disrupt them. They communicated in secret with members in other colonies, courting the charge of treason. Some of them even dared to publish opinions in the newspapers, but never under a name she recognized. Her temples began to throb.

The physician paused. "Best to close off the room until someone arrives to claim him. Has the sheriff gone to contact his kin?"

"Sheriff Johnson didn't tell me his plans."

"I must leave, Mistress Clarke. There are those still among the living that have need of my attention. There is nothing I can do besides share my observations with the sheriff."

Looking up at him, Faith studied the fine network of lines about his eyes. He looked tired. "You haven't been by the tavern in some time."

He smiled without warmth. "I've been busy. I assure you that my absence was not due to any offense on your part."

"Would you care for some refreshment?"

The doctor nodded. The smile this time was genuine. "Rum and don't be stingy."

She walked him to the kitchen where the warmth and welcome dispelled the grimness of the other room. He sat heavily at the table. Without a word, Olivia put a plate of hot food in front of him. Faith poured him a healthy dose of rum as well. Nodding his thanks, he dug in.

His shirt needed mending. A few buttons hung by their threads. Stains best left unidentified peppered his breeches. Examining the man's somewhat haggard appearance, she doubted that Temperance was well enough to see to his care. Martin probably ate where he could or what a servant put before him.

She poured Staunton another measure of rum. "Take your time. You are among friends."

Chapter Two

itus barreled into the room, his hands still dirty from the garden. Breathless and rattled he said, "Miss Faith, a British officer is asking for you."

Hair rose up the back of her neck as her heart began to pound. She stood and smoothed her skirt. "I'll be right there."

Sweat stuck her shift to her back from constant running back and forth from kitchen to dining room. Opening the door into her tavern, Faith forced herself to walk at a well-mannered pace toward the common room. Afternoon sunlight streaming through the windows forced her to squint.

Movement from the doorway startled her. A soldier stepped into the light where she could see him. A finely cut, scarlet coat outlined broad shoulders and long legs, while fashionable, skintight breeches revealed muscular legs that led to highly polished short boots. In his hand was his hat, a finely shaped, black tricorn. Such tailoring did not come cheap; it radiated affluence. He had rank and influence and if he were the officer connected with Bullard, he was trouble.

Faith lifted her chin and met his gaze. His pale eyes reminded her of a frozen lake. Such a hard gaze was meant to instill fear into the recipient. This was no courtesy call. Something about him made her think of a predator, which did her no good whatsoever. Whoever this officer was, he would not eat her.

"Madam." He bowed to her. "I am Captain Stephen Grant, of His Majesty's 17th Lancers. I am here regarding the death of Master Phineas Bullard. I have seen the body. Tell me what occurred."

"I don't know," Faith replied. "My servant found him this morning when he went to check the fire. Bullard was already dead. We do not know what befell him."

Grant raised an eyebrow. "I find that hard to fathom, madam. Were you not concerned when he did not come to settle his account with you?"

"Master Bullard and I had an agreement regarding the use of my private room. Once he arrived, he had no wish to be disturbed. It was not unusual for him to leave without returning to the common rooms."

"An agreement," he said. "So, neither you nor your servants checked on him, tended his fire, or noticed that he had been brutally murdered?"

"I was busy serving guests in the common room. He died in the private meeting room which is separate from the bulk of this house. Guests rent it for private meetings so they will not be disturbed. Master Bullard arrived just before the supper hour. He requested his slave take his meal to him. I sent her to the kitchen while I escorted him and left him to his business."

"He brought a slave with him?" His voice sharpened dropping his hand to touch the top of a polished saber hanging from his side.

"Yes. She was young, not more than fifteen, and delicately built. He called her Stella. I never heard her speak. I directed her to the kitchen and returned to the main tavern."

"What hour was this?"

"Perhaps two hours before sunset. He sent a messenger earlier in the day that he required the room. Titus made sure the room was ready."

"Is this the normal means of reserving your private room?"

Faith shook her head. "Most men check with me a few days ahead or simply ask when they come into my tavern"

"And do they usually stay all night?"

"No, most require the room for a few hours."

"Did he pay you when he arrived?'

"No, he did not."

"Because of your special arrangement?" Sarcasm laced his words. "What privileges did this entail?"

Despite his polite tone, it was obvious that his thoughts were anything but those of a gentleman.

"Use of the room," Faith ground out. "He was a regular visitor." She longed to tell him exactly what she thought of Bullard, but that was dangerous. Taking a deep breath, she waited for him to speak.

"Since you saw him so frequently, perhaps he mentioned any concerns he had?"

"No, he didn't confide in me." The notion was ludicrous.

"Were you aware of any enemies he had?"

Anyone who owed him money, she thought but did not say. "He never mentioned any."

"I didn't ask what he said." Grant watched her intently. The obvious condescension irritated her. "Taverns are a gathering place for many. I imagine you hear all kinds of things from the sort who comes in for ale and gossip."

"What sort do you believe come here?" She stared directly in his eyes refusing to be cowed

He continued in a measured tone. "You do not have the size or clientele of some of the better-known taverns such as the Raleigh or the King's Arms. This place caters to merchants, traders, and farmers, those who talk revolution when they have taken in too much grog."

"I don't serve grog. I run a respectable establishment and have little tolerance for drunkards or fools."

Grant seemed amused by her animosity. His eyes crinkled briefly before he resumed his questions. "Good. Then you will be helpful in solving this crime. I need to see the body and talk to his slave. Where are you keeping her?"

"Surely you can't think that child had anything to do with this?"

"I have seen just about everything since I joined the military, madam. Evil has no particular description. Age has little bearing on what a person is capable of doing. Nor is a pretty face a measure of innocence. Slaves in these colonies are little more than animals. Bullard was not known for being gentle, and those who are ill-treated are capable of anything."

Faith winced. She knew Titus heard every word as he swept the tavern floor. It reminded her that as a slave owner, however unwilling, she helped perpetuate the idea that slaves were not quite human. The thought sickened her. She swallowed the knot that rose in her throat.

Restless fingers drummed the side of his leg. "Where is she? I must speak with her and determine what she knows."

"I haven't seen her since she came to the kitchen last night to take Bullard his meal. I think she returned later to eat in the kitchen."

There was a look of warning in Titus's eyes as he passed Faith with his broom. He would go out to the stable to check on the animals soon. A horrible thought entered Faith's mind. She squashed it, fearing her face would betray unruly thoughts.

Grant's anger was palpable and heard in a sharp breath, "Bullard's slave is missing, and you didn't think it was important to tell me? Madam, this is outrageous! Show me the room unless you have misplaced it as well?" His lips turned white as his tone sharpened. It sounded as if he were biting off the words as his gaze considered her.

"This way. She moved forward and put her back to him as she led him through her business. She took her time as they moved through the public rooms and out back. The captain stayed close at her heels, unnerving her. He remained silent until they reached the door.

"Now tell me, Mistress Clarke." He slowly enunciated her name just enough to irritate her. "What happened here last night?"

"Master Bullard took his supper in here. After bringing him a bottle of wine, I went back to the tavern to tend my other guests. For all I knew, his meeting went as planned."

"Who was Bullard meeting?" Grant asked.

"He didn't say."

"You don't know who met in your private room. You were unaware until this morning that a violent murder took place, and now you cannot find a slave." His voice took a derisive tone. "I wonder that you remain in business, given the care you take of your clients."

Faith glared at him. "Phineas Bullard was an ill-tempered man. He was also powerful enough to cause trouble for anyone whom he bore ill will. No one would wish to annoy him. I left him to his business."

"I am sure you can find a handful of men who will testify to your continued presence."

"I was there until well into the night," she snapped. "I served food and drink until closing."

"Sending your slaves back to the kitchen as needed."

"Olivia stays in the kitchen." She tried not to grind her teeth. "Titus and I take turns carrying trays, as do the boys."

"Any of you could have slipped away and killed Bullard."

"No one living at this tavern killed him," Faith hissed. "Given his temperament, I am sure he had more enemies than lived here."

The look of satisfaction on his face told her he had goaded her on purpose.

Now she was angry. "Is this how you investigate a crime? By intimidation and innuendo? No wonder the colonies are up in arms!"

It was the wrong thing to say. She knew it as soon as the words escaped her mouth, but fear and exhaustion loosened her restraints. Bad enough to have a man murdered without this man saying she or her servants had hacked Bullard to death. The thought made her ill.

Grant's lips tightened as his voice rose loud enough to silence her patrons in the main room. "The colonies and their inhabitants would do well to remember that they are subject to the laws of Britain. Instead, they play at rebellion like reckless children. Yet whom do they run to when trouble comes in the form of the French or the natives? Where have they always run? Mother England." Anger filled his voice as he towered over her. "I have buried good men in these colonies, defending you and yours. Do not criticize the very hand that has saved you time and again, madam."

Faith inhaled. They both were breathing rapidly the situation was fast getting out of hand. They glared at each other like fighters in a ring. Somewhere in the back of her mind an alarm sounded. Enraging the captain would not help. He could have her arrested if he so desired. As much as she disliked him, Faith needed to diffuse the situation. "It was not my intent to malign those who sacrificed their lives to protect these colonies. However, Phineas Bullard could have any number of enemies. No one in this household had anything to do with his end."

His icy control returned. "Bullard was a prominent merchant. I intend to interview all his associates. I will need to talk to everyone staying at this house. Each person will give an accounting of his or her movements last night. It is my hope that checking his accounts and talking to his family will yield answers. His slave must be found. She very well could have killed him then run away."

"Titus," she called, "have you seen Master Bullard's servant today?"

The big man paused, holding loosely to the broom he had been using. He shook his head and kept his face downward and his voice soft. "The last I saw of her was when she was eating in the kitchen. I do not know where she went after that. I was busy in the main rooms helping you mind the liquor."

"So you were." Faith nodded and turned to the captain. "I will ask my cook, Olivia, when she last saw Stella. But I do not believe anyone has seen her since late last night."

Acid dripped from Grant's voice. "Did it not occur to you that her disappearance was a problem, Mistress Clarke? She is an escaped slave, which is a dangerous enough reality for everyone around here. She has vanished. Surely you realize she could either be a witness or a murderer."

"No, I didn't!" she snapped. "I assumed she was with her master until I found his body. After seeing that, I was not thinking about servants but that a man was horribly murdered in my inn." In truth, she had forgotten Stella until he prodded her memory; now she feared what would happen when the girl was found.

"I see."

Faith doubted he did. Even now, she could see the dead man's body with its gaping wounds. She shuddered. She barely remembered the girl, more as a shadow that had slipped in and out of the kitchen, never meeting anyone's gaze. Could that child have murdered Bullard?

"I don't know where she is," she whispered.

His voice was sharp. "She probably ran away, but she can't have gone far. I will mention her when I call on Bullard's family to ask his widow to place an advertisement in the *Virginia Gazette* offering a reward for her return. I also know a man with dogs. If any of her things are with Bullard's, I can put them on her scent. They will find her and place her in the goal."

"Dogs? You would chase a young girl down with a pack of dogs?" She stared at him. "What if she didn't kill him?"

"She was the last person to see him alive. She may be a witness, which means the killer cannot afford to let her live. She knows something or is guilty of a heinous murder. Why else flee into the night?"

To escape was Faith's unexpressed opinion. She kept seeing that small figure bearing the heavy tray of victuals to her master. Pity formed a knot in her throat. "We don't know if she did anything. Is it necessary to hunt her like an animal?"

"It is far better for her to be captured by me or my men. I give you my word that she will not be ill-treated. However, we must hear what she knows. If she did not kill him, she most certainly knows who did. I need to know who met with Bullard, unless your memory has improved."

She flushed. "Master Bullard didn't inform me of his expected company, only that he needed the room and desired not to be disturbed."

"So you have said." Grant shot her a disbelieving look. "You do not know who his guest was. Come now, Mistress Clarke. This is your place of business. Surely you noticed who joined him."

Anxiety was rapidly transforming into irritation. Regardless of his rank, he had no right to treat her as if she had something to hide.

"I did not see anyone else go there. I was busy attending my guests in the common room, which is nowhere near that door, as you may have noted. I had no reason to disturb him." Nor did she want to. "He was obviously meeting someone important."

"Obviously?"

"He demanded one of my more expensive bottles. He requested an extra tankard be brought to him. I doubt it was so he could drink more." The tart remark escaped her unbidden. Faith was tired of questions. She had done nothing wrong.

The wretched man raised an eyebrow at the last comment. For a moment, she could have sworn he was amused.

Turning her back to him, she went to the closed door of her private room. The air had warmed up enough that a few flies buzzed over the corpse. Thank the Lord it was not a few weeks later in spring, or the room would have been crawling with them.

"Dr. Staunton examined the poor man. We covered him out of common decency. His family should not see him like that when they come to retrieve his body. Has anyone contacted them?"

"I will go there myself once I'm finished here, madam. His widow deserves that much courtesy." He gestured to the door. "Let us proceed."

The sickly smell of blood was still in evidence. Faith shuddered involuntarily. Grant showed little reaction. She remained in the doorway and let him enter the room. He walked about and carefully avoided areas of dried blood and spilled wine. He examined the bottle.

"Do you serve this here?"

She shook her head. "French wine is too dear for my pockets."

He spotted the flag where she had left it on the table. "Do you know what this is?"

"I was told it was a flag for the Sons of Liberty, whoever that is."

Grant raised an eyebrow. "Indeed, but I would be foolish to believe you had not at least heard of these ruffians."

Faith knew very little about the Sons of Liberty, but she was sure she was about to find out. She deliberately fed the fire to find out what he knew. "Some have called them revolutionaries, Captain."

His voice sounded vicious for all its soft tone. "Sons of Liberty, indeed. It is but a pretentious title for a band of organized thugs who provoke violence and flout the King's justice. The law is for all His Majesty's subjects, in all his domains. Only a fool assumes otherwise. Look what consequences such unrest bought your compatriots up in Boston. The harbor is closed to all and sundry, and who suffers but the merchants and tradesmen who make their bread on the harbor's activity? Not His Majesty."

"The Sons of Liberty did not close Boston Harbor," she retorted. "It was King George's troops."

"When the laws are broken, there are consequences, Mistress Clarke."

"And how long will the actions of a few radicals cause the misery of many innocent people?" News of Boston's fate had traveled throughout the colonies. She had been shocked at the harshness of the punishment.

Grant's anger filtered through his voice like an icy draft sending a faint shiver down Faith's spine. "It would be wise to remember that defying England will bring nothing but woe to these colonies. Phineas Bullard understood that the colonies need the support and protection of England to survive. His loyalty to the Crown may be what cost him his life. Bullard's killer will be sent to England for trial and hanged."

Faith stared at him. "Why send the killer to England? Have we not courts here?"

"There are courts," he agreed. "But given the unrest of late and the rebelliousness of the citizenry, my orders are that severe crimes such as treason or murder are to be tried in England. The colonists would do well to remember that King George has a long arm and a short temper." Grant stared at her his face devoid of expression. "I must go. If you can remember who met with Bullard, send a message to me either at the capitol or at the King's Arms."

He exited through the garden gate. His saber swung from his hip as he strode off toward the governor's residence. The captain was an attractive man and no fool.

Faith shivered. Both the sheriff and the captain considered her a suspect. Once he looked at Bullard's ledgers, he would know she owed Bullard money. Olivia and Titus were in and out of the kitchen constantly, and both knew how to use knives, as did she. She would have to ask them about last night before Grant did. He would hunt for Stella, but his pursuit would not end there.

Dinnertime approached. She threw herself into the everyday chores necessary to her business. When the boys returned, they helped with turning the spits and carrying victuals back and forth. Men came in for food and drink, to play chess, or discuss matters not discussed at home.

She filled a pair of tankards and turned with them in hand when Andrew ran into her.

"Andrew, easy," she said sharply, eyeing the slosh of ale. It settled, and she gave it to two waiting men.

"Redcoats are here!"

"What?"

"Joshua and I saw them arrive and go in where that man died. There were four or five of them."

Grant had failed to inform her about the search, which she doubted was accidental. Faith gestured to Titus to watch over things before turning to go. A hand reached her arm, and she whirled about, impatiently ready to offer a piece of her mind.

A young man had risen to his feet beside her. His reddish-gold hair looked vaguely familiar, although she was certain he was not a regular client of her tavern. His clothes were too fine to be one of her regular clientele. "Are you in trouble, madam?"

It took her a moment to interpret the words, so quietly were they spoken.

"No, I have done nothing wrong." Faith said this with more conviction than she felt.

"If you have a need of legal counsel, Mistress Clarke, I can be found most often these days in the Raleigh Tavern when the burgesses are not in session. Thomas Jefferson, at your service." He bowed.

His face flushed, and he stammered slightly. She recognized his companion more easily. George Wythe was a familiar and respected lawyer in Williamsburg. Underneath his homely features lay a razor-sharp mind. Jefferson must be one of his students.

Despite her eagerness to leave, she paused to curtsy in return. "Thank you, Master Jefferson. That is most kind of you, but I am sure the matter is of little concern."

Jefferson sat and turned to his companion at the table. The day's papers were before them, as were quills, ink, and fresh foolscap. Faith left the men as quickly as she could without causing comment and hoped no ink stained the table beneath.

Outside, soldiers went in and out of her private room. Inside furniture moved and objects hit the floor warning her they were tearing the place apart.

One of them stopped her at the door. "You can't go in there, ma'am."

"Why?"

"Captain's Grant's orders, madam. No one but the king's men can enter until Bullard has been taken away."

"When will that be?" Faith asked exasperated.

"I do not know, madam. The captain went to inform them a little while ago. I haven't heard anything more."

Neither had she, including Grant's takeover. I hope that Bullard's family would come for him before nightfall. After they took him home, the room would need a thorough scrubbing with lye soap. Considering what lay inside, there might not be enough soap in the colony to make it clean again.

Faith spotted Andrew staring at the activity.

"What are they doing?" he asked.

"Looking for any clues to what happened," she replied with forced lightness. "Hopefully the villain left something behind."

Andrew frowned thoughtfully. "That would be stupid."

"Yes, it would. But so is killing someone in a public place."

"Where would you have done it?"

"Killing someone unless in self-defense is wicked."

They stood together to watch men exit the room carrying bits of clothing and furniture out into the yard.

"Finish your chores." She kissed the top of his head.

Andrew wiggled away. He was getting too big to appreciate being kissed by his mother.

"Check with Titus to see what remains to be done. He did a lot for you this morning. I am sure you and Joshua can repay the favor this afternoon by helping muck out stalls." She ignored her son's wrinkled-up nose. A little dirty work would not hurt him and would teach him to appreciate those who did such work on a daily basis.

By evening, Bullard's family had collected his body, much to Faith's relief. Tomorrow they could clean before letting the room to another guest. Although the idea gave her a turn, she needed the income. Expenses never stopped, not even for death.

Supper consisted of leftover food from dinner. By the time the sun lay low in the sky, Faith was exhausted. Nonetheless, her brain refused to rest. Her desk stood near the main doorway. It was here she took coin from guests and tallied her books. Gold always had value, although she would barter room and board if her prospective tenant offered something useful.

Faith sat and trimmed a feather to use as quill, surprised at the sharp ache of her feet. How nice it would be to just rest for a few minutes and not worry about tomorrow, but there was no hope of that. Too many people depended on her, and the weight was, at times, almost unbearable.

Dipping the quill in ink, she opened to the current page. The accounts in the book told the story of her business. She added the coinage from the night's meals and overnight guests. It would do, as long as she was careful. Her inn did not have the reputation of larger ones. Until today, Clarke Tavern had been steadily building a good name for decent food and respite close to the House of Burgesses.

Bullard's gruesome death had upended that. The last thing they needed was to become a place known for violent death.

Upstairs, travelers had settled to sleep. The horses and livestock had been fed and watered. Soon Olivia and Titus would settle into their rooms above the kitchen. Rubbing her eyes, Faith wondered how her days seemed to end before she accomplished all that needed to be done.

She never remembered her mother feeling exhausted, but then Patience Payne had borne three daughters and three sons, all but one still living. That many hands made for fewer chores. Faith grinned. She speculated which of her sisters was now in charge of plucking the Sunday-dinner chicken.

She wondered what Phineas Bullard's last thoughts had been. Had he been making plans for his trading empire, or had his thoughts turned to his family at the end? Had he known God?

Nearby, Andrew's snores were a bare whisper of breath. His sleep remained untroubled. Outside a breeze made the trees bend and groan. She blew out her candle and headed for bed. Maybe tomorrow would bring answers.

Her mind remained restless as she combed her hair in the dark. Why had Bullard come here? The only advantage was privacy. Given that her inn lay on the outskirts of town, fewer people would have seen him or his killer.

Who had he met? Where was his slave?

Before she slipped between the chilly blankets, Faith bowed her head in prayer and pleaded with God for peace and security for her family and for a young slave girl to make it far away from Williamsburg. Even as she closed her eyes, small noises kept her awake—the creaking of the beds upstairs, the settling of the house, and the soft crackling of the fire in the tile stove nearby. Her dreams showed her the dead man in his pool of blood and then her husband, pale as they washed and dressed him for burial, gone too soon.

Chapter Three

Faith spent the next day busy with her tavern, but as the day dawned bright and peaceful, she realized a condolence call was in order. Leaving Titus and Olivia to mind matters at the tavern, she changed dresses for a trip into the heart of Williamsburg.

It seemed ironic that so much life hummed through the street while her current business dealt in death. Bullard's wife and children would mourn his passing. She dreaded the encounter, but the only way she was going to find answers was to ask questions.

Normally she enjoyed walking and seeing various folk about their business. It was one of the pleasures of town living. On the farm where she grew up, the social outlet had been meeting on the Sabbath, and sitting on the wooden benches had always put her bottom to sleep.

Even though she did not hurry, her long-legged stride made short work of the walk to Bullard's main place of business just off Duke of Gloucester Street. Within the protective confines of an iron fence, the well-groomed yard displayed the tender green of young grass rising up in timid tufts beneath the solid branches of a sharply trimmed hedge The heavy shrubbery provided a space to collect both breath and thoughts. Faith needed time to consider her words. She was unfortunately familiar with the place. Even with Bullard dead, she dreaded going inside. It reminded of how little stood between her and penury.

Near Bullard's shop, a printer's business hummed with activity.

From the doorway, the scent of ink and wax wafted out. The press rattled and groaned as it pressed type to paper. Broadsheets hung drying from lines stretched from wall to wall of the narrow room. A printer half turned and winked at Faith, letting her know that he was more observant than she had guessed.

Blushing, she backed away into the street. Purchasing an advertisement would have to wait. Taking a breath, she stepped through the door of her destination.

Inside, two apprentices waited on customers, a woman choosing ribbons and a few men looking at tools. Faith gazed around her, marveling at the wealth of goods available for the affluent. Ruefully, she considered that she had little more than a few pence on her.

The inside of the store contained shelves of goods from the colonies and abroad. If one had the coin, they could find whatever they required. Her nose detected the aroma of coffee, tea and chocolate. She spotted tankards on one set of shelves and smiled ruefully. She would need to buy more soon. The more men spent later evenings discussing politics over ale, the more likely it became someone would break one.

Faith had neither the time nor the inclination to shop. Cordially dismissing the young man who approached her, she walked to the back of the store. Josiah Smythe, Bullard's brother-in-law, sat at a large desk, adding columns of figures in a ledger. Glasses pinched the end of his long nose as he dipped a quill in ink and wrote into a column.

As her shadow fell over his parchment, he paused, sanded it and put it aside, out of her sight. "Mistress Clarke?"

"Master Smythe," she replied, extending her hand. "I apologize for bothering you."

Frowning thoughtfully, he rose and bowed. "Forgive me for not taking your hand, mistress, but I am covered in ink from doing figures. It is not an intentional slight, I assure you."

"I understand."

His features made her think of an old hunting dog. He smelled faintly of sweat and peppermint. A black band of stiff fabric adorned his sleeve, and his shirt strained a bit over his belly, which was undoubtedly a sign of his wife's good cooking. He had married later in life, but the laugh creases around his eyes and lips indicated it had been a good match. She had seen his wife and seven children at church. It helped explain the sweets in a cup at his table.

He caught her glance and shrugged ruefully. "I keep track of such expenses. Molly doesn't approve of too much sugar, but I don't see the harm in an occasional sweet."

"Fear not. My lips are sealed."

Smythe gazed at her thoughtfully. "You didn't come to chat, Mistress Clarke."

She nodded, unsure of what to say.

"A few days ago, we received word of my brother-in-law's death at your tavern. I helped collect his body for my sister. We bury him tomorrow at Burton Parish. It has been a shock. For you also, I imagine."

"I am sorry."

His face was pale. "I had feared something was wrong when he missed our regular morning meeting. Phineas was conscientious regarding his businesses. I can only think that someone tried to rob him and he fought back."

Faith felt sick, remembering the brutality. "I cannot say."

"My brother-in-law died at your place of business, mistress. You need to tell me everything." The weight of his glance was so hard that she stepped back.

"I found him early that morning. He was already dead. That is all I know." Sharing such a horrible thing here amidst the activity of Bullard's shop felt awkward.

Removing his spectacles, Smythe rubbed the crease that appeared high on the bridge of his nose. He looked tired. "My sister prepares for the funeral tomorrow. She would like to speak with you. Will you accompany me?"

She knew of no polite way to refuse him, so she nodded. Smythe spoke quietly to the apprentices, who had managed to hear everything.

"Mind the store, Geoffrey," he said to the older boy, whose mouth hung agape. "I need to go see Mistress Bullard."

Smythe wiped his hands on his shop apron, removed it, and hung it on a peg. He paused briefly to tuck his shirt and put on a plain, brown, woolen vest. He grabbed his hat, opened the door, and waited for Faith to precede him.

Leaving the subdued shop, they walked toward the Bullard home. She quietly fell in step with him. Dust drifted up from the road and settled on her skirts and shoes. She sighed. There was no helping it. The cobbled streets of Williamsburg offered either dust or mud, and mud was far worse to navigate.

She struggled to keep pace. Although she was taller, his steps were quicker. He turned off on a side street filled with homes and small businesses. She grimaced. Her mother-in-law also lived on Francis Street. She hoped none of the servants was about. Eugenia would not hesitate to demand an explanation, which was a conversation best avoided.

Faith was saved from further distressing thoughts by the slowing of Smythe's steps. He stopped and made way to a gate that separated a two-story, brick residence from the street.

Bullard's home stood a full two stories with a small balcony that cast a shadow on the front door. Large, elegant windows faced front, their expensive glass sparkling in the afternoon sun. The iron gates' geometric patterns contrasted sharply with the rich green of the grass and well-trimmed hedges. It was a residence worthy of royalty. Standing before it, she had the urge to wipe her hands on her apron and check her gown discreetly for wrinkles.

Smythe opened the gate, gesturing for her to go in, before entering and shutting the gate behind them. The snick of metal on metal as he fastened it seemed to echo in the still air. The path was neatly paved with brick in an elegant herringbone pattern that cut through the lawn in a short stretch to the front stoop. Matched pairs of bushes perfectly aligned on either side of the walk. Each mirrored its partner in size, shape, and placement marching inexorably to the elaborate front entryway. They reminded Faith of chess pieces on a board. The manicured lawn and immaculately maintained house increased Faith's unease.

A servant opened the door. He nodded at the two of them.

"Master Smythe." He looked inquiringly at Faith his face too well schooled to reveal his opinion.

"This is Mistress Clarke," Smythe said. "She has come to pay her respects."

The servant opened the door further and let them into the central hall. Light flooded the house, gilding the polished oak floors. The warmly painted walls furthered the impression of opulence and comfort.

"Master Bullard is laid out in the parlor." The maid gestured at the open doorway, where the end of a draped table was visible.

Faith froze. She had not planned to see Phineas Bullard ever again.

"Josiah," a soft cultured voice wafted from behind them.

Although they had never met, Faith had heard of Charlotte Bullard. Rumor said her family were wealthy planters in Georgia. The Bullards' son had gone down to Savannah to learn the business and manage his mother's dowry property. Their daughter was of marrying age. She could not remember any other details.

Charlotte Bullard did not look old enough to have an adult son. Her skin was clear and firm with only the barest hint of creases on the outside of her eyes and in the corners of her smile Her head barely came up to Faith's shoulder.

"This is Mistress Clarke, from the tavern Phineas invested in," Josiah Smythe introduced smoothly. His expression was as bland as a freshly boiled egg.

"Mistress Clarke, welcome to my home." Charlotte Bullard met her gaze briefly before turning and walking through the open doorway.

Faith followed the petite woman into the parlor. She felt as ungainly as a horse in such a cultured and expensive residence.

As befitted a room designed for the receiving of company, the ostentatious room told visitors that the owners were people of affluence. Walls covered in blue toile print emphasized the plasterwork on the ceiling. A richly patterned rug covered the floorboards. On the wall next to the fireplace was a large portrait of Mistress Bullard at a younger age. She gestured, and they sat on wooden chairs with fine needlework cushions.

It would have been a beautiful room had it not been for the dead body on a table in front of the fireplace.

"The servants did an excellent job, don't you think?" Charlotte Bullard lightly touched the heavily embroidered edges of his wool suit.

Faith nodded and tried to keep from gagging. A few flies buzzed about the open coffin, lined in black silk. The cabinet maker had used mahogany to construct the box. Such ostentatiousness shouldn't have bothered her but it did. She could think of far better uses for such fine materials. A small boy waved a fan to keep the flies at bay. The faint scent of decay permeated the room, despite the dried lavender tucked in at his feet and in vases throughout the room. The silver buckles from his shoes gleamed faintly. Faith wondered if those would make it into the ground or be removed just before the lid was nailed shut.

She was thankful when they moved to a smaller room for tea. Charlotte kept up a steady stream of polite talk about weather, crops, and fashion until the tea tray arrived. Pouring for each of them, she offered sugar and passed a plate of delectable baked goods. Faith took the cup out of politeness but could not touch a thing. She felt as welcome as a bug in the cupboard. No one spoke as she set down her cup and smoothed imaginary wrinkles from her skirt.

Smythe stood and paced. "Phineas' affairs will have to be put in order, Lottie. He kept his hands in many pies." He gave his sister a meaningful glance. "It would be best if I dealt with his most pressing business concerns. There isn't time to summon Henry from Savannah."

"His funeral will be tomorrow. The gravediggers have already prepared the spot." Charlotte ticked off tasks to be done then paused a moment. "I trust you, dear brother, to handle Phineas' personal accounts." Their eyes met knowingly.

"I have informed his business associates of his passing. Maria has arrived home in time for the funeral. I believe she should return within a few weeks to our sister's house in Baltimore. It wouldn't do to keep her suitors waiting too long."

"Ah," Smythe answered. "We don't want the bees to move onto another rose."

Faith coughed. They stared at her, realizing that a stranger lingered in the room.

"I should leave you to deal with your grief." She rose and curtsied to the woman of the house.

"My apologies, Mistress Clarke, I had not meant to ignore you. Phineas' passing has left us with many new responsibilities. We are fortunate that my daughter had already planned a trip home." Charlotte offered a sad droop to her lips. "My husband's passing will be a difficult event in our lives. I am not sure how we will surmount his absence, but we will endeavor to carry on, as he would wish. Once we lay him to rest, we can attend his affairs."

Her eyes met Faith.

"I realize, Mistress Clarke, that this is a distressing turn of events for you as well. We will not take you away from your business any further. I hope you can be of assistance to me in a small personal matter."

Faith leaned forward, touched by the request. "What is it you require, Mistress Bullard?"

Charlotte's mouth trembled, but her dark eyes focused sharply. "As I looked among my husband's things that came with him, I could not find his pocketbook. Do you have it?"

Faith stiffened at the implication, "I do not. Anything found on Master Bullard's person was returned with him, unless Captain Grant saw the need to examine it."

"It is very distinctive. I embroidered it in red and gold for him with his name as well. I would be willing to reward you if…"

Faith flushed with anger she dared not express. "I suggest you direct any inquiries toward Captain Grant, who took charge of your late husband's body. I bid you goodbye, Mistress Bullard. There is nothing else for us to discuss, and I must leave you to your grief."

She left the formal room with its delicate furnishings and savage people. A well-dressed slave, perhaps the butler, opened the front door for her, closing it before she had taken two steps away from the entrance. Faith forced herself to walk rather than run. Her desire to break something was strong.

The journey through town and back to the tavern did little to calm her temper. The smoke of wood fires down the street scented the air as meals cooked. She watched some slaves do laundry. Her mind turned to Olivia and Titus.

She had always taken pride in being English and under the protection of English law, but there were no such protections for slaves. They were property with no say in how and where they lived and no hope of anything better. Her throat burned.

Her father had occasionally hired freedmen to help with the harvest, and he had treated them no differently than any other workers. "They are men, Faith," he had said when she had asked him why. "God made them as assuredly as he made us, and no man has the right to own another."

"Where are you?" she asked the sky. There was no warming the coldness that permeated her heart as she contemplated how different her choices had been from her father's. Surely if God wanted her to free her slaves, he would provide the means for her to do so. "How do I manage?"

She trudged home, her heart torn between the world she lived in and the choices she needed to make.

Chapter Four

Sleep remained elusive. After the horrific visit to Bullard's widow, Faith had spent the remainder of the day working out her anger in chores. At least Mistress Bullard had not suggested she had stuck Bullard's missing saber into him, although that may have been next on her agenda.

The recent loss of a husband was no excuse for the woman's behavior. Charlotte Bullard was obviously not paralyzed by grief. Nonetheless, she had a right to all her husband's possessions. Faith wracked her brain for what she could remember. All that came to mind was the horror of the body. She went over the room in her mind, the table, the chairs, and the fireplace. Somewhere were the answers she needed.

She awoke with a start staring out into the darkness. Nothing seemed amiss. It wasn't until she rolled over that she saw a wispy grey fog crawling under the door. Her heartbeat tripled as a damp oily odor permeated the air. She ran out into the main hallway to see smoke creeping through the walls like ghostly fingers, caressing the dry wood like an obsessed lover.

Faith screamed as she ran over to where Andrew slept. She shook him. "Get outside! The inn's on fire." Dragging him out of bed, she shoved him toward the front door. Voices filled the inn as sleepy frightened people reacted to the shouts and the smoke that was drifting through their rooms. Within seconds the stairs vibrated with the feet of her guests rushing out into the night.

Outside she heard shouts, as members of the Night Watch responded to the flames. Fists pounded on the door followed by the shattering of glass as her front and side windows were broken. "Fire! Fire!" There was no time to lose. Once the blaze spread, it could take the whole house in seconds, before continuing through town.

Olivia joined her, hair loose over her shoulders, her eyes wide. Over her shift, she had thrown a shawl; her feet were bare in their shoes. "Out back," she cried. "The spare room's ablaze!"

Andrew's eyes were wide and frightened. Short, harsh breaths emanated from his mouth. They both were coughing from the smoke and scent of ash that permeated the air. "Go where it is safe!" Faith yelled. Red curls danced wild about his head as if they had a mind of their own.

Faith watched him go out the front door with Olivia before turning to the buckets of earth that lined the wall as Titus burst in from the back. His face was stained with soot and dirt. "It's full ablaze!" he cried. Joshua followed him. Both grabbed a bucket before turning to run back out. They weren't losing the inn without a fight. A feeling of relief swept through her at the sight of them. Everyone who mattered to her was all right.

The back of the house was a dark silhouette against the harsh orange and yellow light. Faith watched as the conflagration fed on her house ignoring the cold as it bit her ankles. Her shift billowed as her hair straggled in the loose braid, she wore for sleeping. Pebbles from the rough ground tore into the soles of her feet as she ran toward the fire. Bright orange flames shattered the darkness amidst the harsh roar of burning wood. Fire framed her private room from roofline to floor. "How could this have happened?" Men and boys from the neighboring houses ran to fight the fire. Shaking, she went to join them.

Titus stopped her. "No, ma'am. Stay back here and pass the bucket. Andrew's already lost one parent. He's not losing another."

Faith didn't argue. A pop was followed by a roar. She looked up as a blazing tongue of fire licked up the roof. Huge flames danced over the blackening wood bringing to mind a gaping mouth to Hell.

"Please, no wind," she prayed. If the breeze picked up ash and hot cinders hit the main tavern, it would spread to surrounding homes in seconds. Even with the ground damp from last week's rain, the damage would be high.

A brigade threw dirt and water on the conflagration. Men and women gathered to watch the battle as men from all over town brought buckets filled with earth and water to douse the blaze. Faith watched as folk from some of the nearby buildings brought prized possessions out to the yard in case the fire spread. Sleepy-eyed children watched from behind their mothers' backs as men rushed not only to assist but to prevent the inferno from spreading to their own homes. Wordlessly, she passed her bucket down the line as the fierce heat and smoke kept anyone from getting close. Glass from the window shattered spreading teeth like slivers that shone with feral intensity on the ground. Orange and red lit the sky as more men came to attack the blaze.

Titus' voice called out, "The fire engine is coming!" His body was indistinguishable from the dozens of figures in the darkness.

Faith looked down the road toward town. Williamsburg's fire engine rolled in, its stout wooden body bouncing as it rolled through her gate to stop in the midst of her garden. As it arrived, a swarm of men went over to it to operate the levers and treadles necessary for its operation. A team passed buckets up from a nearby creek to fill its reservoir. Water shot out from the cannon-like barrel on its roof controlled by one of the town's blacksmiths who knelt behind it while grasping the sprayer between his hands. He pointed it at her tavern, dampening the roof to douse any flying sparks. Faith knew her private room was lost but there was a chance they could keep it from spreading. She passed bucket after bucket listening for the sibilant hiss as water connected with the red hot, heat. The pulsating flames lit the night washing the scene in orange and gold. The roar deepened as the roof collapsed; leaving broken timbers caved into the rough bowl of the standing walls. The slow-rising sun spread a hesitant light on the scene. Faith looked across the yard to where the gate stood silhouetted in the darkness. Olivia stood just inside its confines, her long dark hair streaming past her shoulders. Flames gilded Andrew's hair, making him stand out from the crowd. Olivia kept a hand on his shoulder preventing him from getting too close. Lit by the dawning sun as well as the flames, Faith watched the destruction. By daybreak, the walls collapsed destroying what was left of the structure. She rubbed her eyes as they teared up from smoke and fumes.

It didn't make any sense. There had been no fire in that room since Bullard's death. There was no reason for the room to be ablaze. Her mind went over every detail of cleaning the space. No candles, no kindling, nothing to cause a spark. Faith stared at the burning room dumbfounded until it hit her. Someone had set fire to her home. Smoky ash drifted by in dark clouds choking anyone drawing breath. As she coughed and then inhaled, a familiar oily scent permeated her nostrils, like fat being rendered. Faith used tallow candles to spare the expense of beeswax, but never in public spaces. Her meeting rooms all featured the clear flame of beeswax. Tallow candles sputtered and had to be watched carefully. One or two candles would not cause such a powerful odor. It would take several. It didn't make any sense, and then it did, as brutal as a slap. Fear trickled down her spine as she considered the outcome had she not awoken; the fire could have claimed all of them.

Someone threw a blanket over her shoulders. She startled when she recognized Ezra. Her father-in-law smiled tightly. "I came as soon as I heard. I'm relieved that you and Andrew are unharmed." He patted her shoulder and left, weaving in and out of the crowd, stopping to talk to people as they worked. She pulled the blanket tighter, comforted by its solid weight and warmth. A dull black fog of fear mingled with anger filled her head. They could have died.

The black charred logs oozed smoke, burning her nose and throat making her cough. She began to look about the crowd. Some were neighbors who had battled the blaze through the night, others simply came to stare or perhaps admire their handiwork? A flame shot up as a log popped before dying down. Her eyes focused on the wall the room shared with the tavern. It would be so easy for sparks to spread. "Please no," she prayed. The fire engine squealed in agony as it spilled its payload on her roof and the remains of her private meeting room. The hiss of evaporating water sounded angry as if the fire resented the intrusion. Yet the blaze was dying down. As the engine continued to spurt out its steady stream, the flames became patchier leaving a black smoldering mass. The crisis passed leaving only desolate ruins to be picked through.

Faith lost sight of Andrew. She panicked for a few seconds looking about wildly before remembering that Olivia had taken him back to the kitchen with her once the danger had passed. People were dispersing back to their own homes. Staggering slightly, she forced herself off the stump she had been sitting upon and went to thank them. The crowds had thinned rapidly as the fire ebbed. People returned to their homes for what sleep might be had in the few hours left to them. Faith wondered if she would ever sleep easily again. Men still manned the pump but little was left except for mud and ash. As the sky turned silver-gray her feet took her to the kitchen. Using a bucket of water just outside the door to rinse the dirt and soot from her hands, she joined Olivia, dropping the blanket off to the side as she entered.

Lit by the faint glow coming from the hearth, the familiarity of the kitchen eased the tension that wound about her tight as a bow. Andrew and Joshua's voices could be heard upstairs. Coal from the kitchen's fire glowed fitfully, silhouetting Olivia as she knelt to stir it to life.

"Are you all right?" Faith's voice was hoarse and sounded weaker than she would like.

Olivia's eyes gleamed in the dim light.

"I thought I would get a start on breakfast." Her normally rich voice was little more than a whisper. Against the flame, she trembled.

Shivers coursed down Faith's body as well. "Can I help?"

Rising, the other woman nodded. "There's always plenty to do here." Her eyes looked at the ceiling where laughter could be heard upstairs. "They'll come down hungry soon enough and our guests will still expect to be fed just like any other day."

Driven to do something useful, Faith spotted vegetables on the table waiting to be prepared. Picking up a knife, she started viciously chopping onions. Olivia watched her savage attack but said nothing. Faith paused over her work as tears filled her eyes. Rubbing them she noticed a grayish smear on the back of her hand. Olivia handed her a damp cloth smiling weakly.

"That ash is everywhere."

Faith nodded thinking it was only God's grace that everything had not been destroyed. The sound of boys running down the outside steps galvanized her to action. "I need to prepare for our guests. I must look awful." Rising slowly, she left, stumbling over the threshold as she went out.

Chapter Five

The reflection in the steel mirror showed a pale face covered with dark smudges. No one saw that once back behind the door of her room she'd wept. Her eyes still looked puffy, but that could be attributed to smoke. Cold water from the basin allowed her to wash off the worst of the soot and ash. Yesterday's cap was passable so she put it on again. Discarding her smoky shift, she dug around for another one. With a little effort, Faith masked most of the ravages of the night.

The floorboards bore evidence of the night's horror, each covered in filth and ash, a dark reminder of the battle. Picking up a broom, she worked to erase the evidence, but it stubbornly refused to yield the marks of the night's terror.

As the day wore on, Faith found even simple tasks difficult. Clumsiness afflicted her no matter what she attempted. While roasting a rabbit, hot sparks sprayed out almost igniting her skirt, and when serving ale, her pitcher assaulted not one, but two gentlemen. With profuse apologies, she offered free tankards, which appeased them. Finally, Olivia said she and Titus could manage. Faith didn't argue instead, she sat at her desk staring at nothing.

Titus came by what seemed a few minutes later to tell her Captain Grant was out back examining the ruins. Word must have spread rapidly as the timbers burned. Faith slipped out to meet him. A light wind blew ash about as if it were falling snow. The landscape looked bleached of all color. Even the nearby trees had taken a scorching; their tender leaves gray and ghostly.

Grant's cochineal red jacket stood out amidst the blackened ruins. He knelt to examine some debris and rose as he saw her. Faint wisps of smoke still rose from the damp charred logs behind him. Faith said nothing, letting him choose when to speak.

Grant's face looked bleak. "Was anyone hurt?" He seemed shaken by the carnage. Shadows under his eyes told her he had slept as little as she.

"Not seriously, mostly scrapes and minor burns."

"Unchecked the blaze could have taken half the town. You were fortunate."

"All houses in town are required to have fire buckets, Captain. Many have seen the ravages of fire. We stay prepared."

"Good. Any ideas what caused this?" He gestured at the wreckage.

"Tallow."

An eyebrow cocked up in disbelief. "I was unaware that cooking took place in your meeting room."

"No one was cooking in there, Captain. Someone set this fire. Can't you smell it?"

He wrinkled his nose. "It's impossible to miss. So how does one use rendered pig fat to burn down a house?"

"They probably used candles. Enough of them could start a blaze. Once the dry wood caught, the fire would be nearly impossible to stop." If not for her neighbors... Faith shuddered. She absently scrubbed her face, wondering if she had missed some ash.

"Candles?" Grant prompted.

Faith realized he probably wasn't familiar with the colonial custom of using tallow to make cheap lighting. "Not everyone has a plentiful supply of beeswax. Tallow sputters and does not burn as well but provides a light. Many people use it."

"Do you?"

"Sometimes," she admitted. "But I had none in there."

Grant picked up a long stick and walked toward the burned room. Puzzled, she followed close behind. "What are you doing?"

"Looking for evidence. If someone set fire to this room, they may have left something behind. Although anything we find could just as easily belong to one of your neighbors." Grant dug around various spots being careful to avoid areas that still smoked. As he angrily stabbed into the ground, the stick broke. "It is one thing to kill a man in a fight," he hissed. "It is quite another to set fire to someone's home while they sleep, and leave them and their children to be consumed in flames." Stopping, Grant looked at her with eyes blazing ice blue, "Do you have any enemies, Mistress Clarke? Can you think of anyone who would do this?"

Shocked, Faith stammered. "I don't know." She didn't want to imagine such a thing.

"You and your husband's mother are estranged."

Faith gasped, "Eugenia grieves her son's loss. No matter how much she despises me she wouldn't resort to this." She would never endanger her grandson. "Eugenia is a gentlewoman. Surely you cannot think she rose in the night and slipped halfway across town just to enact some sort of petty vengeance." The idea of her mother-in-law getting out of her opulent bed to sneak about setting fires was ludicrous.

"I will speak with her and see what she knows."

That would definitely cause a reaction. "I am sure she had nothing to do with this." Eugenia had helped Jon pay for the right to establish an inn. She would not jeopardize the investment. Faith looked about at the yard, torn apart by desperate men and women fighting the blaze. Track marks from the fire engine wheels scarred the earth. The ground was scorched and covered in ashes and wood particles. Little escaped being marked by the night's trauma. Given how many people had been present, she did not see how there could be anything left of whoever had started the fire. She followed the captain as he poked about the ruins and used his stick to part the bushes and look beneath. Once or twice, he found a rag, a few nails; he even found a few half-melted, candles that he carefully set to the side. Faith watched him work. She had to lift her skirts to keep them out of the soot and mud in the yard.

"This isn't my first fire," Grant bent down to examine a lump of candles. "I think these must have been tied together." He indicated the dark string that was half-melted into the candles. "Your fire starter must have dropped these on the way in or out, elsewise the flames would have consumed them."

Grant continued to look about. The captain asked about the inn's daily routines, from when deliveries were made, to who frequented the tavern for meals. Faith didn't like the implications but she told him everything as he continued to explore. She kept an eye out for more nails. They could be reused. After a while, Grant stood up. His face was unreadable. He asked for a list of what property she had lost. Taking him into her study, he waited while she inked a quill and wrote out what items had been in her private room then he bowed and left.

Afterwards, Faith went to the sitting room where her grandmother's spinning wheel stood. Her strong hands would cover Faith's young hands teaching her the process. Faith ran her hands over it, letting old memories rise to the surface. Hannah Payne had been an island of refuge. Many times she had run to the older woman to escape her mother's relentless criticism and endless chores. While they spun, her grandmother told her stories of the old country, how her family had come to the new world so they could practice their faith without persecution. Out of her daughter-in-law's earshot, her wicked sense of humor emerged., She told stories about the courtship rites of barnyard cats and how horrified her own mother had been when she realized her children had learned the words to several questionable songs they'd heard the sailors belt out on the journey to America. Her death left a hole in Faith's heart, not much assuaged until she met Jon with his laughing eyes and admiration for a girl longing for a little freedom from a strict life.

Her father had given her the wheel when she wed. "It may as well go where it will receive good use," he said as he put it on the wagon.

As her hands moved with the rhythm of the wheel, Faith thought about the Bullards. Their home was opulent, their clothing expensive. As far as she knew, he had only the one store and no great holdings of land. How could they afford such things? Coinage was a rare commodity in the colonies and what one had frequently had to go to pay the king's taxes. "Wretched taxes," Faith muttered. Williamsburg was rife with opinions both for and against England. She never offered one of her own. The wrong words could disastrously affect business.

Andrew needed more than a tavern to run. He should become a lawyer perhaps or engage in some other respectable profession. He was old enough to become an apprentice. Idly, she wondered if her mother-in-law would support it. Eugenia's second marriage had moved her up into the world. Ezra Moore, a pudgy little man with a soft voice and mild manner, was shrewd when it came to finances. Faith had been shocked when Jon had told her how much land his stepfather owned. He dined with prominent families such as the Washingtons and the Randolphs. He could afford to dress Eugenia well. Ezra ate at the tavern occasionally with his associates. A gesture Faith appreciated considering there were far more impressive establishments that would have welcomed him.

Her mind returned to Bullard's death. Was that why someone had set her tavern ablaze? In the distance, she heard the wild barking of dogs which brought the missing slave girl to mind. Faith remembered seeing Stella in the kitchen. The light of the fire illuminated bruises on the child's arms and neck. It had bothered her, but she had said nothing.

Where would the girl have fled? There were not many places a slave could hide, particularly one suspected of murder. Faith stopped the wheel as a thought possessed her. Putting down her wool, she walked out the door and into the back yard of the tavern stopping at the door of the small barn where livestock stayed, where Titus had so generously done the boy's chores the day of the murder. She was greeted by the cow's soft lowing. A few horses belonging to guests nickered.

"Hello?" Faith called, but there was no reply. Her eyes adjusted swiftly to the dim light inside the building. She carefully checked each stall for signs someone could have hidden there. There was nothing. So intent was she that she did not hear the door open and close.

"Mistress Faith?"

She jumped and turned to see Titus. "I didn't hear you come in."

"Why are you here?"

"I wanted to make sure the boys were doing a good job."

Titus frowned. "There is no need to worry over that. Is there anything else I can help you with?"

She looked into his warm brown eyes. "I wonder if Stella hid in here."

Titus didn't blink. "The captain already searched this barn, the privy, and the smokehouse. I don't think he would have missed her." His strong broad fingers curled in the folds of his shirt disturbing the unusual stillness of his body.

Faith flushed. Titus was a terrible liar and she was putting him in an awkward position. She wondered if she would be better off remaining ignorant, but there was no safety in that. "Stella is in danger. You know how folk react to news of a runaway, much less one suspected of murder."

"Is that what you think, mistress?"

"I don't know," Faith admitted. "She looked too frail to prevail against Bullard. But the authorities want to find her."

"Will anything good happen if they find her?" Titus's tone was soft, but she could see the tension in his hands as he grasped the stall door.

Faith couldn't lie. "No, I think not." Stella would be punished, innocent or guilty because she was a slave. Her only hope lay in escape and that was thin at best. Perhaps ignorance was indeed bliss. Turning, Faith squared her shoulders and looked up at Titus with a determined smile. "I believe you are right, Titus. The boys do excellent work. There is no reason for me to poke about here. I have far more pressing matters to attend." She passed him and walked back to the tavern, steadfastly ignoring the yellow rag Titus stuffed into his pocket.

Faith turned her attention to her common room, wiping down tables and serving drinks to the few men inside. She picked up an abandoned newspaper where a notice caught her eye.

Runaway, a Negro girl named Stella, about sixteen years old, property of the deceased Phineas Bullard of Williamsburg. Last seen wearing a yellow dress and apron and shoes. Anyone who brings her to me will have ten shillings. Charlotte Bullard

Faith had read the notices about runaways before and it never ceased to startle her to see human beings listed among shipments and livestock. Where was Stella? Was she cold and afraid? Had someone provided the runaway with shelter from the winter or was she hiding in the woods, trying to escape to freedom somewhere? Faith didn't know. If she discovered Stella, would she turn her in or let her go? A knot rose in her throat. Turning her in was as good as killing her. Her eyes scanned the page for further notices and stopped at a familiar name.

All persons indebted to the estate of Phineas Bullard, late of Williamsburg, deceased. Are desired to make immediate payment, as his affairs will not admit any indulgences. Those that fail to pay may depend on having their accounts put into a lawyer's hands. Charlotte Bullard

There was no money to pay the debt to Bullard. She looked out at the remains of her private room. Faith could not afford to rebuild. Depending on the generosity of Lottie Bullard, it might not matter anyway. All that remained of her private meeting room was a pile of charred and broken lumber. Ash had been tracked in relentlessly, staining the floorboards blackish gray. Titus had offered to scrub the tavern's floor with lye soap. Faith had thankfully agreed. Although no amount of cleansing would erase the images of the past few days from her mind.

Screams shattered the moment, mixed with wild, excited barking. Faith ran to the doorway to see what was happening. A mob marched down Waller Street loosely surrounding a black woman with a rope around her neck like a leash. At first, all that was visible was the yellow of her dress, then the woman's head lifted. It was Stella. Faith stared in horror. Her heart raced as she surveyed the scene. Men and women gathered around yelling as the girl's captors herded her like an animal toward town. Faith winced as a clod of dirt whizzed by to strike a member of the crowd who cursed. Hatred and fear pulsed through the throng like a gathering storm.

"Kill her!"

"Hang the little bitch!"

The road became a nameless sea of faces screaming and yelling. "Lord have mercy!" Faith had never seen anything so vile. Fear knotted her stomach. Her heart raced as the crowd drew closer. They appeared as mindless as a pack of rabid dogs. A rock hit the side of Stella's head, causing her to stumble. Blood ran unchecked down her cheek in a river of red. Olivia joined Faith on the porch. Her jaw clenched as she witnessed the debacle. The blood seemed to incite the crowd further. More rocks flew, most missing their target or hitting others in the crowd. Titus appeared nearby holding a club between them and the mob. It was a futile gesture. Should the crowd spill over into the inn's yard, nothing could stop them.

Faith wanted to look away, but the sheer brutality of the scene froze her in place. "They'll tear her apart."

Olivia's breathing was uneven. Her voice shook. "There is nothing you can do."

"I can't stand by and do nothing." Yet there she was, Faith realized bitterly, ogling the scene as if she were audience to a play. Anger began to outweigh fear. "My father always said if God be for us, who can stand against us." While her heart beat rapidly, she silently prayed for the courage to act.

Olivia didn't reply. Grief flew across her features before returning to the expressionless mask that Faith was beginning to despise. Her eyes remained on the crowd boiling down the street. In her hands was the knife she had been using to chop winter squash. Faith had no doubt she would use it should the crowd attempt to enter the tavern. Joshua and Andrew were just inside the door out of sight. When one of them tried to come out, a look from Olivia sent them back inside although Faith knew they were watching from the windows. She leaned in until she met a pair of dark eyes.

"Joshua, go out back and run to the barracks. Stay away from the crowd. Tell Captain Grant a mob has Stella. Olivia, mind the tavern!" Gathering her courage, Faith ran out toward the street.

Chaos ruled. Stella's long hair hung over her face in dark tangled strands like a rough veil. Another rock struck and her body jerked. Faith approached the crowd with caution trying to get closer without being drawn into the madness. Neighbors stood and stared, taking in the event as if it were a form of entertainment. A few screamed and threw whatever they could lay their hands on, primarily rocks or clods of dirt.

Faith yelled "Stop!" but no one heard. As she moved toward Stella, a rock whizzed by her ear. Another hit her shoulder with a dull thud causing an exclamation of pain. She stumbled and fell. The crowd in the street made it difficult to move or see. Someone grabbed her hard around the waist and dragged her back. Her head rocked back against a man's chest. His breath was hoarse as he labored to pull her out of the street. Gasping, Faith tried to free herself but he wouldn't let go. Faith struggled as panic set in. "Let me go!" She hissed, twisting to get loose. The intruder continued to drag her back into the grass away from Stella and the enraged throng. No gentleman manhandled a lady like this. She elbowed him hard, connecting with what might be his ribs.

"Ouch!" he yelped in her ear. "Be still!"

The muscular arm dug further in as he swung her around putting himself between her and the mob, then turned her about. Faith didn't recognize him.

"Stay behind me." The man turned halfway so he was not blind to the mob in the road. A sinewy arm blocked anyone from attacking her. Faith struggled to move past him toward Stella.

"Do ye want to be killed?" Her savior hissed as he pushed her back behind him. They both looked at the drama unfolding before them. "You little idjit, that mob will tear you apart!" His hand gripped her forearm to keep her safely on the sidelines. Faith twisted her arm but he tightened his grip. His eyes met hers. "Don't be a fool!"

Faith gasped as Stella fell to the ground only to be dragged up again by someone pulling on the rope. It was choking her. "We can't just watch them kill her."

His laugh was ugly. "They'll not do that. That lot will want a hanging. They think that little girl killed her master and they will want her to pay dearly for their fright."

"You're right." It didn't matter whether Stella was guilty or not. She was damned. Faith's helplessness sickened her. The man's grip loosened although he kept a hand on her arm. Surely there was something she could do! A gunshot rang out suddenly.

Her head jerked. Her rescuer's reaction was quicker. He shoved Faith back, knocking her over. "Get down!" Rising up cautiously, she looked about, seeing nothing but the solid back of her infuriating protector. Silence fell over the crowd. Standing on tiptoe, she peered over his shoulder.

Smoke drifted from a pistol held by a British officer on horseback. She realized it was Captain Grant. Backed by foot soldiers, he rode fearlessly toward the mob. Grant's scarlet coat looked almost garish amidst the homespun browns and tans of those gathered in the street. His mount snorted nervously amidst the restless crowd. The reins were looped around one gloved hand, the other held his weapon. Faith spotted the pistol's mate at the ready at Grant's side. He motioned his foot soldiers and they moved forward with their bayonets extended. There was something comforting in the precision and order of troops who were forcibly dispersing the crowd. They offered little resistance. The unruly madness began to fade.

"Disperse immediately or face the consequences," he bellowed. "This colony is ruled by English Law and English Courts. Anyone found disrupting the peace will be arrested and held until trial." He kicked his horse forward and moved into the crowd, meeting the eyes of men and women as they parted about him. Grant's bayonet was sheathed in the saddle, as was his rifle. As he passed, he exchanged his spent pistol for one primed and ready to fire.

A man yelled, "She killed Bullard!" Grant nudged his horse. The large dappled gray moved forward until its nose nearly brushed the accuser's shoulder. She could not read his lips, but she could see that while his left hand held the reins, the right kept the pistol. Neither man moved. Grant's eyes stayed on the man as he spoke. The man retreated, backing away until he melted into the remaining crowd, eventually disappearing. The big horse wheeled about controlled by the captain. People began to disperse, leaving the scene to resume their business. Grant's men on foot infiltrated the crowd and surrounded Stella, who lay crumpled on the road. Faith wondered if she was dead. In moments, only soldiers remained. Two of them grasped her under the arms and pulled her roughly upright. The girl staggered but remained erect. Her eyes were dazed and her face was bloody, but she was undeniably alive.

Grant nodded at his men. "Take her to the gaol. Put Pelham in charge of her care until she can be tried. Clap irons on anyone who causes a disturbance. The court will decide her fate."

Faith exhaled. It was over, for now. Her shoulder hurt, she was covered in dirt, but Stella was alive. The gaoler would keep her alive for now although Faith harbored no illusions about justice. Guilty or innocent she would hang.

Faith saw Grant look into the crowd. She stepped out from behind her protector. Grant's eyes widened with recognition. She met his eyes calmly as she brushed the dirt from her clothes. Faith knew she looked rough, but refused to show fear. There was a question in his eyes. She smiled faintly and shrugged. Grant looked at her sharply as if he would speak, then nodded and turned to his men. At his gesture, they began the short march to the outer edge of town. The Captain walked his horse behind his men as they took Stella to the gaol. His pistol remained in his hand. Faith watched them for a while, shading the sun's glare with her hand. She crushed her skirt folds in her hands.

"Ye be all right?"

"What?" Faith looked up to see her stubborn protector staring down at her. He was only slightly taller than she.

"Ye be all right? You are not hurt?" His gaze swept her top to bottom. Faith would have been offended if it were not for the obvious concern on his face. The man was probably about her age, which made him less than thirty. Pale freckles dusted a long bony face. A distinctively, long nose swept down to an expressive mouth that indicated by its faint creases it knew the warmth of a smile.

"I'm fine," she said, trying to swallow the knot in her throat.. "Far better than that child."

He stared over at the soldiers disappearing down the road with Stella. A faint cloud of dust kicked up and blurred the figures. "You mean the slave?"

"She is still a human being."

"Well yes, but if someone owns you one way or another, most consider you a little less than that." Despite his neutral expression, emotion lay underneath his words. Faith looked at him carefully. He was dressed cheaply, but presentably. His clothes had obviously been made to fit someone else. They hung on his lanky frame. His long, freckled fingers hopelessly stained, which marked him as a printer. Over his breeches and shirt was a leather apron also marked with ink. Her eyes met his.

"Will MacKay." He bowed and she could see his hair was tied back with a piece of frayed rope. His expression was still grim.

"Street mobs can kill you if you are not careful, my lady. I might not be around to rescue you another time."

Faith stared at him for a long moment. She wasn't used to being protected. "Maybe next time I'll rescue you."

He raised an eyebrow. A reluctant smile curved his lips. "Perhaps."

"You're a printer."

"I work for a printer," he corrected. "As you can see," he held up his stained hands ruefully. "Tis a hands-on affair. Twill be six years and seven months before I'm free to begin my own business." It was an indirect way of admitting he was an indentured servant.

She lifted her apron, which was stained with flour, among other things. "I understand. I am Faith Clarke. Tavern keeping is also a hands-on business." Not a day went by when the evidence of her work did not cover her in some manner.

She eyed him thoughtfully. His voice had the lilting musical rhythm that marked him as Irish or Scot She wasn't sure which. His hair was unruly and most of the reddish-brown strands had escaped from the piece of hemp that tied it back. His mouth quirked in a half-smile as he spoke to her. "Should you want to advertise yer fine establishment, you could do no better than the *Virginia Gazette*."

"Which one would you be referring to? There are at least three in operation that I'm aware of." Faith asked dryly. She had no idea which one had recently hired on an assistant.

"The best one, of course," he retorted. "I work for Mistress Clements."

Faith found herself smiling at him without exactly knowing why. Something in her wanted to see that smile widen. It was an odd thought to have.

"I will have to give that consideration," she murmured. Will MacKay looked at her wistfully, perhaps too directly. Faith shivered. It was too soon for her to think of a man as attractive, especially one indentured to another.

Apparently, he had similar thoughts. His eyes broke off from hers and he moved away from her carefully as if touching her was dangerous.

"I must be off, Mistress Clarke. My mistress will be expecting me at the press." He bowed and walked swiftly down Prince of Gloucester Street toward the printer he worked for. Only one newspaper was run by a woman. She pondered Will MacKay. His thin body and pale face, barely touched by the sun all bore witness to the fact he was a fairly recent arrival to the colonies. Poor people came to the colonies as indentured servants. At the marketplace, the well-to-do paid for their passage in exchange for servitude for seven years, more or less. Georgia Clements needed a man to help out with the press since her husband's death. Master MacKay apparently fit her requirements. She could still see him walking back towards Duke of Gloucester Street although he was rapidly becoming an indistinct figure among the many other people out and about. Will MacKay walked upright and proud as if he didn't care what others thought. Faith wondered if that pride would endure the length of his bondage.

Chapter Six

Faith should be in her tavern, tending her patrons and keeping an eye on the liquor. There were victuals to be gathered from the cellar for tomorrow's meals and coin to be counted. But she could not focus on any of those tasks. Her mind replayed the horrifying image of Stella being dragged away. Faith could not bear the thought of the young girl alone in such a grim place. She had never before been where prisoners waited to be tried although she knew it was not far from her tavern.

Well behind the grounds of the capital, the gaol lay on the outskirts of town. Faith carried a container of food and a wool blanket. The late afternoon sun cast long shadows on the ground along the quiet footpath that led to the prison. A breeze stirred the air making the leaves whisper overhead as if they were sharing secrets. Hugging her shawl around her did not help the chill inside. After so much violence and death, Faith wondered when the sun would truly shine again.

There was something grimly unnerving about the place even though she knew it was a residence as well as a prison. The Gaoler and his large family lived there. Drawing closer, her nose picked up the odors of privy, blood and sweat emanating from the simple brick building. No soldiers were visible. These prisoners were under the care of the gaoler and his family. Nevertheless, she was sure someone kept watch. Over the years, the gaol had housed pirates, drunkards, and other lawless individuals. A sturdy fence encircled much of the grounds.

Knocking on the gaoler's door, she was greeted by a child of perhaps twelve. "Is your father home?" The little girl shook her head. Her mother appeared.

It was apparently wash day. The strong smell of soap emanated from the woman. Her clothing was damp and her knuckles raw from scrubbing. A very small child clung to her skirts.

"Greetings, Mistress Pelham. I am seeking the young slave brought here earlier today."

The woman nodded. "She's around back. There aren't many awaiting trial right now, you'll find her quick enough. I'll have one of the boys unlock the door." The door closed.

Faith heard a voice calling, answered by another. Not lingering, she walked down the steps and to the cells behind the house. Yet another boy unlocked the big wooden door that led to the brick courtyard. Stout wooden doors were on either side. Cut into each was a narrow metal grill. Men peered through, eyes glittering in the shadowed light. They could be murderers or thieves. The gaol housed them all.

"She's there." The boy pointed to a cell to the left. Peering into the grill set into the window, Faith's heart twisted when she saw the huddled figure within the dark space furnished sparsely with a pail and loose straw. Although private, the cell was no place for comfort or peace. The door creaked as it swung in casting afternoon sun on the dirt floor.

"Stella?" There was no response. Faith repeated it a little louder and the girl's body jerked as her head turned to look toward the cell's entrance. Faith caught her breath. Even in the shadows left by the lowering sun, she could see blood. It had dried in her hair leaving it stuck up in odd tufts like a wild animal. Stella's face was bruised and smudged with blood from a cut lip. Her clothes were filthy. Blood and dirt-stained her shift. Her bodice was ripped so that it hung off one shoulder. Brown stains on her skirt delivered the unmistakable scent of manure through which she must have been dragged. Her feet were bare. None of her wounds had been dressed. Anger made Faith's hands shake. Sticking her head out the door she addressed the man who had let her inside. "This child is injured. Why haven't her injuries been tended?"

The door shut behind her. Faith shuddered. What would it be like to be incarcerated in such a place?

Before opening her mouth and saying regrettable words, she turned to Stella. "I'm Mistress Clarke. I own the tavern you were at a few days ago. I've brought you some food and a blanket. If you let me, I will tend your injuries." Faith hoped they weren't serious. She could tend minor wounds, but serious ones needed the skills of a physician or apothecary.

Faith yelled at the closed door. She knew that the boy remained even if he chose to remain quiet. "I need clean water, wine, and bandages." The cage stank of blood and urine and there were no blankets in sight despite the growing chill as the sun set. The girl huddled in the back. Behind her, the door squealed as it cracked open.

"That's a murderer, ma'am. She stabbed her master and left him in some seedy inn." The voice sounded young, probably one of the children parroting what he had heard.

Faith resisted snarling. This was a child, even if she seriously wanted to shake him. "I am proprietress of Clarke Inn, which is far better kept than this establishment." She let her eyes circle the interior to convey her contempt. "I know who she is. No one has determined her guilt or innocence yet and all of God's creatures deserve mercy. Captain Grant knows me. Now bring a basin. This child's wounds need tending. She should see a doctor."

Pelham's voice came through the gate. "All prisoners are fed and cared for. I am responsible for all these prisoners. I can't leave you alone with her. What if she attacks you? My eldest is apprenticed to a doctor, he checks on all the prisoners. You want water; there is a bucket right there." Then she saw the fresh pail just inside the door. He must have slipped it in while she looked Stella over. It wasn't the words so much as the way he said them and the faint but unmistakable scent of rum that made her want to take it and throw it in his face. She didn't, practicality outweighed the short-term satisfaction such an act might provide, or so she convinced herself. The bucket was oak and heavy with its load of water. It took effort to pull it over. It took the threat of angering Grant and a large section of apple pie from the food she'd brought to get him to bring her a roll of linen.

One of the gaoler's sons came down and passed a preparation of black snake root inside. "Ma uses this for our scrapes." Faith nodded her thanks as she took the concoction from the boy who scampered away once the delivery was made. Her watcher declined to bring alcohol for cleaning her wounds evidently preferring to drink it. She hoped he choked.

Faith took the remaining food over to Stella. "I brought you some supper." Faith kept her voice soft. Something about the girl made her think of an injured deer she had seen as a child. Too badly hurt to survive, it had gazed at her with all the pain of the world in its expression, right before Papa had put it out of its misery with a bullet. Stella slowly turned toward her. She was not much bigger than Andrew. "Why don't you eat, then I will tend your wounds."

There was no place to sit so Faith settled on the straw nearby as the girl hesitatingly took the crock of food and eyed it cautiously before snatching it close. Faith realized she probably had not eaten in days. Murderess or not, no one deserved to be treated like this. Stella stuffed the food in her mouth as if she feared it being taken away. Stewed rabbit, carrots, potatoes, and biscuits, washed down with water from the bucket cupped in a hand. Her thin shoulders and stick-like arms spoke of few meals. Bullard had been a corpulent and wealthy man. Anger washed over Faith when she considered the disparity. She had seen plenty like him back home and here in Virginia; wealthy, pompous, and privileged, dressed in fine clothes and unwilling to dirty their hands with an honest living. Bullard apparently chose to be blind to the basic needs of those who served him. God might have mercy on his soul but Faith had none.

Stella turned away, guarding her food as she hurried to finish it. She waited for the child to finish eating. Faith kept her distance, not wanting to frighten her further. Her hands wrapped themselves in her skirts as she looked up and out as stars began appearing faintly above the dimming sun. There were no clouds so the rising crescent moon was evident as well as the evening star below. The walls of the gaol prevented Faith from seeing the glory of the sunset, but the faint warm glow of the sky was still faintly evident at its edges. She prayed to find the right words to get Stella to talk. She could possibly hold the key to all the answers Faith so desperately needed. The dinner pail hit the ground between them.

Her eyes downcast, Stella spoke. "Saw you at the tavern." Her voice was lightly spiced with an accent as if she had come from one of the sugar islands out in the Caribbean.

"Yes," Faith replied. "I found Bullard's body the next day. I didn't know what happened to you. I was afraid you might have been hurt."

Stella didn't reply. When Faith touched her arm, she trembled.

"I'm going to clean your wounds now." Moving slowly, Faith took her own handkerchief and wet it and started to gently wash the blood off the girl's face. Stella's eyes were gently tilted at the corner and dark, with long curling lashes. Something about her reminded Faith of Olivia although the girl was a good bit younger. "Summer will be coming soon," Faith began. "I don't know how long you've been in Virginia, but it can be pretty warm." Stella remained silent.

"My cook, Olivia, manages the kitchen. I don't know how she bears the heat."

"It gets hotter in Jamaica," Stella murmured.

"Is that where you are from?"

"Me and Olivia both."

"You know Olivia?"

"She's my sister. Master sold her off just after her sixteenth birthday. I went later, sold with my ma to Bullard."

Faith stopped as realization hit. They were sisters and Olivia had not said a word, given no indication that she had seen her sister. Her mind pictured her cook hard at work in the kitchen, with all her knives carving a variety of carcasses with brutal efficiency. She forced her mind away from the image. She drew in a deep breath. "Your mother is a slave to the Bullards?"

Stella shook her head. "She died on the way over. Master was quite angry about that. He said it was a waste of money."

Anger bubbled up. Faith was beginning to understand why someone would want to kill him. She was beginning to consider it a public service. Pausing in her ministrations, Faith gently swept hair from Stella's face. It was long and coarse, rich and deep in color, like molasses. Faith realized that underneath all the blood and filth, Stella was beautiful. Her face cleaned,

Faith started on her arms. Faith winced at the bruises she could see in the dimming light, some were dark, others were yellowed. Life had not been kind. For all she knew, the child could have broken or bruised ribs. The thought was troubling. The cuts and bruises looked minor despite the swelling, but Faith had seen the senseless savagery of the mob. Stella was lucky to be alive.

"I will ask Dr. Staunton to come by and check your injuries. He has tended my family since we have been in Williamsburg. I brought you a blanket. It's old but quite warm I assure you. The nights are still somewhat chilly but the days will be getting warmer."

"Why are you doing this? Stella's voice was soft, too soft for the man outside the cell to hear.

"I didn't like what I saw in the street earlier," Faith replied, struggling to explain her actions. "T'was wrong for people to treat you like that. They were animals."

"I didn't kill him."

Faith stared at the girl. Stella's eyes were bright with tears but her voice was calm. "They'll hang me, but he was alive when I left that room. I ate supper with your slaves and waited until late like he told me. It got late, late enough I knew the mistress would be angry if I went back to the house without him so I peeked in the door to see if it was time to go." Stella trembled. "I saw him on the floor, with that sword sticking out."

"His saber?"

"It was stuck in his gut, like it pinned him to the floor. He turned to look at me, his eyes all glassy, and then he just died." Stella's voice grew hoarse. "I knew everyone would say I done it. So, I ran."

Faith couldn't blame her. Everyone would assume she killed him because it was an easy solution. Yet Bullard was a stout man, he would be a powerful opponent. How could someone like Stella kill him? Bullard had been cut deep, neatly like a hog being butchered. The details caught her mind. Where had the saber gone after Stella fled? The answer frightened her. It meant the killer had lingered long enough to go back and retrieve the weapon, out there in her yard watching everyone go about their business as his quarry died.

"Who came to see him that night? Was it a business acquaintance?" Maybe Bullard had pushed someone too far. Faith loathed doing business with the man. He had haggled mercilessly over the amenities to go with the room. Pressing Faith over the debt she owned until he had gotten the room for free. Demanding only the best and most expensive from her kitchen and then criticizing the fare. Faith had dreamed about him choking to death. It was easy to imagine someone killing him in a moment of rage.

Stella gave an ugly laugh. "Not the type of business you're thinking about. His regular business he handled at the store. He came to your place for things he didn't want anyone else to know about." She caught her breath as dirt was cleansed from each wound.

Faith continued to work, stroking on ointment with a gentle hand, binding a nasty cut on her leg, hoping her silence would encourage the girl to continue speaking.

Stella took it as condemnation. "I didn't kill him!" The girl's panic-stricken voice tore at her. As the girl sobbed, Faith stopped her ministrations and patted her shoulder trying to offer an assurance she did not feel.

"I believe you, but you could have seen who did. I need you to continue. Tell me everything about that night."

Stella sighed. "He called me to attend him just before we left. He was pleased with himself, like he was getting away with something he shouldn't. Mistress Charlotte was out making calls, so I figured he was up to something. He didn't ask for me when she was about. It made her mad when he messed around with her slaves, not that it stopped him. Nothing ever really stopped him from what he wanted and she didn't really care as long as she got her fancy clothes and nice things. Mistress always wanted to know what he was about but he didn't like her to know all his business."

Faith turned as someone tapped on the door. No sooner had she cracked it open than someone handed her a flask and shut it back. Strong fumes of brandy wafted out as once it was open. Deciding it would help settle the girl, she handed it to Stella who took a long drink, choking on it briefly. The girl offered but Faith waved her off. "You have more need of it than I."

Stella took another gulp before continuing. "I dressed his hair, polished his shoes, and helped with his coat. Then he gave me a bottle of wine to carry. He tucked some papers in his pocketbook and we went to your place."

"I don't recall seeing a pocketbook."

Stella gave a grim smile. "You wouldn't have missed it. It was embroidered all fancy with red and yellow flowers, about so big." She put her hands together flat. "He used it for his coins and papers. It was always stuffed full."

"What else?"

"Besides the sword sticking in him? It was a fancy brass piece he liked to wear. He was always getting that thing polished."

"He was stabbed with his own side piece?"

Stella shrugged. "Sure looked like it."

Faith let Stella continue speaking about their arrival at Clarke Tavern and his sending her to the kitchen to get his supper, but her mind was on the sword. Neither it nor the pocketbook had been in the room when she had entered. The murderer had to have taken them. Could it be as simple as robbery?

Faith looked at Stella who had paused to take a few breaths. "Who visited him that night?"

"Don't know. He sent me back to the kitchen and told me not to come back until he sent for me. I stayed with Olivia, not that anyone will believe me." Stella shook. "I'm going to hang."

Faith gripped Stella's fingers gently. "I will talk to Captain Grant. Surely, he will look at the case fairly. We are an English colony, ruled by English law." Brave words she knew to be a lie, but the truth was too brutal to express.

"Not for slaves," Stella whispered. "I learned that a long time ago."

Faith shook her head in denial. "Justice sees no color, Stella. I will speak to the captain. We will find the truth." She tried to sound confident but knew better than to believe Stella would face any type of justice. Faith just couldn't admit it.

Stella continued sobbing. Not knowing what to do, Faith took the child in her arms feeling tears burn in her own eyes. She almost didn't hear the knock on the door.

The gaoler himself opened the cell door. "Mistress Clarke, it's time you left. You should not be here anyway. I could get in trouble. A gentlewoman should not be in the gaol alone with a criminal."

"She's not an animal." Faith glared. He was a symbol of all that was wrong with humanity. Hugging Stella gently, she rose. Reluctantly, the girl let go and wrapped herself in the blanket. As Faith rose, she said, "Olivia will be by in the morning with food and clothes."

"Who's Olivia?" Pelham asked suspiciously.

"Her slave," Stella said.

Faith winced. She didn't like to think of Olivia and Titus that way. The truth hurt. They had no more rights than Stella and should something happen to her, they would receive as little justice. But how could she afford to free them?

The gaoler waited for her to leave. "No one will harm her here. I swear it."

"No one will save her either," Faith replied as the door was locked behind her. Through the barred window she saw Stella drinking brandy as tears ran down her face.

The walk home in the deepening shadows was long. Her father's face rose in her mind, speaking of the innate evil of owning people. "God created all men equal. It is man that decided that one can possess another, like a cow or sheep." He had been quick to condemn when he learned that Jon's family owned slaves and she had been quick to defend her new husband, even when she knew he was wrong. Faith still felt her father's disappointment although the moment had been years ago.

When she got back to the inn, she sent Joshua with a request that Dr. Staunton attended Stella the next day. As darkness fell and the last patron left, she secured the tavern and retired to her room. As Faith said her prayers, she remembered Stella as well as Bullard's family who had lost a husband and father. Sleep did not come easily.

The next morning, Faith sent Olivia to the gaol. Her return was marked by silence as her steps echoed down the hall and out back. Later, as Faith pulled onions out of the garden, she heard ragged sobs from the kitchen. She rose to help but stopped when she heard Titus' voice as well. His croons became a soft lullaby to his wife whose pain emanated through the kitchen wall. Tears rose in Faith's eyes as she stood frozen in the yard listening to the agonized cries.

Faith found solace in the garden where she busied herself collecting items for dinner. A light breeze teased something white from within the hedge near the back gate. Puzzled, she went over for a closer look, wondering if someone had lost a handkerchief. It took a few minutes to disentangle it from the stubborn branch that held it close. Faith shook it out and realized she held a small child's gown, torn and splattered with dark rusty stains.

"How did that get here?" She stuffed it into her pocket before turning back toward the inn. The kitchen had grown silent but Faith remained hesitant to intrude. She left a few cabbages stacked neatly outside the door before slipping into the back of her tavern.

Supper time had her dealing with an inebriated patriot who insisted on sharing his opinions in song. Unfortunately, music was not among his gifts. By the time Titus got the man out the door and staggering home, it was late. Faith checked to make sure all the fires were out before heading to bed. There were no answers to be found in the darkened tavern or in sleep either.

Chapter Seven

Cleaning up from the fire took days. Faith and Titus spent time poking about the ruins of the private room checking for live coals. Once they were certain it was safe, they began stacking charred debris to one side of the yard. Titus then cut away damaged tree limbs before proceeding to the damaged skeleton of what had been the private room of Clarke Tavern. Faith refused to let the boys enter the collapsed ruin but kept them on the outside picking up burned bits of wood. Ezra sent over men to dismantle what remained.

She was grateful for the distraction when a group of farmers arrived from western Virginia and practically set up shop in the common room. For the next few days, they plied local men with food and drink as they attempted to forge contracts for their wheat and whisky.

Faith went over the room in her mind, the table, the chairs, and the fireplace until she wasn't sure if what she saw was accurate or simply how the room was normally kept. No recollection came of a pocket book or the man's saber. All that came to mind was Bullard's dead body.

Faith pondered what Stella had said. There was little chance that a scrawny creature like her could wrestle Phineas Bullard, much less slit his throat and gut him. No weapon had been found. It struck her as strange that it had not turned up.

Bullard's wife could claim the girl but Faith suspected the only future Stella faced was a noose. Would Captain Grant be satisfied with that? He didn't seem the type to stop at an easy answer, but then he had implied that she or her slaves could have easily committed the crime. He had taken the token of the Sons of Liberty with him, not that there was any sign of who had left it there or when.

Going down to the cellar, Faith gathered the last of the small pumpkins stored over the winter and brought them to the kitchen, placing them along a wall, out of the way until needed. Olivia stood over the long wooden table chopping vegetables that would go into an enormous stew pot with venison and spices to cook slowly all day.

"Did Stella seem upset when she ate with you?"

Olivia checked a rabbit on a spit. Not satisfied, she adjusted it until fat hissed as it dripped down into the hot coals. The cook busied herself about the fire. As she spoke, she checked the Dutch oven where bread was baking, scraping off dead coals and increasing the number of hot ones so it would bake evenly. "No ma'am. She came and got his tray and came back. Said he told her to come back later and they would go home."

Faith looked at the bowl Olivia had placed on the table, surmised her next task, and began handing her ingredients. "Did she know who he was meeting?"

Olivia shook her head. "Not his name although she said she had seen him before. Master dismissed her told her not to come back til 'bout midnight."

"Why didn't you tell me she was your sister?" A knot tightened around her heart as she waited for a response.

The silence grew heavy as Olivia started to turn away. Faith reached out and grasped her wrist gently. "I need the truth."

"What good would it have done? Stella belonged to that man! No matter that he beat and abused her, there was nothing anyone could do." Her eyes blazed. "I'm glad he's dead. Bullard deserves to burn in Hell." She picked up her knife and savagely chopped carrots to bits. Even distressed, she didn't miss a strike.

Faith's voice softened. "For your sake, I will do what I can to see she is treated humanely."

Olivia sounded tired. "No one can help her now."

"I can press Captain Grant. We can take her food, blankets, and clothes."

"Like a charity."

"What would you have me do?" Her breath came hard and heavy as she struggled with emotions long suppressed. Her stomach tied itself in knots as unwanted tears welled in her eyes.

Olivia stared at her. "We're slaves. What do you care?"

"You're far more than that. Surely you know that. You took care of me after Jon died. Both you and Titus comforted him as he lay dying. You treated him like family." Olivia had stayed with her day in and day out when Jon's mother had been too busy making accusations and Faith's mother did not respond to letters, as she had done since Faith married and left the Quaker way of life.

Olivia gaped at her. "You consider me family?"

"I consider you and Titus family. I didn't get a choice about your enslavement, I did everything I could to ensure Joshua would be free." It hadn't been easy. Jon had been incredulous, his mother impossible. But Jon yielded after Joshua saved baby Andrew from a rattler strike, getting bitten in the process.

"There is so much more I want to do, but right now we have to solve this murder. If Stella didn't do it, someone else did. There remains a killer in Williamsburg who is free to strike again."

Olivia finished the carrots and began dismembering a few turnips with sharp chops of her blade. "So, who do you think did it?"

Faith sifted through her memories of that night. With the exception of a few travelers who had stayed with her on previous occasions, her patrons were working men who lived in or near Williamsburg. Some men just came to drink and discuss news with one another. She couldn't remember every face. Men had gone back and forth to the privy during the evening but who had turned and gone to see Bullard?

"Has she told you anything about that night?"

Olivia shook her head. "Stella's pretty shook up. She's saying she doesn't remember, but I'm not sure about that. Stella ate with the boys and then helped me with dishes. We talked a little bit. It was late and we were tired. She went out to see if he was done and never came back. I thought they had gone home until Titus found his body. I'm not sure where she went after that."

Faith decided not to enlighten her that she knew where the girl had hidden for a short time. "How long has it been since you last saw her?" Williamsburg was small enough it was possible that the two women had met at the market or other places in town.

Olivia did not answer. Pain etched her features. Faith touched her shoulder and felt it stiffen. "Don't turn away, I want to help."

Olivia shuddered and took a deep breath. "I hadn't seen her since I left Jamaica. She'd grown so much I almost didn't recognize her."

"I'm so sorry."

"Stella will hang,"

Faith couldn't lie, "I fear she will, but I don't believe she did anything besides run away. We need to find who was with Bullard."

Olivia shrugged. "What good will it do?"

"It gives us another plausible suspect." Faith stood resolute. "She will be no one's scapegoat."

"She'll still be dead." Olivia shuddered. "Nothing you can do 'bout that."

"I can clear her name. Let them know they killed an innocent and God will judge them accordingly." Olivia rubbed her eyes and turned to the fire. Faith left her working in silence.

Restlessness consumed her as she walked back to the common room. Bitterness bubbled up inside. "No one owns family." Once again Faith stood at a crossroads between her conscience and her need to survive. Olivia and Titus were necessary for the inn to continue, but at what cost? "What right do I have to hold onto people for my own benefit?" Frustrated she slapped a door, the stinging of her hand was nothing compared to that within her soul.

While serving the midday meal, a few British soldiers lingered near the hearth. Pouring them ale, Faith struck up a conversation and discovered Grant was at the capital. The initial rush was over and only a few lingered over their food. Leaving her guests in Titus' capable hands, Faith wrapped a peace offering in a clean cloth and set out to meet him. She couldn't take too long; she had promised Olivia some time to visit her sister which was all the comfort she could offer.

Grant stood beneath the curved archway that led to the entrance to the capitol. Late morning light cast shadows on his face. Two other gentlemen stood with him. Their fancy powdered wigs and velvet knee breeches indicated they were gentry. Since the House of Burgesses was not currently in session, there were relatively few at the capitol. Nevertheless, Faith could not put names with their vaguely familiar faces. Although she was certain her mother-in-law Eugenia would have recognized them and known their families, Faith was not a part of that society. Upon seeing her, the captain nodded in acknowledgment. His polite expression changed to a frown when she paused for him to finish his conversation. Grant spoke briefly in a soft voice she could not hear before separating from the men who continued under the arches and into the heart of the brick building. As she stepped closer, he looked mildly curious. "Mistress Clarke, what brings you here?"

Grant knew Clarke tavern was only a short distance away. Nerves tied knots in her stomach; she had little talent in getting people to share information, "I fear I was rude to you when last we spoke and wanted to apologize. The shock of such a horrible incident was most upsetting. I made scones this morning. I thought you might enjoy a few." Faith handed him the cloth-wrapped parcel hoping she did not sound like an idiot. The scent of cinnamon and apples warmed the air. He sniffed appreciatively

"Our London cook used to make scones like these." Grant took the basket from her. "Thank you, Mistress Clarke. This is most kind." Removing one from the cloth he nibbled an end before wolfing the remainder of the piece down. He delicately licked his fingers then wiped them on a handkerchief he had tucked into his uniform. Faith could detect no stain or wrinkle in his clothes. He looked like he had just left his tailor. "But I doubt your only business was to provide me with scones. How may I assist you?" Despite the mildness of his tone, his pale eyes were intent.

Faith flushed. He looked like a hawk assessing a mouse. She would prefer not to get caught in those claws. "Can we talk, privately?"

"Certainly, I have no pressing business beyond protecting our fair city. Perhaps a turn, about the yard would suit your purpose." He turned and waited for her, ever the gentleman. Grant represented the military, the privileged class, and the might of Mother England. Who was she to challenge him? But determination prevailed over cowardice. Faith refused to back down.

Leaves and gravel crunched under the weight of the captain's highly polished boots as they walked together. Small green leaves fleshed out what had recently been the skeletons of trees. It would be a few weeks before the trees filled out enough to soften the austerity of the place. The spring air felt cool against her cheeks. Perhaps that was why she felt like shivering.

Grant lifted an eyebrow in inquiry. Unless her eyes deceived her, he could not be more than thirty, yet already a captain. How had he achieved such a thing? But rank could be purchased if one's family had the coin and connections. That would also explain his excellent tailoring. His watchful gaze did nothing to calm her anxiety.

"I have seen Stella," Faith began, drawing breath. "Surely there is a better option than caging that child like an animal for all to see and abuse."

"No one will abuse her. Pelham is a fair man. She will be fed and sheltered along with the others in the gaol. I have a few men down there to keep an eye out. Murder tends to incite fear and prejudice in people. Those walls keep her safe. Consider what would happen were I to free her; the moment she set foot on the street a crowd would soon gather to administer their own justice."

Faith didn't like to admit he was right. Surely, he knew what sorts of people were locked away in the gaol. The cells were full of drunks, thieves, and murderers, the lowest dregs of society.

"Her treatment is no worse than any other person incarcerated. She will remain there until her trial."

"That is a few months away," Faith pointed out. The courts met in June and December. It would be several weeks before one convened.

"The girl needs to be locked away for her own protection. You saw what happened. Normally decent law, abiding people are capable of anything when panicked. Her chances of survival are better there." Grant's face was grim. "She is lucky to be alive. Had I not challenged the mob they would have beaten her to death."

Faith considered what would happen to Stella outside of the prison. "Do you believe she killed him?"

"We are all capable of killing, my dear lady. The question is, would we? Stella was a pretty girl owned by a pompous, ill-tempered man. The simplest answer is that she took the first opportunity she could to free herself."

"But is it the right answer? Bullard had many enemies. Stella was not the only person who might have wanted him dead."

Grant sighed. "No, she's not. Bullard was rumored to be a difficult man to do business with. But innuendo is not proof. She was there in the private room with him. Even the little I have been able to gather tells me she had good reason to desire him dead."

"Where would she have gotten a weapon? Bullard died violently, cut to pieces. Where would a slave get such a weapon, much less know how to use it? Would Stella have had the strength to fight such a large man? It makes no sense."

"Slaves use knives and sharp implements for all kinds of work. I would wager your own kitchen houses many sharp blades used for anything from harvesting cabbage to slaughtering a hog. There is even an axe close by that your man uses to chop wood. A desperate slave could have grabbed any of those and who would notice them gone 'til morning? Stella is stronger than she appears. There is no tolerance for weakness in a slave as you should know. If she couldn't work, Bullard would have gotten rid of her. She may appear childlike but fear and desperation can lead to actions an individual would normally be incapable of committing. Perhaps he abused her one too many times. Bullard carried a saber like many gentlemen. It wasn't with his body. Maybe she grabbed it in desperation and slew him in self-defense."

Part of her contemplated the possibility, but Faith refused to admit it. "His wife mentioned his saber and wallet were missing. So you believe that Stella took his wallet and then slit his throat and gutted him like a pig?"

Grant's eyes bore into hers. "How do you know so many details about his death?" His voice was sharp.

"I found him. I went with Dr. Staunton when he examined the body. Whoever did that had to have been insane, enraged, or both. It was horrible." Faith felt sick remembering. She doubted she would ever get the images of Bullard's bloody body out of her mind.

Grant waited until her breathing stabilized. "You never forget your first exposure to violent death," he said quietly. "You learn to accept it, but it doesn't make it easier."

"I keep seeing him."

He showed no surprise. "The horror fades in time. I doubt you will forget it, but the mind adjusts to the shock as more experiences come."

Faith found that idea more disturbing than comforting.

"I was not even twenty when I saw my first victim of scalping. I would like to say I took it like a good soldier but the truth is I vomited all over the poor man. My commanding officer was furious." His expression was rueful. "Bullard's death was terrible and nothing will change that. The best I can do is provide justice and hope that will comfort his family."

"Does that help?"

"Sometimes."

"Why are you investigating his death? Surely that is the job of the sheriff or the magistrate?"

The wind blew a lock of hair across his forehead softening his features. He was virtually a stranger. She knew very little about his beliefs or leanings. Keeping the peace was Grant's business but what would he do to maintain order? His gaze considered her for a moment or two before replying.

"Bullard was a loyal citizen to the crown as well as an influential businessman. I knew him as a reliable source of information regarding the leanings of the town. I fear that may have resulted in his death. I have a certain responsibility to find out. His murder inflames passions on every side, but whether the Governor will wish me to continue to handle it or not I cannot say. Unrest continues to spread throughout the colonies. My regiment may be called north to deal with issues there. Boston has been in a state of sedition for months." He rubbed his eyes and Faith realized he was exhausted. He looked down at her and smiled ruefully, "I can see that you are not going to let this rest although why the fate of one hapless slave troubles you so, I do not know. I give you my word that I will do what I can to ensure that Stella is not ill-treated, Mistress Clarke."

Faith believed him. She also realized he did not have time or resources to seek difficult answers. Throughout the town, she had heard the discord of those who supported as well as those who decried the actions of king and parliament. But those issues did not affect her as directly as Phineas Bullard's murder. It had to be resolved or her tavern would never recover. She could not let that happen. "Mistress Bullard mentioned her husband's pocketbook was missing, did you see it?"

"This is the first I have heard of it. No such item was with his body." He looked at her assessing. "I was unaware that you and Charlotte Bullard traveled in the same circles, Mistress Clarke."

Faith flushed. "We don't. But I thought it courteous to offer condolences given the situation."

Grant raised an eyebrow. "Indeed. How much comfort did she take from your visit?"

Faith gritted her teeth. There was no way she was sharing the humiliation. "Mistress Bullard seemed to have her emotions well in hand."

"The funeral is later today. Do you intend to offer your comfort there as well?"

"I do not. I am neither family nor a close friend. It would not be appropriate." She didn't add she had no desire to see Bullard's body ever again. Faith curtsied before he could ask anything further. "Thank you for your time, Captain, I must return to care for my guests."

"Mistress Clarke?"

"Yes?"

"It would be wise to leave the investigation of this crime to those with experience. Poking about Bullard's life is not for an innocent. He was useful but he dealt with unsavory people as well. You would do better to stay in your tavern and take care of your patrons."

"My inn's reputation remains tainted by these events, Captain."

"You are fortunate that worse has not happened. Did the fire teach you nothing? There is far worse you could lose than your reputation, Mistress."

"The fire taught me I could get hurt even if I did nothing. I won't be returning to the Bullard's home, Captain. But I can't just wait for some madman to strike at my family again."

"Your tavern is watched, madam. No one will set it ablaze again." Underneath his measured tone lay cold rage, "It is my duty to protect the inhabitants of this town."

"You've kept watch over us." Faith's voice softened.

"My men have."

"Thank you."

The warmth of the afternoon sun did little to dispel the chill in her soul as she walked home. Everything she treasured felt threatened. While down the road in the gaol, a frightened young girl faced certain death from the hangman's noose. Faith had never felt so helpless and angry. Finding Bullard's killer seemed her only hope of restoring peace to her world.

No one would rescue her if she failed. Those she loved depended on her for support and to keep them safe. Nothing she had ever experienced had prepared her for this. However, nothing had prepared her to run a tavern either. Survival entailed more than putting one foot in front of another. She needed to use her wits, her mind, and any gifts God bestowed upon her to proceed. It was up to her to find the truth.

Chapter Eight

Faith rose early to attend her chores before leaving with Andrew for the nearly mile-long walk down Duke of Gloucester Street to the Market. She carried a large basket to stow her purchases. A light breeze teased hair out from under her straw hat. She paused to tuck it back in as Andrew ran ahead almost out of her line of sight. Shading her eyes, she looked down the length of the street. Even this early the streets were crowded with folks selling goods and those eager to acquire them.

Business was precarious enough without the notoriety that a murder caused. Faith ignored stares that followed her down the street. No one would stay in an inn perceived to be unsafe. Unsavory whispers could ruin her. More troubling was that she still had no inkling of who had attacked Bullard or why. What if it were the work of a random madman? The notion frightened her. What if she or one of the others had stopped in while the murder was taking place?

Faith could not bring herself to believe that a slight girl like Stella could inflict such damage. To cut a man's throat and belly took savagery. It was far too easy to blame a slave. With all the unrest in the Colonies, the murder might not receive the attention it should. Grant admitted he expected to be called north soon. The sheriff stayed busy collecting taxes that many refused to pay. She had little doubt that he already considered the killer found. Very few would lose sleep over hanging a slave.

Faith was no expert but surely it took some skill to slit a man's throat? Despite Grant's assertion, Faith could not imagine a scrawny girl like Stella taking a weapon away from her master and using it to dispatch him. Her mind turned uneasily to Titus, his strong muscled arms effortlessly cleaving wood for the fires. He had shown no emotion to the bloody crime. She refused to consider it. Titus was one of the gentlest people she knew. Neither he nor Olivia could commit murder. She didn't think so anyway, although Faith had often wondered what thoughts ran underneath that stoic face. Unbidden, the image of Olivia cutting up a side of beef came to mind. Uneasily, she shoved it away.

What would she have done if someone had hurt one of her sisters? Her pain regarding Stella had been uncontainable. Faith pushed the troublesome thought away. Phineas Bullard was a stout but powerful man. He would have put up a fight. Neither the sheriff nor Grant had mentioned finding a weapon. All that remained of her private room was charred wood and a crumbling chimney. Stella had seen the weapon on him but it was gone when Faith saw his body, so the killer had to have taken it; maybe he had taken other items as well, such as a fancy pocketbook. Then she recalled Titus had discovered Bullard. What had he seen?

The raucous cry of a rooster reminded Faith to quit dithering and buy what she needed before the best disappeared to women and servants focused on the job at hand. By the time she returned home a few hours later, her basket was respectably full of vegetables, meat, and spices for Olivia to cook. After delivering her purchases to the kitchen, Faith paused to rinse dirt from the street off her face. She had enough time for a few sips of ale, before turning to her daily tasks of airing linens, sweeping floors, and tending to the needs of her guests. She didn't have time to sequester her thoughts until well after the midday meal.

In the days since she had spoken to Charlotte Bullard, Faith had calmed down although the accusation still stung. Bruton Parish memorialized Bullard and then laid him to rest in the graveyard. She sighed, running her fingers through her hair, loosening the knot at the back so it hung crooked. Her mother-in-law probably knew a great deal of gossip about the Bullards. But Faith felt queasy about asking for help.

Jon's death remained an icy impasse between them, unlikely to thaw soon. There had never been much warmth in their relationship. Faith knew that

Eugenia had tried to dissuade Jon from marrying her. Faith being Quaker and lacking any social connections or property had thoroughly dismayed the ambitious older woman. She remained convinced that Faith had married Jon to move up in social standing, unwilling to accept their union was rooted in love. But it had been impossible to explain to her own family as well. Something about Jon had connected with her. She had not realized until after their wedding how much insecurity lay under his boyish charm. He had never had a chance to grow into the man she knew he could have been. All that remained were the connections to his family.

For all her faults, Eugenia adored Andrew. Faith encouraged him to visit because she couldn't bear to cause the older woman further grief. She knew Eugenia Clarke Moore could provide more opportunities for Andrew's future than Faith much as it stung to admit it. Should the inn fail, Eugenia would not hesitate to swoop in and demand Andrew come live with her at their James River estate. Should that happen, Faith would not see him often if at all. Eugenia would make sure of it.

She could not let that happen. There had to be a way to clear her name and the inn's reputation. Already there were whispers, that she might have had a hand in the murder. Whenever she looked, a soldier was in the common room downing ale although they could have been there before Bullard's death. Faith had not paid great attention to everyone who stepped in. Now she wondered who among them was a murderer or thought she was.

Faith made regular payments on Jon's debt despite the fact they drained her finances to the breaking point. She had once tried to renegotiate the loan with Bullard, but the man was unyielding. "I had nothing to do with your husband's death," he had said staring at her coldly from his desk, "He willingly took my coin to open his business, now yours. My debt still requires payment. I am not a charity to take pity for acts of the Almighty. Either pay me back or title me your business. You have no other recourse." With that, he showed her out the door.

Faith sighed; Bullard's death would not erase the debt. If the newspapers were to be believed, her situation had gone from bad to desperate. If Charlotte Bullard demanded the full amount, Faith would lose everything.

As much as it horrified her, she would have to steel her nerves and discuss her situation with Eugenia and then Mistress Bullard. There had to be someone with a better reason to kill the man. The question was who?

At one time, Bullard had been a member of the House of Burgesses. He ran a well-stocked shop in the heart of town. He shipped all sorts of goods to Jamaica and Europe and received plenty more back. Despite her protests, Jon had bought the old inn borrowing from Bullard to do so. As a woman, she had no option but to obey her husband. Only as a widow, was she allowed to own property and to conduct business. She knew she had the intelligence of any man and more than many she had met. Sleep refused to come that night. She arose tired and unprepared for the day.

Olivia went down to the gaol after supper. Faith sent her, knowing there might not be much time left for them to share. She had returned a few hours later, with the silvered tracks of tears still wet on her face. Faith left her alone although she wondered how she had felt when she had first seen Stella at the tavern and realized how she lived. As a cook, she used knives every day. In addition, Olivia had helped butcher hogs and cattle at the Moore plantation. Faith had helped her cut up chickens at the tavern. She was both skilled and efficient. Faith shuddered and put away the thought. She had to believe Olivia and Titus innocent.

Faith wondered if Dr. Staunton had gone to the gaol or not. Given Stella's injuries, someone should check her. Stella had been afraid to talk much, but maybe she would share more tonight. It was late to be making calls, but the sun would not set for a few hours yet, so Faith told Olivia where she was headed and left.

Staunton lived on Botetourt Street, which was not far. Faith had been raised in the country and was used to using her feet for transportation. She knew that his wife would know where he could be found, should he be out when she arrived. Faith wished she had tried to make more time to visit. Years ago, Temperance had contracted a fever while pregnant with her first child. Their child had been stillborn. Worse, the fever had left her an invalid. Temperance had not had a successful pregnancy since. She never mentioned it, but Faith had seen the longing in her face when Faith had brought Andrew with her on a visit once.

The house was pleasant, although not great in size. The doctor conducted his business in a few rooms downstairs and kept the back rooms and upstairs for his wife and servants. Faith walked up the steps to the stoop. A sign proclaimed *Martin Staunton, Physician* above the door. The brass knocker needed polishing. There was a spider's web in the corner of the door frame. She frowned and used a leaf to remove it.

Staunton himself answered her knock. His sherry brown eyes were clear. Shadows made the lines on his face more evident than she remembered. "Mistress Clarke, Faith, come in. How are you and your family? Is someone ill?"

"My family and I are fine. I have come regarding another matter." Faith answered. "How are Temperance and yourself?"

Martin's smile did not reach his eyes. "We continue. Temperance is resting. She tires easily these days. She might benefit from some company tomorrow if you could. She doesn't get out much."

"Certainly, I will call." Faith said, mentally slapping herself. It was little to ask, and it should have occurred to her that Temperance might get lonely. Martin looked exhausted; she wondered if it had been a rough night. "Forgive me calling so early, but I had sent word about the young girl at the gaol. I was hoping you could tell me how she fares?"

He winced, "Your man brought word, but it left my mind what with the Quincy boy falling out of a tree and breaking an arm." He reached for his medicine chest, closed it, and grabbed the handle. "Let's go now before the sun sets."

"What about Temperance?"

He looked at her quietly, "My wife is as well as can be expected. I gave her a tisane that should help her sleep. Her maid will attend her if need be. Now, let us be off to where I can provide real assistance."

With that, they headed to the gaol. Despite his tiredness, Staunton walked swiftly toward their destination. He seemed almost eager to leave his home. Faith had to stretch out her legs to keep pace. The streets were relatively quiet. A man passed on a fine red-brown horse headed west toward the governor's mansion away from the gaol. A sense of familiarity niggled at Faith's brain as she stared at his back. She continued for a few steps mulling who it was. There had only been a brief glimpse of brown breeches, a vest straining at the buttons, a well-worn coat. It was Bullard's brother-in-law, Smythe. Faith turned only to stumble on a loose stone. The man and horse were already out of sight. What was he doing out at this time? Most people were home eating their evening meal or at a local tavern.

Faith felt a stab of longing to be home. There would be cold pie and meat. Bread and whatever remained from dinner. Laughter would be coming from the main room as men discussed their day and relaxed over cards and drink. She had not chosen this life but she had come to appreciate it. As a businesswoman, she had independence. The tavern allowed her to meet and engage with people she would not have otherwise known. As she poured drinks and served food, she listened to their thoughts and ideas and developed a few of her own. The inn had become home, its inhabitants, her family. Dr. Staunton stopped abruptly as a wagon jolted past stirring up clouds of dust on the rutted road. On the other side lay their destination.

The sight of the gaol always made Faith shiver. She could not imagine being incarcerated. The gaoler lived as well as worked here. She knew Peter Pelham vaguely having seen him play the organ at Bruton Parish Church where all the Clarkes attended. Faith had never heard an organ's sounds before moving to Williamsburg. The resonant sounds had amazed and delighted her. Jon had pointed out to her that Pelham always brought a prisoner with him to pump the bellows.

Not surprisingly, it was quiet on the streets surrounding the Gaol. Faith could not imagine anyone wanting to linger. A quiet sense of despair surrounded the property. Dr. Staunton went to the door of the gaoler's home and knocked. A boy slightly older than Andrew answered.

"Is your father present? We have come to tend to a prisoner."

The boy shook his head. His eyes did not meet either the doctor's or Faith's. "He's not able to come right now."

The doctor stared at the boy thoughtfully. "Nonetheless, your mother will know where the keys to the cells are. Tell her Dr. Staunton has come to see a patient. We will go to the prisoner's yard." Stepping out of the fenced courtyard, Staunton turned to the doorway in the long brick wall that contained the cells. Another child, this one older than the first ran up to let them in. "I see your mother found the keys. We need to see the slave girl, my friend." They passed the debtor's cells which housed a few men, then down the exercise yard to where Stella's cell lay.

"She's been quiet today," the boy offered. "All I've seen her do is sleep."

"Sleep can aid healing," the doctor responded. "Nonetheless, we need to wake her in order to check her injuries." He knocked on the bars as the boy unlocked them.

Faith looked past him and saw the girl curled up under the blanket she had brought last night. She looked even younger than the last time she had seen her. Her eyelashes rested like black fans on her cheeks which were pale. Then Faith realized Stella was not breathing.

"No!"

Dr. Staunton leaned over brushing fingers over her neck. He shook his head. "She's dead, Faith. She's been gone long enough for her body to chill."

Tears burned in her eyes as she looked in disbelief. "She seemed alright the last time I spoke to her." Faith struggled to compose herself.

The doctor gently covered Stella's face with the blanket. "Injuries can be difficult to predict. She could have hit her head or been ill. You told me the mob was brutal so it's possible that she had internal injuries. Bullard did not have a reputation for compassion or the sense to safeguard his investments." Staunton looked at Faith with compassion. "You did all you could, her death is no reflection on your care. Dying in her sleep is a far more merciful end than facing the noose later." He rested a hand on the still body. "No one can hurt her now." Faith attempted to swallow the knot in her throat. Seeing Stella's small figure on the ground felt painfully wrong. With a pang, she realized she would have to inform Olivia.

"Tell your father, one of the prisoners has died," Dr. Staunton instructed the boy, who ran back to the gaoler's quarters. When the boy was out of sight, Staunton muttered, "That should get him out of bed."

"Is Master Pelham ill?"

Staunton snorted. "Only if you consider too much rum an illness." Sighing, he qualified the remark. "Peter is a good man and an exquisite musician. But he does sometimes overindulge in spirits. Far be it for me to judge the man too harshly. We all have our demons."

Faith had heard a rumor about Pelham's drinking. She pitied his wife.

Within moments, the gaoler arrived looking pale and unwell. His hair stuck up around his face and he needed a shave. In some ways, Pelham looked not much better than his prisoners with the exception of being cleaner and better dressed. From the way he held his head, Faith confirmed the doctor's earlier speculation. His skin, already a sickly hue, turned even greener when he saw Stella.

"She was alive last night."

Dr. Staunton studied Pelham thoughtfully. "Did anyone come by?"

Pelham shook his head. "I was out most of the day, but my boys or my wife would have said. When I returned, I made sure the prisoners were all in for the night and turned in myself. I let no one in last night."

One of his boys, this one in his teens, shuffled his feet. "There have been a few in and out, sir."

"Who?" Pelham asked sharply. He had reason to be concerned. Prisoners were his responsibility. If the governor felt Pelham was not up to the responsibilities of his job, he could be removed. "I have heard of no one coming to see the girl since Mistress Clarke."

The boy shrugged. "Someone brought clothes and blankets for some of the men awaiting trial. Somebody brought rum to a few others. Pretty much the usual for what goes on here." He paused thoughtfully. "A black woman came by to see her." He nodded toward the cell. "She gave me a slab of apple pie to get in. After that one ate, they sang and prayed for a while. I didn't see the harm in it."

Faith spoke. "I bathed her wounds and provided her with a clean blanket last night. That woman was my cook Olivia brought her more food." She decided not to tell them of their familial connection. Her eyes burned with unshed tears as she thought of Stella dying alone in the straw.

"You would not have noticed an internal injury, Faith. And even if I had been able to come, I may not have seen anything amiss either."

"I'll send one of my boys to inform the captain," Pelham said dolefully. "Do you know if anyone will claim the body for burial? It will need to be handled soon." He turned and walked away his doughy face dripping sweat.

Staunton buttoned his cuffs and replaced his coat. Some of the lace on the cuffs was torn and frayed, unusual for the ordinarily immaculate physician. Faith felt it indelicate to mention, perhaps he had been too busy to notice. He picked up his medicine chest. "Come, Mistress Clarke, there is naught we can do here."

Naught indeed. In a matter of days, Faith had witnessed two deaths and been unable to accomplish much of anything. Frustration welled up making her speak without thinking.

"Do you think her death was natural?"

"Eh, what?"

"She looked well enough when I saw her last, beaten but not dying."

Staunton looked at her with ancient eyes. "I doubt you have seen many deaths, Faith. I have. I doubt this is anything more than a tragic accident. Slaves die of injuries all too frequently. For all our refinements, we have yet to accept that humanity comes in many shades." His voice sounded faintly bitter. "You have no idea of the suffering of those unfortunate not to be born white. They suffer. They die and yet are not even provided the dignity of a dog."

Faith was speechless. She'd never seen Martin so angry. She had no answers for his accusations. She had seen the auctions in the market. A slave was property and as such subject to the rules and dictums of his or her owner. No one really spoke of the fact that they were people who suffered and felt pain just like their owners. "What needs to be done now?" she asked.

His lips twisted. "I doubt a thought will be given to a decent Christian burial for this child." He raked his hand through his hair, already looking untidy. His hat was on the ground beside him. "Don't fret, I will take care of it." Dr. Staunton looked tired. "Forgive my words. These are the ranting of one who is terribly weary. This is not your fault. Indeed, you have behaved more honorably than many. I need to go home and tend to my family."

Staunton strode out of the exercise yard. Faith had never before noticed the tired stoop in his back. As he left, a prisoner called out to him.

"Doc, have you time to look at my boils now?" This was followed by a chorus of pleas from the cells surrounding Stella's. Some asked for treatment, others for rum or women. It did not cease until Pelham pounded on the iron gate with a stick and demanded silence.

Staunton looked at Pelham. "Have any of these poor wretches been attended to by a physician?"

"Those who can afford one or have family to pay one," the gaoler admitted. "I tend to the worst afflicted."

Staunton nodded. "I can do nothing for that poor child; let me attend those who can be helped." He turned to Faith. "This is not the place for a gentlewoman. Mistress Clarke, go home. There is nothing here you can do." Moving outside of Stella's cell, the doctor gestured to Pelham to open another.

One of Pelham's sons led Faith out of the cellblock. Neither spoke. Stella's death lay like a heavyweight, unspoken but almost unbearable. Faith kept seeing her as she was last night, terribly frightened but alive. How could she be dead now? With a chill down her spine Faith realized the one potential witness to Bullard's death was gone. Once again Death came when least expected.

Chapter Nine

A warm breeze blew through the open doors bringing the sounds and scents of new life. Between the serving of drinks and sweeping of floors, Faith stayed busy in hopes of keeping her mind off of Stella. Too often images of the dead girl flashed behind briefly closed lids. Grief rose in a wave until she could shove it back. Work provided a needed distraction.

Olivia had not been surprised at her sister's death. Had Faith not noticed the tightening of her lips and fisting of a hand in her apron, she would have thought Olivia felt nothing. The cook offered no reaction to Faith's expression of sympathy. It was not until a late evening trip to the privy that she heard sobbing from the rooms above the kitchen. Faith walked all the way up to the base of the steps leading to the York's rooms, torn by the heartfelt cries. Feeling like an intruder, she returned to the tavern hoping no one noticed the hoarseness in her own voice. She struggled to choke back tears, as she filled drinks before sending Joshua back to the kitchen for stew and bread.

The next morning, Faith ignored Olivia's puffy eyes. After her offer to cook breakfast was politely refused, she took on more public tasks, freeing Titus to go back and forth to his wife. Although she lacked his intimidating size, she could guard the liquor cabinet and pour whisky. When anyone acted up, she gave them her best impression of her mother's reproving glare, usually seen when she believed Faith was being idle.

Within days, the weather warmed to almost summer-like heat, which meant more folk were traveling. When it was not raining, townspeople were out and about as gardens were planted and gossip exchanged over fences. From time to time she could hear the town crier broadcast news on the streets from where it was discussed in all the taverns. Behind Clarke Tavern, lettuce spread over the warm brown earth in a pale green profusion of color. Carrots sent up feathery tips as well. Watching Andrew and Joshua plant potatoes, Faith sighed happily. She loved spring. Signs of continuing life gave her hope. There had been too much death and darkness. "Please God," she whispered. "Let life be good again."

With the influx of travelers, there were times when both women worked in the kitchen preparing meals. Sweat ran down Faith's back as she prepared yet another chicken for roasting. She longed for a cool drink but dare not leave the fire unattended long, lest something burn. Her lip stung, making her realize she had bitten it, an old habit she'd yet to break. Olivia came in from gathering peas and stared at her flushed face.

"You best take a break before the heat gets you. Dining room is mostly clear and probably will be for a few hours. I can take care of things now."

Faith didn't argue. She was happy to escape the oven-like interior of the kitchen. She was halfway to the tavern when she heard Olivia's voice. "Mistress, your skirts!"

Looking down, she realized they were still tied up around her waist, both to keep them out of the fire and provide a little cooling air. But no one in the tavern needed to see her legs. Such a shocking display would only degrade her tavern's already dimmed reputation. Once back in her room, she took a moment to wash her face and tidy her hair. A few hours tending the fire and tendrils had snaked out from around her cap. Outside the door, tankards clanked amidst the murmur of her few remaining guests. There was comfort in the normalcy of it, yet she knew everything could change in a heartbeat.

Faith struggled with the reality of Stella's death. How could she have missed the signs of serious injury? The girl had seemed bruised and frightened, not mortally hurt. "People die," she murmured. But this felt wrong. Olivia and Titus's outward stoicism tore at her. Faith understood that slaves generally did not reveal emotions to their masters, but she liked to think of herself as a friend as well. But how could one friend own another? Her family would be horrified to realize that she now owned people. Faith did not know how she had gotten into such a mess or how to solve it.

By the time supper had been served and the dining room cleaned and readied for tomorrow, she was exhausted. Yet there were still accounts to settle. Titus and Joshua minded the few men that remained playing cards and finishing their drinks while Andrew worked on sums on a slate. Steps in the hallway made her pause to see who had come in so late. The setting sun rimmed the horizon a bright copper. A few remaining rays burnished the hair of an older man. It took her a moment to recognize one of her mother-in-law's servants.

He bowed.

"George, what brings you here so late?"

"Mistress Eugenia desires you to join her for tea."

Faith was unsurprised that Eugenia would not permit so minor a thing as conflict with England to adjust her habits. Taking tea was unpopular in many quarters in Williamsburg. In Boston, this past December a band of locals dressed as Indians had dumped enormous quantities of the stuff into the harbor. The British had not been amused. Faith quit serving tea. She was not going to involve herself in a potentially disastrous conflict, but a quiet bit of defiance provided some petty satisfaction.

Alienating her mother-in-law would be a bad idea. Eugenia still blamed her for Jon's death, despite her desperate efforts to save him. The fact that it was Eugenia's own fault she was absent at her own child's death was irrelevant. Her vicious diatribe before the funeral shattered an already precarious relationship. Faith avoided her whenever possible. They had not spoken in weeks although she sent dutiful greetings when her father-in-law visited the tavern. Perhaps this was an olive branch although she had her doubts. "When would Mistress Moore like me to call?"

"She expects you tomorrow afternoon, Mistress Clarke."

Faith rolled her eyes. Did it not occur to the woman that she might have other things to do, like run a tavern? She smiled at the servant while trying not to grind her teeth. "One moment please." She walked back to the kitchen to let Olivia know of tomorrow's errand. She should be helping her, she knew, but furthering the tension with her mother-in-law would be costly in many ways. Eugenia would not hesitate to further blacken Faith's reputation. Olivia knew it too. She had lived too many years in Eugenia's house before she and Titus came to the Clarkes.

"You had best go," She commented as her strong hands kneaded dough before setting it to rise.

"That will leave you shorthanded," Faith fretted. "Dinner can be busy."

Olivia looked at her. Her dark eyes possessed a knowing look. "I can manage and with the burgesses not in session for some weeks, it's not that busy. Don't use me as an excuse to avoid Mistress 'Genia." Olivia's voice turned to cajoling. "She doesn't bite so much as bark."

"But her bite is not to be forgotten," Faith muttered as she went back to the main house. Truth be told, Olivia could run the tavern without Faith. The pity was the law would not permit her to do so. Staring into the steel mirror in the hallway did not improve her mood. Hair straggled out of her cap which was sliding to one side. Her shift was sticking to her in odd places. Grease stains from cooking and serving dotted her apron and her face was flushed. "I look like a servant." But then she *was* a member of the working class and her dress reflected that. Faith had no time for fancy dresses and powdered hair. Laces and jewelry would only impede her and nothing could persuade her to tightly lace her stays. She smiled ruefully. Rumor had it that Martha Washington favored simplicity over the excesses of the upper class, perhaps she was not alone. Although she doubted Mrs. Washington worried much about keeping a roof over her head.

Turning, her eyes she caught sight of Andrew carrying in a load of wood. Her son's curls were escaping the ribbon that clubbed his hair behind his head while his shirt crept halfway out of his breeches. Tucked in his vest was a treasured fife. When not pressed to work, he liked to slip away and blow tunes on it back behind a stand of trees where he didn't realize she knew to look.

"Why was George here? Is Grandma coming?" he asked hopefully. Eugenia was indulgent with her grandchild. Visits meant trips to the store and a chance to ride one of the Moores' excellent horses as well as a break from chores. She didn't blame him for longing for their company. Any child would. Faith just wished she could provide some of the same things the Moore's did.

"Grandmother Moore is not here," she responded. "She sent him to ask me to tea tomorrow."

"Tom Olmstead's father says that tea drinkers are traitors to the colonies."

Faith ruffled his hair gently before he squirmed away. "We are subjects of King George, whether we agree with his rules or not. Pray we find a way to resolve our conflicts soon. Your grandmother is no traitor. She just likes to drink tea. Maybe you can visit her soon."

He was getting taller. In a few years, he might well tower over her. "You will need to help Titus and Olivia tomorrow." Faith sighed, "I am sorry to be leaving you all busy, but your grandmother would not understand a refusal."

Andrew would love to go with her, she knew but two people could not be gone when a good many men came in to grab their large meal for the day. The inn required more people to assist but Faith could not afford wages and she refused to take another slave even if the Moores offered one.

George had not moved from where she had left him. Faith wondered if he had breathed. His breeches and hose were skin-tight without a wrinkle or flaw. Brass buttons marched up his heavily embroidered ivory satin vest like well-trained soldiers. His freshly curled wig was brown and smelled faintly of cinnamon. His face wore the polite blankness of a lifelong servant although hidden thoughts glimmered in his eyes. But she had heard of his ruthlessness at cards. Faith wondered what thoughts he held behind the quiet façade.

"Tell your mistress I will be pleased to attend." Then thinking about the dusty walk back to the Moore residence, she said, "Get yourself a drink before you go, either Titus or Joshua will tend to you."

"Thanks, mistress." A brief smile transformed his face before he turned to the main room. Then the servant hesitated and turned back. "Mistress Clarke."

"Yes." Faith's mind had already shifted to other items such as whether or not she needed to go to the cellar for another bottle of wine.

"Word came to us when Master Bullard perished in your establishment."

Faith stiffened. There was nothing she could say although she was sure that Eugenia had said plenty.

"Mistress Eugenia and Master Ezra are very concerned. That fire was no accident he says. Bullard was a business associate and had influence with certain persons. The Governor called him a friend." Swiftly, he added, "He had enemies as well, folks who he betrayed one way or another. While some may delight in Bullard's death, others might well seek vengeance. His death puts you in danger. My master could help if you permitted. His connections are many."

"Has he discussed this with you?"

"Servants hear things, madam. Most folks forget we exist, but our eyes and ears work as well as anyone's."

Faith suspected he was right. Since the murder there had been times she felt watched but by whom she did not know. George waited for her answer. "Then I had best attend to tea." Although she knew she would rue it.

"I will inform Mistress Moore of your decision."

"George. I would not refuse any help your master offered. It was kind of him to lend assistance during the fire."

The servant bowed and stepped across to the common room for a pint before striding out the door and down the street. Staring after him, she wondered how his clothes remained immaculate in the dusty streets. She suspected it involved a carefully cultivated relationship with an excellent laundress.

Eugenia did not casually invite one to tea. Her teas were designed to build her social standing and gather all local gossip so she could make use of it. What could she possibly want? On the practical side, what could she wear that would pass inspection under Eugenia's critical eye? Faith grimaced. She would have to tighten her stays and wear one of her pre-tavern owner gowns that Jon had gotten her. There was no other solution.

The day was wearing on. She needed to see what assistance Olivia needed. Faith knew she was fortunate to have a skilled cook. There was no way that Faith could have operated the tavern without her. Yet, her conscience reminded her that Olivia earned no wages for her hard work. Her father would call that unjust and unchristian. Faith sighed. She would have to do something despite fears of her own potential penury and the reaction of her husband's family.

A visit to the kitchen revealed stew bubbling merrily providing needed steam for the pudding also being prepared. Bread baked in the huge Dutch oven. Titus' snares provided rabbits spitted over the fire. Perhaps the greedy rascals would take heed and stay out of her garden.

After determining that all was in order for the afternoon meal, Faith returned to her ledgers. Numbers had never been her great skill, although her father had educated his daughters alongside his sons. He had forward ideas regarding education, so Faith could do sums, read and write. She also knew a smattering of Latin and French. Faith bit her lip and dug into her work. There were new debts to be paid for flour, sugar, and bacon. A horse had thrown a shoe that had required the services of the blacksmith. Fortunately, he was willing to trade his services for use of Faith's barn for the animals that would not fit in his small barn. Good English coin was hard to come by. It was easier to barter.

A quiet cough brought Faith out of her accounting-induced daze. Captain Grant stood in the entryway. So involved had she been with her sums, she missed the opening of the door. Faith stuffed loose hair back under her cap. Capping the ink, she sprinkled sand over the page, before blowing on the page so it would dry without smearing. Grant said nothing as the quill was wiped and placed in its holder. Amusement flashed in his eyes as he bowed.

"Mistress Clarke." Removing a lace-edged handkerchief, he unfolded its ivory edges. "I fear your labors have left their marks upon your face." His eyes crinkled slightly as he daubed her nose and the side of her cheek gently. His touch was light and made her skin tingle.

Faith took the delicate piece of linen and completed the work, wincing to see the ink stain ruin it. Flushing, she finished cleaning off the offending ink, stopping when he nodded. The fabric burned in her hand. Seeing it still bunched in her fingers, Faith offered it back. As he took it, Grant folded it gently with the smears inside and tucked it away.

"Surely you didn't come just to attend my nose?"

"Indeed." Something about his gaze made her shiver. His eyes were as clear as a winter sky. "Tell me about your visits to the gaol."

"Why?"

One of his eyebrows lifted. Faith wondered how to interpret his behavior. On one hand, he was attractive and at times charming, on the other he thought her capable of carving Phineas Bullard like a Christmas ham. She didn't know what he was thinking.

"I brought Stella food and a blanket the other night. I was unsure how she would be tended in such a rough place as the gaol. When I saw her injuries, I tended to her wounds as best I could and sent word to Dr. Staunton to come see her. He has tended to my family and staff since our arrival in Williamsburg."

"Very thoughtful, especially considering she was not your slave."

Faith sent him a sharp look, unsure how to interpret his tone. Grant's face was devoid of expression. She longed for some indication of what he was thinking. "She was a frightened young girl. Someone needed to look after her."

"That was not your only visit."

Sadness washed over her. "I went the next day with Dr. Staunton. She was dead when we arrived." Faith clenched her hands into fists at the memory. "I didn't know her injuries were so severe." Grant said nothing as she struggled to compose herself. Tears would not bring Stella back. When she could look at Grant again, his face was oddly compassionate. He reached out a hand, and then drew it back as if suddenly recalling his purpose.

"From all appearances she died in her sleep, wrapped in the blanket you provided. I doubt she felt any discomfort. As for her injuries, some were older than the past few days." Grant's voice hardened. "I had my surgeon take a look. Bullard or someone abused her. Her passing may have been a blessing of sorts."

What kind of life would make death a relief? Faith felt no comfort in the idea. "To die alone and frightened in a cell..."

"People die in worse circumstances every day. Battle, disease, and misfortune will strike us all one day. But this is not the only reason I came. Bullard was likely stabbed by his own blade. Stella had no weapon with her so it was either hidden here or elsewhere. I would like to search your establishment again."

Faith shrugged. What could he possibly find? "As you know, my private room burned to the ground. Search if you wish, but I believe someone would have noticed a sword by now."

"A bayonet, yes but the type of sword worn by gentlemen daily could lay unseen in tall grass or in a woodpile. They are delicate and deadly, not difficult for a man or a woman to handle." He smiled gently as if to take the edge off the implication. "Bullard's was silver-hilted with a leather-bound silver scabbard, quite fancy. My men know what to look for. If anything remains that relates to Bullard's murder, they will find it."

"They are already here?"

"I don't require permission to search your property, Mistress Clarke, but I wanted to extend the courtesy of informing you."

"You wanted to see if I would refuse." It was an effort to keep her voice calm.

"You did not which gives me more reason to believe you did not have a hand in this crime. But someone murdered Bullard while you entertained guests nearby. It would have been easy to leave and execute an inebriated man unused to savagery." His eyes met hers, "Anyone could have done it. A sharp blade cuts through flesh easily as I'm sure you and your cook know. I don't imagine she was happy seeing her sister abused." He smiled grimly at her gasp. "There are many secrets in this town, not only those that can be revealed by good ears in and about the Gaol. I intend to keep looking until I find out who killed him and why."

"What makes you think it was more than a robbery?"

"It takes hate to cut a man like that. Bullard could be ruthless with those who did business with him, but you already know that, don't you?"

"My husband," Faith began.

"Foolishly borrowed money from Bullard and when he left you a widow, you inherited his debts with this tavern. He was not a man known for his generosity. I imagine making payments has been quite a challenge." Grant could have been discussing the weather given the pleasantness of his tone. Faith wondered if he looked so benign in battle before slaying his adversaries. The faint scars on his face and hands indicated he was no stranger to engaging the enemy.

She met his gaze feeling as if they were fencing and his foil was poised to sweep in to disarm her. Faith smiled without humor. She was no delicate lady to be cowed into submission. The past seven months had taught her to pretend courage she never felt. Boiling rage warmed her as she replied, "I have always paid my debts without resorting to spilling blood. Search as often as you please, Captain, and pray continue your investigation to the end. Far too many, blame whomever is convenient. Finding the truth requires a great deal more effort."

"Fear not, Mistress Clarke, I will find out what happened and administer justice." He bowed before he left, walking swiftly away in his shiny black boots down the hall and out to the ruins of her private room.

Faith returned to the ledger seeking where Jon had written. She remembered the letters from the landowner in England but little else, other than the fee he had paid for the right to operate the tavern. Jon's sudden death had pushed her into survival mode trying to run a business as well as raise a son. She had not looked too deeply, once she realized he had poured all of their assets into the business and left nothing in reserve. She stared at Jon's sloppy handwriting, so similar to Andrew's. "Why did you do this?" However, her husband was no longer alive to answer. Faith had to succeed. The tavern was their only source of income; their only hope of survival.

Chapter Ten

Morning light flooded the parlor, gilding the painted walls. The walnut secretary's grain stood out illuminated by the powerful glow. A gift from Eugenia, Faith suspected that it had been replaced with something from France. She loved its rich, dark grain and utilitarian features. The desktop was folded up to allow access to the table linens and cutlery kept in the drawers below, a convenient step or two away from the main room. Following breakfast, Faith slipped in to note a guest's payment for lodging.

No sooner had she dipped a quill in ink when Olivia entered, followed by Titus carrying a suspicious load of flounces. Olivia directed Titus to lay the dress and petticoats on the bed in her bedroom next door. Faith followed trying to determine what sort of insanity was transpiring. Joshua came in with a pitcher which he set down by the basin before swiftly exiting.

"I'll keep an eye on things," Titus said, amusement glinting from his eyes as he made his escape. The door echoed as it shut behind him.

"What…?" Faith felt like a rabbit felt caught in a snare.

Olivia moved a chair to the center of the room.

"You want to look your best for Mistress Genia. She puts great store in appearances."

In short order, Faith was stripped down to her shift. "Take off your stockings."

The stockings she was given shimmered. "Silk?" Faith asked, wondering where they came from.

Olivia smiled mysteriously. "Could be." She glided over and assessed her charge with a critical eye.

Before Faith could protest, strong hands pulled the strings on her corset, taking the wind out of her lungs. Olivia shook out the petticoats making them swirl in a wave of cotton. Meekly, stepping in, Faith held her arms out and allowed the other woman to drape her in silk and lace. Every rustle reminded her that she was about to enter another world where the cut of one's gown and the way one held their tea meant something. A place where she had never felt comfortable.

Her legs collapsed, sending her into the waiting chair. Olivia tsked as she removed the mob cap and eyed Faith's hair, "You are not going to tea with hair like this." Pins rattled as Olivia pulled them out and dropped them into a bowl.

"Ouch!" The comb wasn't much better, gliding through her hair until it became caught, where her merciless would-be, ladies maid would tug it out. Faith wondered how much hair she would have left once Olivia was done. Soon her hair was piled in a heavy mass on top of her head with the exception of a few selected strands that hung down to frame her face and curl down her nape.

Spotting the smoking curling iron on the stove, Faith's eyes widened, "Is that necessary?" Over her left shoulder, Olivia lifted the iron checking it with a damp finger. It hissed like an irritable snake which seemed to please her. She continued her implacable walk over to Faith.

"Stay still."

Feeling the heat near her cheek, Faith froze. The other woman worked swiftly, tugging slightly as she positioned hair exactly where she wanted. Faintly steaming curls fell to Faith's shoulders. Unsure of where the iron would be next, she maintained the stance of a statue; the tugs and brief sensations of heat were her only clue. Her head felt light and fuzzy.

"Mistress, you need to breathe."

Faith inhaled and exhaled rapidly.

"Slower. I do not want to have to haul you off that floor after all this work."

Faith gripped the seat with her hands and focused on breathing slowly letting the air go in and out of her chest. Gradually her head cleared. Done with the iron, Olivia produced a cap festooned with ribbon that she pinned in place with a few well-placed jabs.

Standing up, her feet skidded as they adjusted to embroidered slippers she had not worn in ages. Faith grabbed the chair to steady herself "I am as ready as I will ever be."

Olivia smiled in satisfaction as she eyed her project. She knew what Mistress Genia looked for in a guest. Five years in the Moore household had served her well. If Faith would hold her head high and act like she belonged, Eugenia Moore would quit bullying her. Her old mistress only respected people who would not back down. Long ago, the woman had saved her life, which made Olivia more willing to forgive flaws in attitude and behavior. Mistress Genia had been the first white person to treat her decently.

Olivia grew up on a sugar cane plantation in Jamaica. When she turned fifteen, she had been sold and put on a ship to go to the American Colonies. The horror of the trip had left her a traumatized skeleton, nevermore the carefree child of the islands.

A local planter bought her along with a half dozen others. Deemed too small to do heavy work, she was put in the house and finally the kitchen. Olivia had been learning more complex cookery when her skirts ignited. Her panicked run caused the well-spread flames to engulf most of her body. Field hands heard her screams and ran to beat out the fire but it was too late. For days she laid in horrible pain in the slave quarters she shared with eight other women, one of whom attended her. The master came in and shook his head. "There's no saving that. She should be put out of her misery."

Olivia would have welcomed the shot. The pain was unimaginable as blackened skin sloughed off, revealing the raw tender flesh beneath. She lingered between pain and fever for days not remembering who or where she was. Sometimes Olivia thought she was still on that horrible ship watching those around her die in their chains. When she awoke, a strange white woman stood over her. Olivia whimpered as the woman lifted her arms and turned her back and forth examining every inch.

Eugenia Moore stared down at her, a frown between her brows. "You are conscious now, which is good. The fever has broken. We scrubbed all the dead skin off. But it will take time before you heal and it will be painful. I am your new mistress, Eugenia Moore, and I will ensure you have the care you need. There will be scars, but you will heal." She smiled grimly. "But now you will always remember to tie up your skirts when you are around fire."

Olivia's throat was raw. She could not speak above a rasp. She slept waking only periodically for brief periods when someone would pour broth down her tortured throat. Day and night blurred.

Mistress gave her laudanum for the pain, gradually reducing it over the course of days. "Laudanum dulls pain but leaves an addiction that is a slow cruel death. I am weaning you off so that in addition to burns, you will not become an addict. If the pain is too great, there are other things we can use to help you."

Olivia refused to ask. The next day she got up moving her stiff and painful limbs so the scars would stretch and let her move. Olivia bit her lip bloody to avoid crying out. At night, tears fell in the anonymity of her pillow. She might be ugly, but she refused to be a cripple.

It amazed Olivia that the mistress attended to her, standing over the slaves and fussing over their technique. As the days passed Olivia realized her new mistress didn't believe anyone could do a task to her standards. Eugenia permitted her to return to the kitchen albeit under the direction of Edith, the house cook.

Olivia knew she would never marry, not with the scars that covered her body. The Moores allowed their slaves to wed as they wished, which was rare, so while many of the women talked and flirted with men in the house and fields, she focused on mastering her skills as a cook. Edith was patient and was willing to teach her what herbs made a roast more succulent and how to place bread so the drafts wouldn't make the loaves fall. As the weather turned cold, both women worked on curing meat for the winter.

It took two weeks for Olivia to realize that the large smiling man that kept bringing game into the kitchen had been smiling specifically at her. She had been incredulous when the other slaves began teasing.

"Wonder what Titus is hunting in the kitchen?" one of them would whisper with a knowing look.

Another would look at Olivia and wink. "Must be something small." The never-ending innuendo, coupled with smiles and winks nearly drove her insane. She pretended as if she were unaware of the growing wave of gentle jibes.

One fine fall day she went to get water and gather herbs before the frost got them. After filling her pail, she placed it down at the edge of a row and began filling her basket with strands of rosemary and parsley. When she looked up, Titus was at the end of the garden holding it.

"That's mine."

He nodded agreeably and took her basket out of her hand when she went over to retrieve her water. Carrying both in his huge hands, Titus started walking back toward the kitchen. Avoiding her attempts to snatch them back, his steady pace continued. Olivia had no choice but to scramble after him as he steadily ignored her icy stares and attempts to get her things back. She might as well have tried to wrestle a bear.

Finally, she glared up at him, "Stop! You will get us both in trouble."

"For what? Carrying a bucket of water?" He smiled gently at her, the idiot. "I carry bigger buckets than this to water Master Ezra's horses. He doesn't mind me helping you."

"Well, I do." Olivia had to crane her neck to meet his eyes, "I don't need no man to help me with my work."

He set down the bucket and wiped the sweat off the back of his neck. Titus was tall and broad-shouldered. Olivia imagined he could have any girl he fancied.

"I know you don't. I've seen you work. You work harder than anyone around here. But why not let someone help you? It lightens the load." His eyes were the rich golden-brown of oak leaves framed by long, curly black lashes most women would envy. His hair was cut short, so short it barely curled. His attractiveness made her madder.

"What do you want?" She knew it could not be her. Those sorts of illusions had been dispelled by anyone who had seen her during her convalescence.

"Oh, my own farm and a few kids. The right to do what I see fit when I see fit and a house with real glass windows I can look through and see God's beautiful world."

Olivia laughed. "And how will you get that? Have you forgotten what you are?"

He laid a large gentle hand under her chin and tilted it up. "Now that's a pretty smile, even if your words aren't too kind. Everyone needs a dream, something to hope for when your soul gets dark and painful. What do you dream about?"

"I gave up dreaming a long time ago."

He shook his head. "I don't believe that. I've seen your eyes go all soft and far away when you are picking herbs for the kitchen. Sometimes you hum a little tune that sounds like it came from the islands. I used to hear them down on the docks in Savannah when I was a boy. Your mind is somewhere else."

Titus had been watching her, and Olivia hadn't noticed him catching her daydreaming. Olivia flushed. "Haven't you got anything better to do than spy on busy people?"

"It's not spying to admire what God has created. You are always working. I just wondered what goes on behind those pretty eyes."

"I'm not pretty!" His syrupy words made her want to slap him. Whatever he wanted he was not getting.

"Why? Because you have marks on your body? That has nothing to do with your soul, Olivia. You are a strong woman. All of us have scars. I have whip scars on my back from when I was a boy before Master Ezra bought me and brought me to Williamsburg to handle his horses."

"Men don't look at souls," Olivia replied bitterly, her fingers bunching in her skirt. Titus was making her nervous. She could bully the other men into leaving her alone. They thought she was cold and aloof and she liked it that way.

"Then you have met some stupid men. You have the most beautiful eyes I've ever seen. There is fire and spirit in you. I admire you for coming back from what would have killed most people. There is nothing ugly about you."

Olivia's throat was tight with emotions his words evoked, feelings she had worked hard to shove away. Titus shouldn't have said such things. It gave her hope. She didn't need hope. It was far better to deal with reality. Reality didn't make promises that could not be kept.

"You don't know what you're talking about."

"Yes, I do."

Olivia glared at him. He had no idea how badly she was marked. "You don't know what I look like." She took a step only to have him stop her and stare down.

"You're wrong about that. I know exactly what you're hiding under all those clothes."

Olivia froze. "How?"

"Mistress Genia had me help bring you home. You were in bad shape, out of your head. I carried you up to your room and helped her settle you." His eyes were soft,."You weren't much more than skin and bones, but I knew you were going to pull through. You had too much fight in you not to. You bit me." He showed her his thumb. The digit had a faint whitish scar on it. Titus looked at it and her tenderly. He closed Olivia's shocked open mouth with a finger under her chin. "I don't care about the scars, Olivia. I know you have doubts but I can wait. I've got time, but I don't ever want you to think that I would reject any part of you. You are a beautiful woman and I intend to marry you."

Shock washed over Olivia like a large wave leaving her trembling and uncertain. Feelings she had pushed down rose to the surface threatening to blind her.

Setting down the basket, he reached over and wiped her tears with his huge thumb. "I didn't mean to make you cry."

Olivia sniffled. "I don't cry." She used the back of her hand to wipe her face, mortified that it was wet.

"Let's get you back to the house before they send out a search party. You're never late."

She walked back with him, her mind whirling. Titus had thrown her off balance.

As the days grew into weeks, the wretched man continued to see her every day. Master Ezra let him. Olivia couldn't believe it, but she had seen the master smiling and sending the large man off to the kitchens. Was he crazy? No matter how rudely rebuffed, he kept coming back for more.

Titus wore her down with his cheer. Before Olivia knew it, she agreed to marry him. It wasn't until after she wed that she realized that the love of a good man could make any woman beautiful. Titus's unrelenting happy spirit made her past miseries fade away. When she lay with him, they were in their own world, nothing else mattered. No one was more surprised than Olivia when she became pregnant within a year. They remained with the Moores until Eugenia decided that Jon needed slaves. Under the weight of her nagging, Master Ezra had sent them to his stepson as a wedding gift. When the Clarkes relocated to Virginia and bought the inn, Olivia realized neither Faith nor Jon knew how to run a business. Jon Clarke had all the common sense of a cuckoo bird and too much pride to admit his shortcomings.

The purchase of the inn meant Titus and Olivia could work together. Faith insisted they needed proper last names, so Titus took his from the nearby York River. Their fate rested in the hands of a Quaker woman who hated owning slaves. Faith insisted on Joshua's freedom which Master Jon said was impossible. Fighting continued until Joshua pulled baby Andrew away from a rattlesnake, resulting in him receiving the impending strike. As he lay for days fighting the poison, Jon relented and applied to the governor to free the boy and it had been granted. For that act alone, Olivia would help Faith Clarke. Although she hadn't freed them yet, Titus believed she would. Faith was only beginning to assume her full responsibilities as a tavern owner. Right now, her mistress looked grim as Olivia prepared her to visit the Moore's.

Faith plucked at her skirts, trying to rearrange them to hide an almost invisible spot just below the bodice, and sat straight as a board. Her body had changed since she last wore a fancy gown, even a day gown for tea. She was leaner and her breasts had gotten smaller, enough that her gown ran the risk of being shocking in its disclosures. A lace kerchief helped cover what her dress risked revealing.

Released by Olivia, Faith hurried towards the door. Painfully tight stays forced her to stop. Stopping to take the shallow breaths available; Faith proceeded out to the carriage at a much more ladylike pace. Negotiating the door with wide skirts took a little thought, but Faith managed it without losing too much dignity. The weight of elaborately dressed hair pressed down on her neck. Stomach flutters made her wonder if she would be sick.

Eugenia's town home was a short ride from the tavern. Even in the carriage, a certain amount of road dust drifted upward. Faith felt fortunate that there was little traffic once they left Duke of Gloucester Street and entered the more gentrified section of the city. The air was warm and mild. Not warm enough for the amount of exposed skin a lady's dress entailed though. Faith pulled her dark wool cloak around her as a defense to the breeze on skin unaccustomed to such exposure.

The carriage slowed to a stop at the front of the house. Ezra purchased this house for Eugenia after their marriage or so Jon had said. He had been a youth at the time and unsure how he felt about having a father again. Her father-in-law had insisted all the Clarke children, male or female received a good education. Ezra insisted on paying for Andrew's schooling as well. Faith didn't know what she would have done without her father-in-law's assistance in ways great and small. Faith suspected his influence was why more and more gentlemen ate at the tavern. But now she had to face Eugenia in her lair.

Faith walked slowly down the walkway to the front entrance. It was a familiar, if awkward ritual although she had not been to this house in nearly a year. Jon had teased her about her nerves. Unbidden his amused gaze rose before her, his warm brown eyes gentle even if not very sympathetic.

"It's only tea, Faith, a civilized ritual where gentlefolk gather for tea, refreshments, and polite conversation. My mother doesn't eat guests and her refreshments are very good."

Faith knew he was right, but he never felt inadequate or heard the comparisons Eugenia had made when measuring Faith against the other girls he could have wed. More likely, he chose to ignore them. Jon adored his mother. His easy charm could cajole both of them into lighter moods.

Now there was no one to act as a buffer between two decidedly different women.

Faith was surprised when Eugenia herself opened the ornate door to let her in. Perhaps the butler had had an attack of apoplexy? She could not think of any other reason her mother-in-law would stoop to answer her own door. Faith murmured a polite response to the older woman's greeting and followed her down the hall being careful to walk slowly so as not to overrun the smaller, more delicately built woman. Eugenia had been a beauty in her day and it was still evident in her soft, regular features and delicate skin. Faint lines marred the porcelain surface, evidence of a strong will barely checked. Light powder tinted her hair to a fashionable shade of lavender.

Sunlight streamed through the window illuminating the parlor in clear golden light. The ornate marble fireplace held no fire today. Faith remembered prior visits when the air had been scented with pine logs. The room was richly papered and a portrait of a much younger Eugenia hung on the wall. Silhouettes of her children hung between the windows. Faith's eyes automatically went to the one of Jon. A few strands had escaped from his club that day curling over the top of his head. Her eyes stung briefly. Many memories had faded but she could still summon the flash of his smile and the look of those wild curls. Andrew's hair did the same thing.

Already seated was one of Faith's sisters-in-law, Martha Moore. She was wed to one of Ezra Moore's sons from his marriage before Eugenia. She saw nothing of her father-in-law, although a faint scent of his pipe perfumed the air. Next to his favorite chair by the fire, a newspaper was folded, the bottom edge torn.

It had been over fifteen years since Ezra Moore's first wife had died from a chill a few short months before Eugenia's husband's fatal fall from a horse. Within a year they had found each other and combined families. Faith was acquainted with both Daniel and Zachary, their wives, and children though various family gatherings. She was not well acquainted with their sisters long since wed and moved away. She knew that Zachary engaged in shipping while Daniel preferred to farm the generous plot of land he had been given when he wed a well-placed widow. Martha was petite, shorter even than

Eugenia, but curving into a plumpness that was attractive. Soft wisps of dark hair slipped down from a finely starched mob cap framing a round face used to merriment. Seeing her eased Faith's tension. Martha smiled when she spotted her, showing off a perfect Cupid's bow mouth and pearly teeth.

"Faith! It has been too long. Come sit and talk to me. What a lovely gown!"

Eugenia chimed in delicately, "It was a quite popular style two or three seasons ago."

Faith flushed as she took her seat. A self-satisfied smile crept across her mother-in-law's face as she fussed with the teapot and cups until they were arranged just so on the tray. Eugenia's dress of rich blue with white lace and bows perfectly mimicked ones currently worn by fashion dolls in shop windows all along Duke of Gloucester Street.

Martha continued speaking as if she had not heard Eugenia. "Daniel has come to trade at the market. He is considering planting indigo and is seeking advice. I have many calls to make while I am in town. You must tell me all the news you have heard at your tavern."

Faith carefully arranged her skirts as she composed her thoughts. Martha thought the tavern was a grand adventure. Her father owned land on the James River and had gifted a generous portion to his only daughter. Having never been without money, Martha had no idea of the risks involved in running a business although Faith thought she would probably be good at it. Martha ran her home with the precision of a general. It was always clean, comfortable, and welcoming, a refuge to all who entered. Daniel adored her. It did not seem to bother him that his bride was a good seven years older than he, not that she looked it. Her pale skin showed nary a line, although her eyes had a faint crinkle when she smiled. Her plump fingers displayed no calluses or cuts, only the rings her husband had graced her with. Martha put her efforts towards raising and educating their five children, two of whom remained at home.

Faith looked at the friendly face of her sister-in-law. "It has been a while since we last spoke. How is life in Charles City?"

"I stay busy." Martha laughed lightly. "There are always travelers to house and feed. Daniel insists on feeding all and sundry that might drop by. Men come in for a drink and conversation with one another. Many times, they bring newspapers to argue over and discuss. If I am fortunate, they bring their wives so I have someone to talk to."

Faith smiled. "Men are not much different at Clarke Tavern. They eat, drink and argue there as well."

"What say they about all the troubles in Boston? My Aunt Sibyl lives near Concord. She grows fearful of all the soldiers she sees about the town. Samuel Addams stirs the crowds against England. They become bolder each day in their protests."

"We are British citizens," Eugenia reminded her. "These colonies belong to King George. It would be wise to remember this before they bring the wrath of all England down on our heads." Her expression turned sour before she smoothed her face to avoid wrinkles. She looked like the perfect hostess; her skirts artfully draped her back as straight as a pole. A new ring graced one of her bony fingers, joining the collection already encircling various other digits on display forced over faintly swollen knuckles.

"But what of all the taxes the parliament has put upon us?" Faith blurted out. The words tumbled out before she considered the consequences. It was not wise to speak impulsively in this house.

Eugenia's eyes held all the warmth of a dead fish. "We are dependent on the goodwill of Parliament for trade and protection. These colonies cannot produce the kind of goods we receive from Mother England." She patted her skirt, which featured delicately embroidered flowers, and smiled over her teacup at Martha, choosing to ignore Faith's impudence. "I must take you to see the shipment of French fabrics Ezra has recently received. All the most cultured ladies have rushed to have gowns made up. There is none like them in all of Williamsburg. Only the most discriminating shops will have a chance to acquire them."

Martha looked apologetically at Faith before answering Eugenia. "Perhaps after I've checked on the children. I will need some new gowns made. Daniel will expect me to entertain his associates while we are in town."

Faith knew that Daniel Moore had recently purchased a home not far from the governor's palace, although she had never been inside. He and Martha spent much of their time cultivating people useful to them, there was little time for poor relations. Her mind drifted as the two women chatted over what balls were coming up and who wore what. What young ladies were being courted by which gentlemen and who had indulged in too much syllabub at the last dance at the Raleigh Tavern.

Faith found most of it a dreadful bore. She did not reenter the discussion although her thoughts ran along the line that sometimes Mother England seemed a tremendous bully. Martha filled in the silence with light chatter about fashion and the planting of crops on the plantation. It appeared that plans for cotton and tobacco were already going forth. Life stayed busy along the James River. Faith knew about crops and the danger of frosts from her childhood in Pennsylvania although her father's crops ran more to potatoes, pumpkins, squashes, and grain. She smiled at Martha's stories about her children and their dogs.

"Daniel seems intent on having as many hounds as we have children." She laughed. "No one can approach the house unannounced. They are heralded by much baying and barking!"

Eugenia passed around a tray of delicate cakes. Every move Eugenia made was deliberate and graceful. She had been educated in such things; unlike Faith, whose childhood lessons had emphasized tending sheep and hens alongside weeding the family garden. There had been books, too. Her father and mother had believed in education for all their children. Eugenia had not liked that Faith read books that she considered more suitable to a man's mind. Being here brought back painful memories. Her hands shook despite her attempts to steady them. Jon was no longer here with a quick joke or comforting look to ease her discomfort. The silver spoon slipped off her saucer to land in her lap. She looked up to catch the exasperated look on her mother-in-law's face.

Nice to know I'm living up to barbaric expectations, Faith thought wryly. Martha either had not noticed or more likely chose to ignore the interaction between the two other women. Instead, she discussed the latest fashions in from London. "The newest dolls have come in. The fabrics for summer are exquisite! I love the printed chintzes. I believe I shall have a couple of lightweight gowns made up." Martha nibbled a tea cake. Edith, the cook, was an exceptional baker. She was also kind. During visits when Faith had first married, her nerves made it difficult to eat. Edith had always arranged to have fruit and biscuits available for when Faith would come down later, starving.

Eugenia spoke to Martha about the children, her face suddenly animated. Listening patiently to discussions about college, apprenticeships, and potential suitors, Faith startled when talk turned to the subject of Captain Grant.

Martha laughed, "I have seen the dashing young captain. He is quite popular with the ladies here at Williamsburg. His mother's father was a baron. I think his father has land in Scotland and rumor has it has a nice grant of property in the colonies, too. He would be quite a catch for one of our Virginia girls."

Eugenia leaned in convivially. "I have heard he has visited the Randolph Household, as well as the Lee's. I could name a few other prominent households where he has been seen."

Martha chuckled. "Connections with either of those families would take a man of ambition far."

Faith didn't know why the thought of Grant seeking a well-dowered bride bothered her. It was the logical thing for a man of his position to do. It was a relief when the topic changed to the choices of ribbons for hats and gowns. Time in the elegant parlor seemed to drag. No amount of sipping tea or pretending to nibble one of Edith's tiny cakes helped. Faith responded politely to questions about the weather and how Andrew was growing.

Martha's two oldest sons were young men now. Inside Faith felt a sinking sense of despair over how little she could offer her son who was as gifted and bright as any young man in the colonies. Martha and Eugenia were enmeshed in discussing the success of her sons, one a lawyer, the other a minister, both deep into their respective studies. The next child, a daughter, had caught the eye of the son of a local merchant.

"His father is a member of the House of Burgesses," Martha cooed. "It would be a most advantageous match. But then Lettie is only sixteen. There is plenty of time before she weds." Martha went on to discuss the two youngest whom she had brought with her to Williamsburg.

"They grow so fast. It is impossible to keep young George in breeches and Susan is walking already. She will be ready for proper schooling soon. I have hopes of finding a worthy tutor while I am here, someone skilled in teaching the proper refinements of a lady."

Eugenia waited for the conversation to lag. Her pale hands were artfully placed in her lap as she posed. Leaning toward Faith, she said, "Lady Dunmore has arrived in Virginia. Once she is settled, there will be a ball and other events to celebrate her arrival."

Faith knew of Lady Dunmore's arrival in Williamsburg a few months ago. Everyone did. Why was Eugenia discussing it? "I am sure there will be," she said politely. "Lord Dunmore must be glad to be reunited with his family after such a long separation."

Eugenia's serene smile was belied by the cold, calculating look in her eyes. Faith felt like a mouse being eyed by a hawk. Her mother-in-law never addressed her casually nor did she invite her to tea. Faith waited for the trap to spring.

"Ezra and I will attend a ball given in her honor in a few weeks' time. There will be many people there with whom it would be advantageous to connect. Several well-connected gentlemen will be in attendance. I would like you to come with us."

Faith had not been to a ball since before Andrew's birth. She had neither the clothes nor the coin for the type of wardrobe expected at such an important event. "I don't see how that would be possible." Panic's sharp claws drew down her insides. How could she attend a formal ball? It was impossible for someone of her means.

"You need to make connections if this tavern is to be a success," Eugenia said impatiently. "It would be foolish to ignore the opportunity to make social connections. The tavern is my son's legacy to his only child, provided that it can be run by someone with intelligence. Williamsburg has many taverns. You are a relatively young woman, not unattractive when you put forth the effort, young enough to consider a second marriage eventually. You need to think of Andrew and not be so selfish. An older gentleman might be happy for a companion, regardless of her origins. Even if you fail to make a respectable liaison, connecting with some of the better families in Williamsburg could do much to persuade them to patronize your business. Farmers and tradespeople do not have the coin that some of these people do. Had you not allowed your private room to burn you could have persuaded some of them to have rented it. Now you must make do with what you have left. This debacle over Bullard is more evidence of your incompetence. If you are not careful you will lose everything. You think only of yourself and naught for your son or the Clarke name!" Sniffling dramatically, she rose before stomping off to another room slamming the door behind her.

Faith sat dazed. She stared at Martha. "I cannot do this." She started to rise, leaving before her emotions got the better of her.

Martha put a plump hand on Faith's arm. "She means well, Faith. Eugenia is trying to help."

"Why would I place myself out like a mare at auction? I have no desire to remarry regardless of her opinion nor do I have the means to dress for a fancy ball." Humiliation and embarrassment flushed her face.

"You need to go, Faith, not only for yourself but also for her. She is right about building goodwill for your business. Not even Eugenia can force you to marry. This murder has upset her. She fears for you and Andrew. You need to build a civil relationship with her for your son's sake. I have a dress or two that can be made over for you. I will send them over. Do you have slippers and gloves?"

Faith nodded. They were packed away, but she did have them.

She looked at Faith kindly. "Acquiescence in such a small matter could do much to mend what is broken between you."

"I don't know about that."

"Don't let your pride override your sense. Eugenia travels in the best social circles. A little of her goodwill could do wonders for your tavern, a business Andrew will inherit one day. Think of him. You can do this."

"Thank you," Faith whispered.

"Go make amends. It's time there was peace between the two of you."

"I don't know if that is possible. No matter what I do, it goes wrong."

Martha sighed. "She says likewise." At Faith's dumbfounded look, Martha smiled wryly. "She doesn't know what to do with you. And she is terrified you and Andrew will end up destitute." Martha reached over and touched Faith's hand, her plump white fingers soft over Faith's calluses. "Let her help you. It would do her much good and could benefit you as well. Andrew needs both of you. In the end, this discord only wounds him."

Faith rose and moved awkwardly in the direction her mother-in-law had taken. She had no idea what to say. She never knew what to do around Eugenia.

Her mother-in-law had not gone far. Faith followed the sound of voices. Ezra had apparently come in. She could hear the deep timbre of his voice but not the words. He was patting his wife on the shoulder. He looked over and saw Faith. His spectacles gave him the appearance of an absent-minded owl.

"Faith, dear, how are you?"

Eugenia continued to make sniffling noises although Faith was certain she listened to every word. "I am well enough, Ezra. How are you?"

He smiled, the light catching his glasses. Shrewd gray eyes lay partly concealed by glass lenses. "Trade becomes more challenging with the blockades Mother England puts up, but we manage. I am hoping that the arrival of Lady Dunmore is a sign that we can settle and once again trade peacefully."

"That would be beneficial for all of us," Faith answered. "We should do what we can to welcome the governor's wife to Virginia."

Eugenia turned around slowly. Her eyes were puffy. Her lips trembled as she caught her husband's eyes before sniffing dramatically as she turned toward Faith. "Then you will attend her welcoming ball?"

"Yes, Eugenia. I am grateful for your efforts on my part." Faith did her best to sound sincere even if she wanted to grind her teeth. Eugenia's playacting annoyed her no end. She reminded herself that this was for Andrew who needed her to make amends although her heart said she had done no wrong.

Eugenia sniffled. "I must attend to my toilet. Please join Martha until I am presentable." Faith knew the other woman would return when she had once again perfected her face with powder and rouge. Ezra walked her back to the receiving room. As he turned to enter the door, a small piece of paper swirled from his coat pocket. She caught it before it slipped away, catching a flash of a name that sounded biblical before her father-in-law took it from her hand.

"Thank you. I would be searching the house for it later." He stuffed it back into his coat pocket before gesturing for her to proceed with him within.

Martha looked up as they entered. Faith nodded and saw her relax. Martha poured her father-in-law a cup and offered him the plate of cake.

Ezra signed happily. "Edith works magic in the kitchen. I don't know what we would do without her." His eyes twinkled. "Don't let my wife know, she worries about how many sweets I eat." The cake disappeared in two bites and then he shared stories about trading for rum and sugar. Faith said little, choosing to listen as her father-in-law regaled them with the adventures of his favorite dog, Judith. Eugenia slipped in quietly before sitting and dominating the conversation with gossip regarding the impropriety or poor attire choices of her neighbors. It made Faith's head ache.

Over an hour later, she walked home. Eugenia had made it clear the carriage was no longer available. It provided time for her to compose her thoughts, which were numerous. Visits to Jon's family were beneficial, she knew, but even after ten years, she still felt like a stranger among them.

Chapter Eleven

Faith recognized the Bullard house as she walked by. The compact yard was tidy with neatly trimmed hedges and clipped grass that outlined the walkway. It was a large brick house that dominated the street both in size and elegance. Steps led up to an imposing door. Pausing by the gate she admired the iron-wrought gate and fence separating the yard from the street. Suddenly the front door opened and a house slave ran outside bouncing off the frame and nearly tripping down the steps. Faith's laugh turned to concern at the panic on his face.

"What's wrong?"

"Mistress Charlotte collapsed. We can't wake her. I've been sent to get Mistress Moore. She helped before when she had one of her sick headaches. I pray she is home."

"I know she is. I just left there. I am Mistress Moore's daughter-in-law."

"Please go to my mistress. She needs care."

Faith hurried toward the still open door as the man ran down the road. Following the maid, Faith continued to the receiving room where the most noise was coming from.

Charlotte Bullard lay on the floor, her flowered dress arranged neatly about her. A girl, no older than twelve, fanned the air around her with a feather while a well-dressed lady hovered nearby straightening the unconscious woman's gown while delicate sobs made her shoulders shake. Faith knelt down taking in the pale face and crossed arms stopping the young lady from placing flowers on her as well.

"She's not dead."

The woman sniffled. "She looks so pale."

"Rice powder does that, but I believe she has simply fainted." She smiled. "I am Faith Clarke, an acquaintance of Mistress Bullard."

"I am Prudence Wright, her niece. I came just this week from Baltimore for an extended visit." Her hands continued to arrange gown and petticoats. "Chintz wrinkles if you're not careful."

Faith rolled her eyes. Rumpled clothing was hardly a priority. She looked at the woman on the floor. She didn't spot anything indicative of illness. A pulse still beat at her throat.

"What happened?"

"We were enjoying tea. Then she said she couldn't breathe and passed out." Prudence's lip trembled. "I've tried to wake her but to no avail. Surely some ailment has taken her."

Hoping to avoid histrionics, Faith spoke firmly. "She's breathing and her heart is beating strongly. She would probably be more comfortable in her own bed. Perhaps some of the servants could help?"

Prudence rose and sat primly in a chair. Moisture dribbled off her chin. Sniffles followed a few distinct hiccups. "We were talking about visiting my family while the weather is pleasant. I guess that will need to be postponed: Momma will be most disappointed."

Faith heard the sound of another person arriving. Before she could turn about, Eugenia's voice became clearer.

"Where is Mistress Bullard?" Bustling into the room, Eugenia began giving orders, "We need to get her upstairs to bed where she will be more at ease."

Her sharp glance settled on Prudence who hastily jumped up and went in search of servants to carry their mistress.

"What happened?" Eugenia had grown up on a plantation near Fredericksburg. Her family had always tended to their sick. Her knowledge of medical treatments was extensive.

"I don't know. Her niece said she fainted during tea."

Eugenia frowned then leaned down to look at Charlotte. "When I spoke to Lottie yesterday, she seemed to have accepted Phineas' passing. Following the funeral, most of the relatives left once they realized there was no profit in remaining. It may be the stress of dealing with a violent death or her maid has pulled in her stays too firmly. Regardless, it doesn't appear all that serious. Let's have her carried to her room." Eugenia turned to the two menservants who had appeared. "One of you takes her legs, the other under her arms. Gently, now let's get her to bed."

She looked over at her daughter-in-law. "Your presence is not needed."

Faith silently counted to control her temper. She forced a smile, "I was asked to come." Further acrimony was prevented by Charlotte Bullard's niece breaking into tears.

"She collapsed right in front of me!"

Eugenia's tone was placating. "I am sure she will be fine after a little rest. I have a tisane I will send over for unsteady nerves. It will help her through this difficult time. Perhaps you would benefit from a sip of wine. My son's wife can attend you."

Prudence nodded while snuffling daintily into a delicately embroidered handkerchief.

"I will ensure that she rests comfortably."

Prudence looked at Eugenia's stiff back ascending the stairs. "She seems so powerful. I don't know what I would do alone."

"Eugenia has always believed strongly in her own opinions." Walking quietly over to a side table Faith poured a small amount of wine and handed it to the hapless woman.

"Stay with me. I cannot bear to be alone." Taking a generous swallow, Prudence gasped. "I don't think this is wine."

Faith sniffed the bottle, "No, it's rum, but it too has medicinal purposes." If nothing else it would dull the edges of her upset.

"Very well." Prudence downed the rest in a single gulp, coughing slightly as the strong liquor went down her throat. She picked up the bottle and poured some more. "My nerves could use some settling."

"It may do more than settle you if you are not used to it."

Warily eyeing the stairs for signs of Eugenia's return, Faith sat down by her. "Your tea is getting cold, why don't you finish it?"

Prudence lifted the cup and took a delicate sip. She was a pretty girl with pale brown curls and dark brown eyes, probably no more than sixteen or seventeen. Her ivory dress was sprinkled with a pattern of flowers and leaves reminiscent of a flower garden. She began to calm under the influence of a sympathetic presence. Between gulps of rum and delicate sips of tea, conversation flowed out of her.

Faith patted her hand and listened absently, making appropriate sounds as the girl spoke of the difficulty of acquiring proper mourning clothes and the increasing cost of getting goods from Europe. It was not difficult to steer the conversation around to the subject of her recently departed uncle.

"Aunt Lottie was going through everything. She had already put a maid to sorting his clothes. She was going to go through his desk herself. I don't know who will handle it now."

"Surely his business partner, Mr. Smythe, can go through his ledgers."

She shook her head vigorously. "He came by yesterday to do that, but she refused him. Aunt Lottie had to make sure nothing of a personal nature was involved. He was very unhappy. You know he is her younger brother, of course." She hiccupped and raised her glass. "Wonderful properties this has. I must write and tell my mother how greatly it settles the nerves."

Faith nodded, watching with some concern as the liquid drained. Prudence continued speaking, "Uncle Phineas conducted all sorts of business in trade. Sometimes we entertained his associates here, but most often, they went to the taverns. Generally, he took them to the King's Arms. He was quite fond of Mrs. Vobe's establishment." Prudence rested her head against the back of the chair.

"Perhaps, you should lie down," Faith suggested. "It has by all accounts been a trying day." She was beginning to wonder how long the girl would remain upright. Faith reached out to steady her. Frowning, she looked at the girl's flushed face and wondered if a hint to her maid should be dropped. At least she was no longer teetering on the edge of hysteria.

Prudence set down her cup almost missing the saucer. "I believe I will." She stood, waving slightly before straightening her back. "It's always important to act like a lady. 'Tis been a most trying afternoon, Mistress Clarke. Forgive me if I excuse myself." She held the chair back with both hands as her face took on a bemused expression.

Alarmed, Faith rose with her, but Prudence shook her head. "I'll be fine. Please make yourself at home." She wobbled down the hall and up the stairs, pausing at the landing to sway like a leaf in the wind. Faith watched Prudence's progress wondering if yet another of the Bullard family was in danger of collapsing. When she reached the top, she swung with her hand on the doorframe and disappeared into a room.

Upstairs Eugenia gave orders with the authority of an empress keeping the staff occupied with the care of their mistress. The main floor was deserted which provided the perfect opportunity to look around uninterrupted. If Bullard were like most men, he would have a place to conduct business at home. After peeping into a few doorways, she found an office. The elegant room had a marble fireplace and wallpaper imported from England. A fine woolen rug covered the floor and a carved wooden chess set graced the table. Edging inside, she closed the door behind her. A hinge squawked, making her almost jump out of her skin.

Several sheets of paper lay on a small desk in the corner. Walking over, she began sifting through them. Her eyes scanned the script, hoping for some scrap of information that would aid her cause. Faith knew she was prying, but there were too many unanswered questions about Phineas Bullard.

"Forgive me, Lord," she murmured as she leaned over the stack. The majority of the papers were letters, written in the elegant script of the well-educated. Most seemed concerned with various business concerns and discussed shipments of cotton, sugar, and other goods. One stuck out askew as if it had been laid down in haste. The writer sounded angry. *"Unconscionable actions earn unprecedented action. May God have mercy on your soul. You, sir, are a scoundrel and a dog, unworthy of all with which you have been blessed. I demand that you immediately inform me of the location of David and Felicia Verity or face the consequences."*

The letter alarmed her. Someone had been very angry with Bullard although she wasn't sure why. The handwriting looked familiar but from where she did not know. Her guest book was full of signatures from all across the colonies.

Footsteps headed down the stairs. Unless she moved quickly, servants would discover her, just when she was finding something useful. All that remained on the desk were more letters and a ledger of accounts. The ledger was smaller than most, designed to fit in a pocket or kept private. Flipping through it she noted a series of names and a list of amounts but unlike the letters, the reason for the payment was not indicated. "How odd." Bullard struck her as being meticulous about his money. Frowning she noticed both her father-in-law's name as well as Jon's brother, Louis in the ledger. The little book indicated dates of delivery as well. She frowned; the last one had been a few days prior to Bullard's demise.

Faith needed to examine his papers further, but how? She had not worn pockets and carrying papers would draw attention. Steps drew closer in the entryway. Mere seconds remained in which to act. One letter would not be missed, so she grabbed the one that sounded so alarming and stuck it in the only space available, down the front of her dress, and pulled her kerchief closer over her shoulders and breasts. She stepped away just as a maid entered. Faith fanned her face and turned, assuming a bland expression.

"I was feeling a bit faint," she said. "I hope Mistress Bullard is recuperating."

The maid shook her head sadly. "I knew that stuff was not good for her, but she had to have it."

"What do you mean?"

"Laudanum," the maid hissed. "She takes it for her nerves." The maid leaned in to whisper in Faith's ear. "I've seen it before when my brother broke his leg falling off a roof. It's not a drug to be played with. It's easy to develop a craving that won't go away."

Faith shivered. She had heard of laudanum but knew only that it deadened pain, not of its deadlier effects.

"Faith, what are you doing in here?" Eugenia demanded coming in behind the maid, blocking the exit. Her color was high, whether it was from exertion or rage was unclear, but she instantly recognized the tone. Eugenia's voice became shrill when angry. Faith was familiar with it and as her mother-in-law approached her body tensed in response.

"I needed fresh air." It sounded like a poor excuse even to her. Faith prayed that the letter was not visible but she dared not look. The maid exited silently from the room much to Faith's envy. She was more likely to evade a cannon than Eugenia's wrath. Given a choice, she would have taken the former.

Eugenia's eyes narrowed. "That is more likely to be found outside. The lady of the house is indisposed and our presence is discourteous. We need to go." Wordlessly, Faith followed her mother-in-law outside, hoping the paper in her bosom did not crinkle as she walked.

Once they left the house and were into the narrow front yard, Eugenia wasted no time in turning on Faith, "How dare you! No one but the rudest of individuals goes into what is obviously a private room! I have long known you came from common stock. That has been evident from the first but now you embarrass me in the eyes of my neighbors."

"Far more embarrassing to shriek like a seagull in the street," Faith shot back.

Eugenia's eyes took on a rabid glaze. "You are nothing but an insolent wretch who tricked my son into wedding you. You are nothing, nothing without him. My Jon should never have died!"

"I was at least there when he passed," Faith responded sharply. It was a cruel thing to say, and she knew better but she was tired of Eugenia's anger. His mother could not have known when she went to the Moore plantation to escape the summer heat that Jon would fall ill. Word had been sent, but Eugenia had not returned in time. That was not Faith's fault.

Color bleached out of the older woman's face as the jibe hit home, and then began purpling as defensive rage conquered reason and gentility, "I could have saved him! He died under your care. His death is on your hands. Go back to your wretched tavern. It's a pity the fire did not consume you. You have no place in this family. You are not one of us."

"You embarrass yourself with such behavior." With effort, Faith kept her voice even. No one had the right to vilify her care of Jon. His death remained a raw wound, one she refused to discuss with Eugenia.

Faith opened the gate and slammed it behind her, hearing it clang discordantly when it struck the post, hurrying away from her mother-in-law's vicious tongue. Faith was not proud of her behavior but Eugenia brought out the worst in her. Her ribs worked like a bellows, trying to take in air but not getting enough. Stopping when she couldn't breathe, her ribs felt like they were stabbing internal organs. Faith vainly attempted to swallow the knot in her throat that only grew larger. Tears that would not be banished trickled down her cheeks. Faith put her hand on a fence post and prayed for peace of mind.

"Mistress Clarke, Be ye all right?"

Faith jumped as a shadow fell over her. She struggled for a moment to come up with a name. "Master McKay," she choked. "What are you doing here?"

He looked at her curiously and handed her a cloth scrap that was his handkerchief. "I live here. My mistress lets me stay in a spare room in the attic."

Faith realized there was nothing familiar about her location. She had left the fine houses of the well-to-do behind. They were in the shade of an oak tree on a narrow well-tended street. Her hand rested on a simple wooden gate that led to the garden and yard of a sturdy brick residence. Close by she could hear the sounds of horses and wagons which told her Duke of Gloucester Street was near.

McKay stared at her, concern evident on his face. He no longer looked quite like a half-starved colt. His hair remained unruly and dark auburn. The sun had begun its work on that pale skin, causing his nose to peel and his face to freckle. Faith found her voice as she realized the silence had gone on too long.

"Georgina Clements, who operates the *Gazette*?" Faith remembered that Master Clements had died over a year ago. She and Jon had attended the funeral since they were acquainted through church. She had heard that Mistress Clements continued the business. Will MacKay was apparently her assistant, given that the two Clements boys would still be too young to have mastered printing.

Will looked her up and down before coming to a decision. "My mistress is inside. I think you had best come in before you fall down." Leading her inside the gate, he kept a hand under her elbow after she stumbled over a loose stone. Will lifted her up the steps and set her down on the front porch. "Mistress Clements, we have company." Not waiting for an answer, he opened the door and assisted her inside and down the hall to a small sitting room. Will indicated a chair so Faith sat. The wood creaked beneath her, making her a little uneasy.

Within a few minutes, they were joined by a middle-aged woman with an authoritative manner. Dark hair streaked with gray was barely visible beneath Georgia Clements' cap. Her gown was a soft blue that matched her mild eyes which focused on Faith. Her mouth was a delicate rosebud that must have caused hearts to flutter when she was younger.

"Surely you did not find this lady out in the street."

"Actually, I did," he answered with a faint grin. "Mistress Clarke was gracing our gate when I came back from delivering our latest missive."

"Faith Clarke, it has been a while. You continue to operate your husband's tavern?"

"That would be me," Faith admitted weakly. Her breath was coming back although her nerves remained rattled. Uneasily she realized she must look like a complete mess.

Neither mentioned her swollen eyes or damp cheeks. "Come join us for a spot of tea," Mistress Clements said before bringing a sturdy redware pot into the room along with scones. Faith's stomach growled. She had eaten little at Eugenia's.

"It's not British tea. I will not support the tyranny that King George has pressed down upon us." Mistress Clements explained. "It's made with peppermint leaves from my own garden. It is refreshing and thankfully not an item to be taxed."

Faith agreed. The flavor was different than she was accustomed to, but the warmth and scent were pleasing. Will buttered a scone before putting it on a plate and handing it to her.

"You should eat," he said as he buttered a couple more for himself. It was becoming clear why he no longer looked half-starved.

Faith thought about pointing out that her stays would not allow much in the way of food, but remained quiet. He was trying to be kind.

Will MacKay's thick, straight brows were almost black, as were his eyelashes. His nose was long and straight, too large for beauty, but it was offset by a wide and generous mouth. That mouth was tight right now as he contemplated her.

"I am not a man raised with delicate words and phrases. When we last met, you tried to enter an angry mob. Now you are outside my door in a sorry state. You have no brother or husband that I know of to protect you so I must ask. What troubles you to the degree that you weep?"

Grateful as she was for his concern, Faith needed no protector. "I can manage my own affairs." Men might believe they had the right to tell women what to do, but women generally had more sense than to believe that intelligence fell entirely along gender lines.

Will sighed, "You're determined to muck about in Bullard's death, aren't you?" He waved a hand at her face. "It's all through the town how he died. Mayhap you are not my responsibility, but I do not want ill to befall you." His smile was beguiling. "If you will not let a poor Scotsman protect you, will you let him help you instead?"

Mistress Clements chuckled. "Let him help you if only so he will sleep at night."

"Do you have a copy of the newspaper?"

They both laughed. "Plenty," Georgia said. "Here." She handed her the folded sheets.

Quickly Faith flipped to where she thought the torn corner on Ezra's paper had been. There were the usual missives regarding the sales of land and horses, cockfights. Then she saw it, a notice that someone was leaving Virginia between the seventh and fifth and wished to settle accounts. It was signed by Micah Adamson."

"Who is Micah Adamson?"

Will shrugged. "As long as they pay in coin, I don't worry about the name they give."

"Ezra kept this notice. I don't know of any Adamson's in Williamsburg."

"Perhaps the man owes him money or he owes them something?"

Faith considered it. "Maybe. Still, it seems strange. Why say between the seventh and fifth? Would it not be more correct to say between the fifth and seventh? What business could my father-in-law have with him?"

Georgia interrupted, "He likely was in a hurry and didn't consider it. Most men don't think it polite to discuss business among us ladies. They think we cannot understand such complex matters."

Will winced. "Perhaps it's more a desire not to be a bore."

Georgia's eyes twinkled. "It's more than that but as I'm sure our guest has discovered, there are advantages in being underestimated."

Faith couldn't help but smile. She knew what the older widow meant. Suddenly feeling more relaxed than she had in some time, she decided to trust them.

"I am only doing what I must to protect my inn and my family." Slowly, Faith shared about Phineas Bullard, the fire, and why she had been running. They listened without interruption.

"The British think you killed Bullard?" Will asked, leaning forward.

"I don't know. Suspicions cloud the reputation of the tavern and I cannot lose the business. I don't know why anyone would commit such a horrible act and why at my tavern of all places?"

Mistress Clements spoke, "It takes great hate to repeatedly stab someone to death like that. It seems a bit convenient that the only witness died in her sleep. The gaoler is a fair man but he doesn't notice everything. Now Bullard's wife is conveniently ill. Trouble keeps piling up."

Will agreed, "You are dealing with someone dangerous. He's not leaving anyone who will talk. The fire was a warning."

"Or a way to destroy evidence," Georgia added.

"Captain Grant is investigating," Faith said. "He has been all over the tavern with his men."

"But you don't trust him," MacKay noted, "which makes you smarter than most. He's an officer in the British army. His job is to keep the peace, not necessarily find the right criminal." There was an underlying bitterness in his tone. "What England cares about is the legal oppression of the colonies. Is not the treatment of Boston evidence of that?"

"What has happened in Boston?"

Mistress Clements explained. "It's not common knowledge yet, but I've heard from a ship fresh from England. The parliament has voted to close the port of Boston."

"Close the port?" Faith was stunned. To close the port would be to cut the town off from the rest of the world.

Will nodded. "It's only the beginning. Once they've accomplished this, there will be other punishments for offenses real or imagined against the crown. We will never be free to make our own choices while Britain holds the reigns."

"You speak as if we were another country."

"We are," Mistress Clements said. "We're Americans."

Faith stared at them. She had never thought of herself as other than an Englishwoman, but she was here in Virginia, one of the American colonies. Did that make her an American? It was a disquieting thought that she was not ready to contemplate.

Talk turned to goings on in the House of Burgesses. Georgia Clements stirred her tea. "Mark my words; they will react to the news of Boston."

Will nodded before adding his own comment. "The governor will not like that. He's got a temper."

"Isn't he a Scot?" Faith said demurely.

Will growled.

"She has you there." Georgia Clements was amused. "His lordship is a Scot and a hothead, far more so than his predecessor."

"Yes, but don't blame the Scots for his high-handedness. We had naught to do with it."

Faith laughed and felt the stress of the day melt away. This was tea as she had never experienced it. The conversation diverged from proper subjects like weather to remarks on the governor and parliament that bordered on treasonous. She didn't know what to think. After a particularly colorful tale involving a renegade cow charging down Prince George Street, she laughed until her sides ached.

"I need to get home. It's nearly suppertime."

Will walked Faith home. She almost refused, wishing for time to sort her thoughts from the disaster of tea at Eugenia's, to the collapse of Lottie Bullard and the ever-present memory of Phineas Bullard's murder. Tree branches leaned over fences that secured yards casting shadows over the ground. Some bloomed while others displayed tiny yellow-green leaves that would later broaden as the weather continued to warm. After a time, she was grateful for MacKay's presence.

Despite the growing lateness of the day, a crowd gathered outside a tavern. Faith stared at the thickening crowd. Something felt different, harsher. A light breeze brought odors of a foul bodily nature. She jerked back, her nose wrinkling in disgust.

"We had better turn around," Will said grimly.

"Why?"

"There's a slave auction happening."

Squinting, she saw figures moving in an odd, jerky fashion. Puzzled, she moved forward to get a better look only to be blocked by Will MacKay.

"What's wrong with them?"

"They're in chains, so there is no chance of escape. They've probably just come off a ship from Jamaica or somewhere down the coast. What poor wretches survive are dragged off to towns like Williamsburg to be sold like pigs or cattle." His bitterness surprised her. Will's breath was rapid and drawn between his teeth as if he had taken a hard blow to the gut.

Faith avoided town when she saw announcements of sales. She preferred not to think of them.

"They are human beings," she said weakly.

"Not under the laws of these colonies. Those wretches are treated worse than dogs by those in the trade. The bloody ships should be blown out of the water. There is naught but misery on those vessels." Will's lips were drawn so tight they were nearly white. Hard lines ran down the sides of his nose as he looked down the road.

Faith swallowed. If she died, this would be what Titus and Olivia faced. It was time she quit hiding from the truth. "Let's see if we can go around." She walked slowly but resolutely down the street thinking about Olivia who came into town early on Wednesdays and Saturdays to buy food and supplies.

She had last seen her in a cotton shift and skirt, her hair covered with one of the brightly colored head wraps she preferred. It was unbearable to consider her or Titus doomed to such wretchedness. Her willful blindness disgusted her. "Hiding from the truth solves nothing," she muttered as they tried to skirt the crowd.

MacKay looked at her in surprise. "Aye." Taking her arm, he hurried her along as the crowd pooled and thickened.

Giving the auction a wide berth, they slipped by just as a cacophony of noise exploded around them. One man stood on a wooden platform calling out the particulars of the poor wretches lined up for sale. Faith's lips tightened as she took in the ropes that bound the hands. Some had the additional indignity of ropes about their necks used as guides by the men handling them. Faith felt sickened. Will MacKay's hand tightened on her arm as he pulled her through the outer fringes of the crowd.

Snippets of conversation invaded her ears. "How much stamina do you think that buck has? Do they speak the King's English?"

She wanted to scream. They looked like skeletons. The stench that arose from them made the bile rise in her throat. Most wore rags that barely covered their most private parts. Most of the women didn't even have adequate clothing to be modest. It was obscene. Faith started to turn around.

"What are you doing?" MacKay hissed.

"No one deserves to be treated like this! Something has to be done." Faith's hands balled into fists.

"And what do you think you can do?" Will replied brutally. "This has been going on for years. It's legal. All you will do is get yourself arrested and then where will you and your son be?"

"It's wrong. Surely, the Burgesses could do something." Faith saw the auction with new eyes. It was horrible.

MacKay's answer was swift. "Most of your fine gentlemen in this town support the slave trade either directly or indirectly by purchasing these men and women. These wretches are chained in the holds of ships for weeks on end until they reach port. Cattle are treated better."

"How do you know this?" she whispered. Their eyes looked dead and empty of hope.

"I've been on a slave ship. I'll never go on another. There is no crime imaginable that could deserve such a fate."

Faith hurried, her breath catching rapidly in her throat. It was too much to bear. Within the throng were people she recognized from church and around town, waiting to bid on the lives of the wretches before them. Even as Will and Faith escaped down the street, the images of those slaves danced before her eyes.

Faith hurried toward the comfort of Clarke tavern. Avoiding the front entrance, she went back to the kitchen where strangers would not see the tears streaking her face. She scrubbed at them in irritation. Olivia looked at her in surprise.

"Mistress Faith?"

"I am fine." She was not fine. Faith wouldn't be fine until she had made sure Titus and Olivia would never have to endure what she had just seen. Will MacKay came in behind her. He saw Olivia and froze. Faith saw the comprehension and disgust wash over his face as he looked at her. There was no need for words.

"Mistress Clarke," he said coldly, "I will leave you to the care of your slave." He turned on his heel and left, slamming the door behind him. Both women could hear the thundering of his feet as he hurried down the steps and away from the tavern.

"What in the world?" Olivia exclaimed.

"I deserve it," Faith said. "And far more. I've let you and Titus remain slaves when in fact, no person should own another. I've let fear color my perception of right or wrong and I don't have the luxury of doing that. I am sorry. There is no excuse for what I have done." Her heart was pounding unevenly in her chest as the words spilled out. Words she had kept inside and ignored too long. But fear in and of itself was not reason enough to not act. Faith knew this, had always known it but had been too great of a coward to face the reality of her own convictions. A life without integrity was no more than an empty husk and she intended to have more.

Olivia's face was unreadable. She continued her work in the kitchen as

Faith unloaded feelings she could no longer hold in. She would never forget what she had just seen. Never had misery been painted so vividly before her eyes. It burned in her brain.

Faith continued before caution caught up with her, "Freeing slaves requires the governor's approval and proof of meritorious service. It's past time I petitioned for your release. I should have done it after Jon's death."

Titus had come in with a load of wood for the cooking fire. He stood there listening. His sherry brown eyes met hers, "Mistress, you haven't got any money."

"I know," The thought terrified her, but if she stopped to think, she would never do what needed to be done. "I may not be able to pay you much. But I do have a conscience and I will not suffer to own slaves after what I have seen today. God will provide for us. He always has." With that, she dragged herself to her room to pull herself together and to consider how she would accomplish the impossible.

Chapter Twelve

Two letters lay on Faith's desk. One belonged to Phineas Bullard, stolen during her impromptu visit. The other was a letter to the governor pleading for the freedom of Titus and Olivia York. She felt ill-equipped to deal with either one.

She had begun the latter before going to bed. Since then it had lain there as she had agonized over the right words. The governor turned down most petitions. He would not grant manumission without a compelling cause. The faces of the slaves being auctioned like cattle haunted her. Faith slept poorly. She could not forget the look on Will McKay's face when he had realized she owned people. The shame would not go away.

"Why should I care what an indentured servant thinks?" she muttered. Because he was right, her inner voice whispered. She had not spoken to Will since his discovery of Olivia and Titus although she had seen him with armloads of the gazette under his arm going up and down the streets. Remembering how they parted hurt. She wished he had a better opinion of her. Right now she didn't deserve one.

Picking up Bullard's letter, she squinted at it once more. Despite wracking her brain, she could not remember where she had seen the elegant yet spidery script. Holding it next to her ledger of account signatures didn't help. It resembled no one's that she had done business with.

"Who do you belong to?" More importantly, who were David and Felicity Verity? She had never heard of them.

Outside, birds sang in the thickly leaved trees shading the rear of the tavern. Already, the marks of the fire had faded to faintly scorched bark.

The remains of her private room had long since been cleared away, every nail saved, every scrap taken away. The worst of the burn marks on the outer wall had been scrubbed and painted over by Titus and Joshua. Yet Faith still felt she could detect the charred smell of burned wood when she was close by. Perhaps she was being fanciful.

The boys were out weeding the garden while Titus chopped wood. Walking down the hallway to the back door, she watched them hoe peas. Andrew jumped as a disgruntled black snake shot out from between his feet, disturbed from what had been a pleasant nap. The light from the sun set her son's hair ablaze as he hopped about, avoiding the wily serpent who soon slipped under the wooden fence to another yard.

Hearing the front door open and close, Faith turned. Two men wanted to wet their throats after a long ride to town. She was happy to oblige. One was dressed like a parson. Over a few tankards of ale, voices murmured. The parson's voice rose slightly, "There are messages for everyone in God's word."

Faith filled two tankards and placed them before the men. "Could I offer you a meal?" In no time, they were tucking in some of Olivia's chicken stew. She stepped out of sight to wipe sweat off her brow. The morning's rain had left the day steamy as well as hot. She was amazed that the men were not roasting in their attire. Besides doffing their hats, the men did little beyond unbuttoning their jackets. The parson removed a copy of the scriptures and laid it on the table. His words ran through her mind firing an insane idea. Joshua came in and began clearing a nearby table. "Watch the room for a moment."

He stared at her bewildered as she left him to tend to the men.

Faith almost ran to her bedroom and began searching frantically. "Where is it?" Her mother would be mortified that she couldn't lay hands on her own Bible. Her foot hit something under the edge of the bed. Peering down, the leather cover of the Bible she had been given as a wedding present appeared. Dragging it out she rapidly turned to the passage indicated in the scrap her father-in-law had kept. Micah 7:5 "Do not trust in a friend; do not put your confidence in a companion. Guard the doors of your mouth, from her who lies in your bosom."

Out in the main room, Faith heard more men come in. Titus would need her assistance shortly. She stared at the text again and its warning. What did it mean to Ezra? "What are you up to?" If he held to his regular pattern, her father-in-law would soon enter. For the past few weeks, he had taken to coming in two to three times a week for dinner. He met with men unfamiliar to her, only two or three at a time. Their voices ceased whenever Faith approached to refill a tankard or bring more food. No matter how she tried to linger, Ezra kept sending her on errands, fetching special wines, or once to replace a dropped plate.

A knock at her door disturbed her thoughts. "Yes?"

"Pa says he'll need help soon." Joshua's voice sounded muffled through the heavy wooden door.

"I'll be right there." Setting the bible down on her clothes chest, she dusted off her hands and went to lend her assistance with the dinner crowd. For a few hours, she ferried food back and forth from the kitchen and watched men devouring Olivia's fine cooking. Once she could draw a breath, she realized Captain Grant had come in and taken up what had become his regular place where afternoon shadows rendered him less noticeable. He too, had taken to coming in frequently although his appearances varied as to time and day. She smiled as she cleared his plate, "More wine?"

"Certainly, mistress." He held her gaze and smiled, daring her to say more.

Faith wondered if he came to watch her or some of the more vocal patrons. She considered suggesting he try the *Raleigh Tavern* which was popular with those espousing the patriot cause, but decided against it. A little voice inside her head suggested that having him there undoubtedly had a calming effect on guests who might otherwise have been tempted to be rowdy. She had no cause to complain. Grant paid for his ale in English coin and sat quietly in a corner away from the fire watching like a bird of prey.

Her days and nights fell into a regular pattern of work leaving little time for investigation.

Once Martha delivered the promised gown, any spare moments Faith could claim ceased. Sewing occupied most of her spare time. Between

Olivia's and Faith's needle skills, the necessary alterations were soon complete.

A few weeks remained until Lady Dunmore's welcoming ball. Faith had heard nothing from Eugenia, but when Martha paid her a call, she clearly expected her to attend. So, she sewed and tried to remember forgotten dance steps. Even though Jon had once taught her, she knew better than to try the minuet. But the country or contra dances were manageable. These dances were not judged as critically as the other, more formal styles. Since dancers began with the highest-ranking members, Faith knew she was safe from looking the fool early on.

The lengthening days provided Faith more time for bookkeeping. Although accounts were by no means fat, they were getting by. She still made payments for Jon's loan, but she had heard nothing about Charlotte Bullard. Mr. Smythe received her coin with politeness but said nothing about his sister until Faith enquired.

He paused and looked up from his accounts, all neatly written in the ledger before him. "Dr. Staunton attends her regularly. He believes that Charlotte can be eased away from laudanum."

Faith nodded with what she hoped was sympathy although she wanted to know how long she had been using laudanum and from whence did she get it? Although she imagined any of the apothecaries carried it.

Josiah Smythe had lost weight since Faith's last meeting with him. His shirt hung from his shoulders and his waistcoat sagged. It was missing a button as well. Faith was surprised at this omission. His wife was an excellent seamstress, not one to let her spouse look less than well kept. His vest was also a tad short although made of fine materials. Perhaps it had once belonged to Bullard? When his gaze met hers, Faith flushed in embarrassment. His eyes were shadowed, but a ghost of amusement hung in them.

"I'm well enough, Mistress Clarke, and will be even better once I get these accounts sorted out." He pushed back from his desk and stood up, pushing loose strands of hair behind his ears. "Your accounts are up to date so you have naught to fear. I still have much to do in the wake of my brother-in-law's death, so if you do not mind, I will close the shop a bit early."

Faith nodded and let him walk her out the door. Hearing it shut firmly behind her she wondered what he had learned from his brother's books. Next door she heard the sound of the press. Mistress Clements was printing another edition. For a moment, she paused outside the door. Faith wanted to step inside but was hesitant to face Will. Sighing she turned and walked away, never seeing him move from the shadows to watch her.

The day of Lady Dunmore's welcoming ball began with wispy humidity fogging the landscape. The sun rose sleepily in the sky, a pale bright ball that made candles unnecessary. Faith pulled on her clothes and went out into the yard to feed the chickens. The hens stalked the grass for fresh bugs as Solomon the rooster strutted about his harem watchfully. Faith smiled as they scurried under her apron looking for extra food. Finding a few eggs, she went into the kitchen. The scent of hominy arose from a pot on the stove along with the rich scent of frying bacon.

Titus and the boys were already eating. Faith smiled. The boys laughed as he finished a story about a cat chasing a mouse under a lady's skirts. The big man constantly told tales about fishing and things he saw in and about Williamsburg. Faith doubted he missed anything that went on in town. They looked up at her as she entered. She motioned for them to remain seated, serving her own plate before joining them. Although she knew most folk would frown on the idea of eating with servants, Faith did not care. She regarded Titus, Olivia, and Joshua as family. She only hoped they would stay once they were freed.

Coffee perfumed the air, filling it with a rich comforting scent that made the earliness of the hour that much more bearable. Pouring herself a cup, Faith added a little honey and milk indulging a little before taking a sip. She sighed happily, "Bringing this stuff in was a wonderful idea."

Titus grinned, "Olivia is one smart lady. After all, she married me!"

He got a smack from his beloved which Faith ignored. The obvious affection between the two warmed her heart even as it reminded her of happier times in her own life. She watched a quiet smile flit across Andrew's freckled face. He needed to see what was good and right and meaningful.

There had been too much grief in this house. Without Titus and Olivia, he would have missed the joy.

Titus rose and stacked his dishes, as did the boys. He eyed them. "Best get that cow milked and the chickens tended early before Mistress Faith gets prettied up for that ball."

Faith rolled her eyes. "I would rather be here."

"Not after all the work that's been done on that dress," Olivia said, "You go and make Mistress Genia happy. Bout time there was peace between you two."

Faith agreed and if it meant suffocating in a dress that left her chest exposed and her nether regions swathed in so much fabric that getting through doors would be difficult.

"Why is Grandmother angry with you?"

Faith paused trying to find words that would be fair, "People grieve in many ways. Your grandmother loved Papa very much and it hurt her when he died and she was not here. Sometimes when people are hurt, they act angry and it takes time for them to..." Faith fumbled for words.

"Get less angry?" Andrew supplied. Faith nodded. He leaned over to hug her before leaving for school. Joshua pretended not to notice. He was nearly thirteen and affection embarrassed him. Not that it stopped his parents from providing it.

"Don't worry about your grandmother, she needs time." At least Faith hoped that was the solution. Quietly, she prayed for peace within the Clarke family. She was sick of conflict.

The day flew by leaving little time for thought. Faith scurried from kitchen to main room tending guests and plying them with drink. After dinner had been served, the men took over. Giving Titus the key to the liquor cabinet, Faith went to prepare for the ball. She could hear him instructing the boys. Joshua was sent to the apothecary for chalk for his father's heartburn. Andrew wanted to go along which got a chuckle.

"Oh no, little man; there is too much to do for both my helpers to go to the store. You feed the horses while I make sure we got enough on hand for everybody to drink tonight."

Faith knew the tavern was in good hands. She tried to ignore the growing knot in her stomach. A ball at the capital was a major event, especially since it would officially welcome Lady Dunmore to Williamsburg. As such, the room would be crowded with wealthy and important individuals. The idea of hobnobbing with them was terrifying. Olivia fussed with Faith's hair, washed earlier that afternoon so that it would be fresh for the ball. Powder from the many wigs made her eyes water, so they had agreed that it was pointless to use it. Wigs were too ostentatious for Faith's taste. She preferred to be who she was. Nonetheless, her hair needed to be appropriately dressed for an event meant for the gentry. Olivia muttered something that sounded rude in French. Faith raised an eyebrow, "I know I'm frustrating, but is such language necessary?"

Olivia sighed. "Beg pardon, mistress, but this hair is something else. It does not want to hold a curl."

Faith grinned ruefully. "No it never has. We could just stuff it into a cap." Pity Olivia couldn't attend the ball. Her hair curled beautifully and it had a sheen that she privately envied.

Olivia gave her an icy stare. "Mob caps do not belong at the ball. All the members of the House of Burgesses and their wives will be present. You will be there with Mistress Eugenia and Master Ezra as well as their sons and their wives." As if Faith could forget. Her father-in-law was a member of the House of Burgesses. She was not going to embarrass him even if it meant having her hair tortured. Faith closed her eyes and pretended to be somewhere else. Her eyes teared from all the tugging on her head. Hearing Olivia's menacing mutters, she refrained from further comments although she wondered if she was going to end up bald.

"This hair *will* curl." Perhaps intimidated by Olivia's steely resolve, Faith's hair did submit to being curled and tied with silk ribbon in a soft blue-green. The reddish-brown tendrils were brushed up fashionably high with side curls cascading artfully down the sides and back. Thanks to whatever pomade Olivia had used, it did not move. From there they moved to the herculean task of dressing.

Faith's soft lawn shift cascaded down to her knees. She pulled on fine silk stockings she had knit herself from thread purchased in town. They were tied at the top with ribbons to keep them from falling. Over this, went her stays, which Olivia ruthlessly pulled tight, followed by petticoats. Faith wondered if her ribs had cracked in the process. Her spine felt pressed intimately against her navel. The gown was an exquisite mass of seafoam green silk with a low tight bodice and sleeves with ruffles that went to the elbow. It made Faith think of ocean waves. The skirt opened in the front to show the fine fabric of her petticoat, which was a soft blue-green.

Lastly, there were the shoes, made of silk with delicate clasps. She remembered embroidering the flowers and leaves on them one spring after Jon had surprised her with them. She had not worn them in a long time. Thankfully, no mice had gotten into her trunk. Standing in them, Faith wobbled slightly, adjusting to the delicate heels. Olivia stepped back hurriedly, but Faith caught herself.

"How do women manage all this?"

"They don't always," Olivia replied. "Wide skirts are only for formal occasions. They wear narrower ones for every day."

Faith shook her head. "Wearing this every day would be madness."

Once she was dressed, it was time to wait for the Moore carriage, which would take her to the governor's celebration. It felt ridiculous to ride to a place easily within walking distance but who was she to question Eugenia? In contrast to the shadows of evening, the huge brick building blazed with light. Across the grounds, she could already see that people were gathering for what would undoubtedly be a grand event.

Faith wore a lightweight cloak, primarily to keep dust off her finery. It felt odd to be celebrating after Lord Dunmore's dismissal of the House of Burgesses. Yet most of the town was gathered to formally welcome Lady Dunmore to Williamsburg. Perhaps in addition to dance and libations, calmer heads would prevail.

No one spoke during the short ride and she entered the ballroom in tow of her husband's family. Candles placed throughout replaced the light of the setting sun with a more mysterious and elegant illumination. Once her cloak had been dealt with, she proceeded with the Moore's up the elegant staircase to the rooms where the ball would soon begin.

Although Faith realized the room must be huge, it did not feel that way due to the crush of elegant gentlemen and their ladies. Sconces on the walls augmented light from the central hung chandelier. The silk of gowns and embroidered coats shimmered. Her ears hummed with the tones of dozens of conversations. It was both fascinating and overwhelming. Faith stopped to take a breath and immediately lost sight of the Moores. She looked around frantically but could not distinguish one guest from another with any distinctiveness. Between the dimness of the candlelight and the rich hues of all the gowns and coats, everyone looked alike. She was adrift in an immense sea of silks and lace. Squinting slightly, she turned about hopelessly.

"Mistress Clarke, are you lost?"

Faith turned and looked up into a familiar pair of pale blue eyes framed by dark elegant brows. "Captain Grant," she whispered, relieved to see a familiar face. He looked remarkable with an embroidered silk coat of robin's egg blue and matching breeches. His silver knee buckles glimmered. Delicate ruffles of lace cascaded down his sleeves and collar. He wore a formal wig as did most of the men, but on Grant it did not look foppish. Faith flushed with the realization she was staring.

"I appear to have lost my companions." There was no point in admitting that she felt like a minnow set adrift in the ocean. The opulence of the whole affair was overwhelming.

"Come, let me help you find them," he said, offering an arm. A dimple appeared as he smiled.

Something in Faith melted as he led her into the depths of the ballroom. A harpsichordist played a minuet as men and ladies danced the intricate steps. Others were gathered on the outer edges talking and taking time to share news. Grant avoided a group of men in one section, Faith recognized one or two members of the House of Burgesses.

"They do not sound happy," Faith ventured.

"They do not," Grant agreed. "Dismissing them just gave them more reason to be angry. Their belligerence makes them act foolishly with little thought to the consequences." He looked down at her. Faith's eyes were large. She had never been to such an event. "But this is not the place for the rumblings of government. We are here to celebrate the arrival of the lovely and gracious Lady Dunmore to our fair capital. Let me introduce you."

Faith didn't have time to react before Grant had maneuvered them over to a crowd of people, most of whom she recognized as being rich and powerful. Her father-in-law materialized from the crowd. "Greetings, Captain." He bowed formally, although his smile did not reach his eyes.

Grant responded in kind, "Greetings, Master Moore. I am pleased to see a reasonable man amidst all the impetuous few."

Moore laughed. "Impetuous? You might be surprised at how well reasoned many of those you call rebels are."

"Reasonable men do not contemplate treason," Grant murmured.

Moore looked at him. "That's a harsh term for those whose only wish is to be treated the same as other British subjects."

Grant's eyes narrowed for a brief second before replacing it with a mask of geniality. "Be careful or I might begin to believe you have become infected by their high and mighty talk."

Moore smiled benignly. Another mask, Faith realized as she looked at her father-in-law with more attention than she ever had before. "I listen to everyone, my dear captain. It's what a wise man does. Come now; let us talk of more happy things. This is a celebration, after all."

"Indeed it is. Shall we meet one of the fairest ladies in all Virginia?"

Moore replied, "I believe you have another already on your arm."

Faith blushed as Moore leaned over and whispered, "Be careful," before he disappeared into the crowd. Suddenly the crowd parted and she was beside Captain Grant facing a lovely woman with the fair unblemished skin of the upper class and a painted silk gown that probably cost more than a year's wages.

Dimly, Faith heard Grant's baritone. "Lady Dunmore, may I present Mistress Faith Clarke?"

Faith curtsied. Charlotte Murray, Lady Dunmore, acknowledged the gesture, "It is good to meet you, Mistress Clarke." There was a soft whisper of

Scots in her voice. It brought back the memory of Will MacKay. Faith pushed it aside. His angry dark eyes still seared through her as she remembered their last encounter. She was at a ball and likely would never attend one again in her life. It would be wise to make the best of it.

"I hope thy journey was pleasant."

Lady Dunmore smiled. "Your speech is not that of a native Virginian. Do I take it that, like me, you have arrived from another place?"

So gently phrased was the question, Faith did not take offense. "I was born in the Pennsylvania colony. My husband was born in Virginia."

"And where is your husband? I am anxious to meet him."

"He died last summer," Faith answered after a brief pause. There was still a faint sensation of sadness but she did not feel as overwhelmed as she had only a few months ago.

Lady Dunmore's eyes met hers. "I am sorry for your loss." Her gaze was clear and direct when she gazed at the younger woman. There would be no sickly-sweet sympathy from her for which Faith was grateful. Something in Lady Dunmore's expression told Faith that she, too, knew something about loss. After a few moments of polite conversation, Lady Dunmore was pulled away by more of the gentry. Her silvery laugh could be heard over the music and murmurings of the gathered crowd.

Stephen Grant turned to Faith just as the music began again. He bowed. "Could I have the pleasure of this dance?" He pulled her onto the floor without waiting for a reply.

Listening carefully, Faith recognized the tune. She danced to this song with Jon, a long, long time ago. With that memory, the pattern of the steps came to her and she relaxed. She could do this without making a complete fool of herself. Remembering the shared laughter of that moment brought a smile to her face. As they joined the others on the floor to make a pattern, Faith knew Jon would have been proud.

As the dance drew to a close, the Captain walked her over to where Eugenia was holding court. Seeing all the rich and powerful of Williamsburg gathered was a unique opportunity Faith was not going to waste. Straightening her skirts and pasting a smile on her face, she began making the rounds, smiling and replying to all the required social niceties, but still managing to slip in an occasional sympathetic comment about the recently widowed Mistress Bullard and inquiring about her well-being and the unfortunateness of her husband's demise. Most people responded with basic courtesy although Faith noted some did not respond or averted eyes. A few tried to hide an expression of distaste at her choice of topic. Standing with the other gentlemen, she spotted Dr. Staunton, holding a drink. He caught her eye and offered a brief bow. She dipped a faint curtsey in return before the crowd converged, making her lose sight of him.

A plump lady she recognized as the wife of one of the burgesses whispered to her gently, "It would be wise not to mention Bullard too often in gentle company."

Faith widened her eyes innocently, "Have I spoken out of turn?"

Miriam, Faith remembered, her name was Miriam Baker, frowned at her. "You may not be aware that Master Bullard had a somewhat unsavory reputation in trade."

"I had no idea," Faith murmured encouragingly. Mistress Baker leaned forward to whisper confidentially. "I have it on good authority that he engaged in the capture and sale of freed slaves."

Faith was puzzled. "How can you sell freed slaves?"

Miriam looked at her with jaded eyes. "Without proof, freed slaves can be sold like any slave. There are those who capture and sell others to traders who take them far away from Williamsburg, their families, their friends. Once they are bought, they disappear, never to be seen here again."

The idea was both appalling and sickening. "Surely, the law," she began.

Mistress Baker shook her head, "Slaves can be acquired easily and with little argument from the law. My cousin Nettie lost her favorite wigmaker that way. He vanished without a trace. His possessions are still at the shop."

Faith wanted to ask more, but Stephen Grant pulled her away to dance. When she turned to look back, the woman had melted into the crowd.

Plied by syllabub and Captain Grant's charm, Faith found the evening flying by in a blur of music and candlelight. Despite her best efforts, there was less and less time to question other people. She found herself laughing more and more easily as time passed, her nerves forgotten on the arm of the dashing captain. Whether it was the infusion of more liquor than she was accustomed to or the rare opportunity to feel young and worry-free, she did not know, but her cares fell away. The candlelight shimmered like a profusion of fireflies. The well-dressed and well-heeled milled about the ballroom. Faith took a turn on the floor with her father-in-law and later her husband's younger brother Louis, a student at William and Mary. Every few turns, Captain Grant returned for her. Soon she was out of breath.

"Shall we retire from the floor for a moment?" He inquired after observing her flushed cheeks and heaving chest. Faith nodded, unable to speak. Although her stays made her posture perfect, they made dancing a challenge. Grant's gentle hand under her elbow led her to a less crowded part of the ballroom where it was relatively quiet. Leaving her in a candlelit corner, he returned with two tall, creamy glasses of syllabub. She considered holding the cold glass up to her cheek but its high head of foam made her reconsider. The frothiness of whipped cream and sugar floated on her tongue before the wine slid down her throat. Looking at the deepening shadows that threatened to envelop them, Faith realized it was already well into the night. She should return home soon. Tomorrow reality would return and with it her responsibilities. She sighed.

"What is it?" Grant asked. Candlelight created soft bright halos around the room. Whether from chandelier or sconce the room glowed as if lit by magic. The trim on Captain Grant's fine jacket glimmered; his finely styled wig looked pearly, although Faith preferred the darker strands that were escaping from underneath it. She had never understood the necessity of wearing false hair. Her fingers itched to stroke the strand back off his forehead but that would be too bold.

"You are staring," It didn't bother him much.

"My apologies, Captain," Faith whispered. She dropped her eyes demurely. Grant looked amused.

"Perhaps you should call me Stephen, if you are going to dance with me throughout the night."

Faith blushed. "Then you would have to call me Faith."

"Faith," Stephen mused. "Is not Faith believing without having any concrete evidence to do so?"

Her eyes met his, which were intent on her face. "What is it you believe?"

"I believe you are a rare creature. One I would like to know better if fate allowed." Shadows covered half his face but something in it looked sad.

"You think fate would dictate otherwise?"

"I think that circumstances set us upon one path while showing us the promise that lays down another."

"I don't know what you mean." Faith turned her face up to him. Even with her above-average height, he still towered above her. The kiss was completely unexpected. Her lips burned with the memory of it long after he stepped back. "I fear we both suffer from too many libations and the seductive qualities of a moonlit night." Despite the lightness of his tone, he was breathing heavily. "I will return you to your family."

Chapter Thirteen

Grant's sudden desire to separate bewildered Faith. Bewitched by the sudden intimacy, she was unprepared to hurry through the crowd. His long strides made it difficult to keep up, especially with the encumbrances involved in fancy dress. As she stopped to catch her breath, their clasped hands parted and he disappeared. No one had ever kissed her like that. Jon had never cared for touching and it was rare he even pecked her cheek. The captain kissed like he enjoyed every second and had not really wanted to stop. Mindlessly, she wandered through the ballroom barely avoiding the latest round of couples dancing. While her feet moved, her mind was still on those fleeting seconds when his lips touched hers.

Faith needed a few moments to compose herself. Finding the stairway, she quietly slipped down to the first floor passing only a few servants ferrying refreshments up the broad staircase. Downstairs she caught the faint whiff of tobacco from small groups of men gathering in rooms usually used when the burgesses were in session. Faith paused to catch her breath and wipe a few beads of sweat off her brow. The humidity made the vast room feel oppressive.

Distraction dominated as Faith stepped outside to cool her cheeks and collect her senses. Hearing a group of late arrivals approach, she scurried down the entryway steps and slipped into the shadows. The courtyard surrounding the capital was lit by lamps that illuminated the entryway but left much of the courtyard cast in shadow. Eschewing the smooth flagstones leading to the gates, she stepped into the soft grass hoping to avoid notice. The night sky was a panorama of jewel-like brilliance as if someone had cast a lifetime's worth of diamonds into the heavens.

The cultivated grounds within the walls surrounding the building offered a haven away from prying eyes. A handful of couples utilized some of the shadowed alcoves for a few stolen private moments. Stones lining the path made a soft scraping sound against the soles of her shoes emphasizing how few lingered here. Faith needed time away from prying eyes to compose the rioting emotions set off by the captain's kiss followed by his abrupt departure. She didn't know what to believe. Walking idly about the courtyard provided time to settle her thoughts, Faith was surprised to find the main gate unattended, the stout wooden door ajar. Curious she stepped out to see if she could spot anyone about.

Outside a few horses nickered as they waited patiently for their owners to finish their celebrations. In the darkness, it was impossible to tell one carriage from another. Fancy carving and embellishments disappeared with darkness playing the great equalizer of rank. Behind her, the muted sounds of music and voices emanated from the capital. Before was the velvet quiet of night mildly stirred by the voices of coachmen and animals.

Carriages were already pulling up in readiness to take their charges home. Faith stepped forward to see if she could see the Moores' vehicle in the darkness. She squinted, hoping to catch a glimpse of the matched grays that she remembered George handling hours earlier when he had dropped them off.

The soft scraping of footsteps did not alarm her. Likely it was the gatekeeper returning from whatever drew him away or another party going who like her needed a breath of fresh air. It would be embarrassing to be caught staring out the gates, it was time to return to the ball. As she turned to offer a greeting, a dark blur surged forward, the moonlight revealing a gloved hand as it slapped her around shoving her out the gate and into the road.

For a moment Faith lay stunned on the hard gravel hearing nothing but the sound of running feet. The silence was broken by a yell and the sharp crack of a whip. Somewhere near a horse cried out. Her chest burned as she tried to draw breath. Struggling to her knees, the road vibrated beneath her hands. She heard the sharp thuds of pounding hooves followed by the rattling of wheels. Barreling around the outer wall a carriage raced toward her. Faith realized she was about to be crushed. Adrenalin kicked in as she struggled to rise to her feet to reach the safety of the curb. Hampered by yards of skirts and petticoats, she stumbled. Her heart beat rapidly but her body acted as if it were suspended in molasses, moving too slowly to escape. Time itself slowed as the carriage rolled toward her. Every second lengthened as she watched death descend. Her feet slipped on the leaves that littered the ground as she struggled to stand in her ridiculous shoes. As the vehicle neared, one horse rolled his eyes and shrieked, rearing in surprise. Moonlight reflected off his raised hooves. Their sheen made Faith think of an executioner's blade waiting to fall.

A figure darted out from the shadows and grabbed the nearest horse by the bridle. "Whoa!" The man yelled as the horses fought the harness. Faith watched him throw his weight opposite the animal in an effort to slow it. She rolled frantically away from danger and back against the comforting bricks of the capital. The gravel scraped skin from her hands and elbows. Her cheek stung from a flying shard. Faith felt dazed, dizzy, and stunned to be alive.

No driver sat in the carriage. As the horses slowed to a stop just a few feet away, Faith pushed herself up looking at the man who had saved her life. It was Will MacKay.

His dark clothes allowed him to blend in with the night. Will said nothing but eyed her as she remained half sprawled in the road. His face was pale but his hands remained firmly on the reins of the still nervous animals. The coachman was swearing under his breath as he ran down the street toward his wayward vehicle. "Crazy animals, what has gotten into them?"

Will whispered urgently, "Are ye hurt?"

Faith drew in a breath surprised that she could. "I don't think so."

The animals smelled of fear and sweat. Looking up at all the raw power before her, a shiver of fear went down her spine. But for the grace of God, she would have been crushed beneath those hooves. Someone had deliberately pushed her in front of them.

A light spilled out of the capitol and she heard an exclamation. "There's been an accident, someone's in the road!" Soon Faith was surrounded by people trying to pull her to her feet. She let them, slowly becoming aware of growing pain in her knees and legs. Blood trickled down her fingertips. Ezra Moore appeared out of the darkness. He put his hand under her arm and helped her inside. His face was grim in the lamp light. Faith turned to thank Will, but he had disappeared.

Faith didn't realize how bad she looked until she caught the shocked look on Eugenia's face. Looking down, Faith saw that her gown was ruined, torn, and stained with dirt and blood. She staggered slightly and Ezra tightened his grip. "Best you sit down and let your wounds be tended."

Faith was relieved that he had taken her to a small chamber off the ballroom. Now that shock was wearing away, pain and embarrassment were taking over. She half fell into a chair and closed her eyes, wishing for a speedy way home.

"I need a basin and some clean cloths," Eugenia ordered. The older woman sat in a chair next to her and began examining her. "Look at me." When Faith didn't move fast enough, Eugenia's cool fingers lifted her chin and began examining her face. "You're bleeding, but it looks like a scrape. Fortunately, your face is unmarked. Show me your hands."

Faith turned her palms up. They were skinned and covered in mud and gravel and had begun to hurt. "Can I please go home," she pleaded. "I hate to ruin the evening." She heard the wobbling in her own voice and hated sounding so frightened. Her assailant could still be near. Even now he could be lingering to see how successful he had been. She looked up to see her father-in-law eyeing her speculatively.

Eugenia ordered a basin of hot saltwater. When it arrived, she pushed Faith's hands down in the basin. Faith yelped but didn't yank them out. Tears welled in her eyes.

"Salt will help clean the wounds," Eugenia said. "I will clean and wrap up your hands then we will take you home. With your cloak wrapped around you no one should realize you've had too much to drink."

"I was pushed."

"You had no business wandering in the street; if not for Ezra you would have caused major embarrassment to this family. Thankfully it is late and we can discreetly get you away."

Faith wanted to protest but Ezra shook his head. "Let's get you safely home."

Eugenia demanded the Moore carriage be brought to the front, ordering a messenger to be sent to Clarke Tavern to prepare Olivia for her mistress. Faith let her. She could not stop shaking.

"Get some rum," Martha ordered her husband. Daniel disappeared back into the ballroom without a word. Martha removed her shawl and placed it around Faith.

"I've ruined your dress."

Martha shrugged. "Daniel will buy me another. I'm more concerned about you."

Dr. Staunton pushed his way in amongst the gathering of Clarkes and Moores. "I heard that someone was hurt." His clear tenor cut through the tumult and seemed to calm the excitement in the room. He kneeled before her taking the damp cloth from Eugenia. His strong hands examined her scrapes, checked her breathing, and looked at her eyes.

"I see no evidence of an imbalance of humors. Are you feeling dizzy or feverish?"

Faith shook her head. "I will be fine." Although she liked Dr. Staunton, she tended to believe her father's observation that as many had died from a doctor's care as had benefited from it. She hated being fussed over. "I just need to go home."

He leaned back and eyed her thoughtfully. "I see no reason for you not to continue to your home, Mistress Clarke. Although I will advise you that too many spirits will lead to a poor head come the morning. I am glad you did no worse than fall."

Faith never intended to touch syllabub again. She was certain she was pushed, but was too tired to argue. She heard Eugenia order Louis and Ezra to help her to the carriage. Louis fussed about getting dirt on his clothes. His nasal voice buzzed like a mosquito in her ear. Ezra ordered the coach to return later to retrieve Louis, Martha, and Daniel. As she collapsed into the seat, she saw Captain Grant on the curb, Prudence Wright clung to his arm. Faith frowned and then sank back as her head began to spin. Her last view was of Grant watching as the carriage pulled away into the black velvet darkness. Shadows soon obscured his features masking emotions that raced over his face.

Olivia and Titus met them at the front door as Ezra and the coachman helped Faith inside. She winced as she went up the steps and into the inn. Olivia's hair was braided for bed, although she remained fully dressed. A knot formed in Faith's throat as she realized the other woman had been waiting up for her. Titus gently took her arm from the coachmen and led her to a nearby chair. Eugenia's voice cut through her mental fog telling Olivia to bring ointment and bandages.

"Have you agrimony or snakeroot?"

"Not on hand, mistress. We haven't needed it."

Faith knew Olivia had her own preferences when it came to healing herbs having raided the cupboards often enough to tend Andrew and Joshua's scrapes.

Eugenia sounded exasperated. "What do you have then?"

"Chamomile," Olivia replied calmly. "But it looks that her injuries have already been tended."

"Dr. Staunton was at the ball." Eugenia's voice was thoughtful. "I did not see Temperance there, but her health does not allow her to attend these events. Those wounds will need to be redressed tomorrow. I will send the proper herbs with George. Perhaps she had better get what rest she can before the new day is upon us."

Olivia said nothing. She waited until Eugenia left and then helped Faith strip down to her shift and ease her down on the bed clucking at the swiftly rising bruises and scrapes.

"You look like you tangled with a bear."

"No such luck. I nearly got crushed by a carriage."

Olivia looked at her sharply. She listened without comment when Faith told her what had happened.

"Why would someone push you in front of a carriage?"

"I don't know. Apparently, my inquiries have upset someone."

"I'll tell Titus to check and make sure the doors are secure. Whoever killed Master Bullard does not care if more blood gets on his hands. You need to keep your eyes open." Olivia laid a cudgel by the bed.

Faith looked at it, then Olivia, who shrugged. "A little insurance never hurt."

"I will be careful, but stopping is not an option. Bullard wasn't quiet about the stranglehold he had on the inn. I'm sure more than one person thinks I had a hand in his end."

"You weren't the only one who owed him," Olivia said. "I've heard that plenty of folk borrowed from him only to regret it later."

Faith wasn't surprised. Servants tended to know more than anyone about what went on behind the doors of Williamsburg. She wondered who else was under Bullard's considerable thumb. Her head spun and her stomach heaved.

"Do I need to get a basin?" Olivia didn't wait for an answer but placed a pan on the floor next to the bed just in time.

Faith moaned. Olivia took a damp cloth and sponged her forehead. "This evening has just about done you in, mistress."

Faith nodded. She couldn't remember the last time she felt so horrible. Olivia put her to bed. Tomorrow would be soon enough to investigate. Tonight, her bruised and aching body had reached its limits. Her mind was like a spider frantically spinning webs trying to make sense of what had happened. No matter how tired she might be, it would not stop. She looked up as Olivia gathered the ruined dress.

"Thank you," she whispered.

Olivia's eyes met hers. "Take care, mistress. There be some dangerous folk out there."

Chapter Fourteen

Thumping filled Faith's head as if a wayward drummer had taken residence between her ears. It was tempting to bury her head under the pillow and pretend the day had not arrived. Every joint and muscle in her body felt obligated to scream. Andrew entered; bearing a steaming beverage. He stared, his eyes widening slightly. Faith sat up, struggling to ignore her sadistic internal percussionist.

Wordlessly, her son handed her the mug.

"Thank you." Her tongue felt coated in fur.

"Your breath is horrible." Andrew's nose wrinkled in disgust. It was clear he wanted to bolt from the room.

"Allow me a few minutes to wash and dress and I will smell more civilized," Faith snarled. She shouldn't have raised her voice. Her head almost exploded. Moaning, she looked down at the cup. Praise God, Olivia had sent coffee. Raising it to her lips, she prayed for relief.

"Olivia said to tell you she has camphor for your bruises. She said you fell in front of a carriage. How did that happen?"

"I was pushed." Talking was difficult. The drummer in her head picked up the tempo. Andrew could be an unrelenting inquisitor if he chose and his expression showed no mercy.

"Who pushed you?"

"I don't know." The smell of food from the main room across the hall made her feel like gagging. Presenting a pleasant demeanor to her guests was going to require a minor miracle. "Please give me a moment or two to put myself together." God was listening; Andrew left without further words. His umbrage was as visible as a storm cloud. Faith felt guilty for being short-tempered. Her aches and pains were not his fault. Faith knew Olivia was going to be barraged with questions, but the cook could handle him. Faith was unsure if she could at the moment.

The daylight streaming into her room told her she had been in bed too long. Rising, she bumped about looking for clothes. Someone, probably Olivia, had taken away the ruined ball gown. A pitcher of water had been left by a large bowl. Discarding the bandages on her hands, she washed ointment off the scrapes grimacing at the sting. Cleaning her face made her feel marginally better. Faith dressed and carefully combed through her hair before pinning it up and stuffing it into a mob cap. The small silver mirror on the wall reflected a haggard creature that looked like the survivor of a terrible illness. Thus fortified, she went forth hoping no one would be foolish enough to wish her a good day as she staggered outside as her need for the privy became desperate. Fortunately, no one bothered her. Even the chickens avoided her. They busied themselves picking worms out of the rich red earth and shaggy grass.

Once urgent business was concluded, Faith paused on the back stoop praying her body would recover quickly. Avoiding thoughts of all she needed to accomplish, she looked at her garden. Amidst the growing vegetables, weeds had sprung to life. Like many others, hers contained a combination of vegetables, flowers, and herbs. A bumblebee buzzed by her ear as it hummed its way to a patch of dill. The large insect landing caused the plant to shake sending droplets of dew cascading to the ground. The momentary distraction made her smile.

A brief breeze teased tendrils of hair across her face bringing with it the comforting scents of hot bread and meat. Her stomach had settled and eating no longer seemed a crime against nature. Entering into the kitchen, a large bowl of strawberries dominated a table. Impulsively, she popped one into her mouth savoring the delicate sweetness and flavor. Watching the other woman work made her feel grateful for all she did.

"I don't see how this inn could survive without you,"

"I would like to stay here with you mistress," Olivia replied.

The subtle reminder of the other woman's position felt like a slap. It was true that she could send Olivia away, but that was not going to happen.

"This is your home."

Olivia did not respond, although the tension emanating from her body told a different story. She tended a spit, and then stirred something bubbling in the black iron pot that hung over the ever-present fire. Already, the room was uncomfortably warm. Even with the open door and windows, the heat would be hellish by midday.

"Go ahead and say it," Faith said. "I prefer you to speak your mind."

Olivia remained silent, but Titus coming up behind her did not, "You are a kind person Mistress, but we are your slaves. If anything happens to you, we are property just like the house and furniture."

"The governor does not lightly free slaves. I have been searching for the best reason to present to him and his committee. It has to be one that he cannot dismiss. Manumission is a delicate and tricky process."

Titus stared at her. His sherry brown eyes were thoughtful. The big man set down the pile of wood he had brought in before turning to meet her gaze.

"The letter is on my desk. I will read it to you if you wish. Or for that matter, Olivia can read it as well."

Olivia dropped a wooden spoon on the floor. Her face was pale.

"Eugenia told me she taught you to read the labels for herbs and medicines in her distillery. I am glad she did. An education is a priceless gift. One everyone should have." She began sweeping up crumbs from the table into her hand. Most slave owners feared educating slaves, but then many of those same men disapproved of the education of women as well. Her father had taught her mother to read and do sums after their marriage and both had been insistent that everyone should have the chance for education. *I haven't forgotten that Papa*, she thought. Deep inside remained the lessons her family had instilled. She was determined to remain true to her beliefs regardless of the opinions of those with more wealth and power, despite the inevitable cost.

"You need to eat," Olivia said, putting down a plate. "You look rough."

Faith sat down, drank a tankard of clear water, and worked on a few corn cakes before joining Titus in feeding the morning crowd. Entering back into the tavern, she heard the sounds of voices and feet in the common room.

"Drink!" The cry was taken up by a number of men. Others called out "meat, food." Amidst the clamor, voices underneath sounded like they murmured, "Down with tyrants," but the overriding noise made it difficult to tell.

"Best tend those gentlemen," Titus said, striding out past her with a tray in his hands. He made it look easy as he slid tankards to waiting men, picking up empty ones on his second round. "We had better feed them before all that liquor hits," he murmured as he went to take care of his load.

Dropping off the drinks she had just poured, she hurried back to the kitchen. "What remains to be done?" Olivia gestured to more food waiting to be served. Faith grunted as she lifted a tray up and went back in. Keeping up with the tavern's business took all her energy. By mid-afternoon, her headache had faded, but her body protested after all it had been through. Stubbornly she continued, serving patrons and taking payment pasting a smile on her face that hopefully did not look as artificial as it felt.

A short while later Titus looked her over. "Mistress, you look ready to collapse. Go rest and let me handle who's left. There's only a few here and we've got time before supper."

Offering him the key to the liquor cabinet, Faith trudged away from the public rooms and sat at her desk staring blindly at ledgers doing nothing. She awoke with a jerk when Andrew called her name.

"What's the matter with you?" He frowned as he looked her up and down.

"It's been a long day, son." She said drily, thankful that she had not toppled into the floor.

"This day is just like any other: work, work, work. That's all we do."

Her patience snapped. "What would you have me do? This tavern is what feeds and clothes us."

"Grandmother doesn't work like this."

"Her life is different."

"Why?"

"She married a rich man," Faith snapped. She regretted the words as soon as she said them.

Andrew's expression darkened. "So could you."

"Women are not cattle to be sold to the highest bidder."

He looked confused. "I didn't say you were a cow. I said you could find a husband to help take care of us."

"I'm not ready for that." Faith wasn't sure she ever would be. She had become accustomed to making her own choices and had no interest in submitting to a man's will. "We will do alright without adding a family member. Now, is there a reason you called me besides concerns about your workload?"

"Aunt Martha's here." He left before she could respond.

The small woman, accompanied by her footman, peered with fascination into the main room. Some of the occupants cheered and invited her to join them.

Smiling, she demurred and slipped into Faith's parlor, while her servant braved the crowd for a drink. Settling in one of the nicer chairs, Martha eyed her sister-in-law shrewdly.

"How are you?"

Faith grimaced, "Black and blue, but I've nothing to complain about."

"Has the fair Captain Grant been by?"

"No, he has not."

"He caused quite a stir, given how he monopolized you at the ball."

Faith blushed. His behavior had been unexpected. She had tried not to think too much of it. The ball had been a wonder until its ignominious end.

"He cuts quite a swath through the ladies, you know."

Faith did not. The pity on the other woman's face troubled her.

Martha sighed. "Has he made any promises to you?"

Faith shook her head. "No."

"Perhaps it is just as well. The captain has been spending a lot of time at the Bullards'."

"He's been investigating a murder."

"More likely investigating a dowry."

Faith looked at Martha sharply wondering what she meant.

"Prudence Wright danced with him continually after you left. She is seventeen, the only child of a wealthy landowner in Maryland. Her father is Charlotte Bullard's older brother. That young lady is the toast of Williamsburg this season. She would be quite a catch for an ambitious man."

"She acts like a child," Faith protested. She remembered how little help she had been when Charlotte Bullard had collapsed. She displayed the intellect of a feather duster.

"He's been over there one or two times a week. I don't think it's all about Phineas' death. The Bullards are cozy with the governor. Those are powerful connections. Aligning with them would give him a great deal of money and influence." Martha paused. "I mean no offense, you are quite pretty. But you have no wealth or great social standing."

"It's the truth," Faith replied bleakly. She felt sick. She knew most men married to advance themselves. Jon had been very pleased with the land her father had given them, especially with the money he got from selling it.

"Thank you for telling me." Her mouth formed the words although she didn't mean them. Martha Moore was a shrewd judge of character who missed nothing. Faith knew her sister-in-law's warning was well meant.

"I will tell you what my mother told me a long time ago. A handsome man is not worth losing your reputation. He's not going to marry you." Martha put a hand on Faith's. "I wish I could tell you differently. But I took some time to learn about his background. Captain Grant is a soldier, a second son. He will inherit no property, no title. A good marriage is a necessity for him. It will always be on his mind."

Faith bit her lip. "Have you heard anything specific?"

"I called on Lottie Bullard a few days ago. Prudence's father will arrive soon. Grant is expected to ask for her hand."

"I see." Faith tried to pretend the burning behind her eyes was from tiredness.

Tactfully, Martha turned the conversation to more mundane topics. Joshua glided in with coffee, undoubtedly sent by Titus, who missed nothing. Faith let her companion lead her into talking about crops and ribbons. "That boy is getting old enough to be valuable."

"He's free."

"I heard that. You could use a few more slaves to help out around here."

Faith sat up straight. "I'm not buying slaves and I intend to free the ones I have."

Martha stared at her as if she had sprouted another head. "You can't afford that. No one can."

"That doesn't make it right."

"Our economy depends on them." She talked as if Faith were simple. "There would be no tobacco, no cotton, and no indigo without slave labor. We care for them, they work for us. Negros are incapable of caring for themselves."

"There are plenty that do, within just this town," Faith replied evenly.

Martha sniffed, and then changed to a less charged topic. She left not long after.

Faith sat in her chair. Today brought no comfort whatsoever. Martha considered her naive. She liked her sister-in-law whose warm, friendly nature had frequently been balm to her wounds. The other woman had come to warn her about Stephen Grant. Faith had known better than to hope, but last night had been magic until its cursed end. As if waiting for a cure, dull throbbing returned to her head, or maybe it was her heart, trying to learn how to beat again.

Chapter Fifteen

By the next day, the physical aches and pains had diminished to bearable. Faith managed breakfast, freeing Olivia to go to the market. It opened two days a week so the women alternated who would go. Once she returned, they made plans for the next few days' meals.

Titus emptied the chamber pots and mucked out the stable stalls. Then he went fishing, returning with a catch that Olivia battered and fried for dinner. When the boys returned, Andrew from his tutor, Joshua from the Bray school for free and enslaved children, they washed dishes and helped with the feeding and care of the animals, both theirs and the few steeds boarding with them. When Faith stepped into the stable, she noticed an addition, a mare with a blaze on her face.

"Who is this?" she asked Titus when she spotted him within the stall brushing the new arrival.

He looked surprised to see her and paused before replying. "Master Moore picked this lady up at a sale. He wanted to keep her here a day or two."

That made no sense, not when she knew Ezra had a fine barn not half a mile away. "Why would he do that?"

"I don't know, Mistress Faith. You would need to ask him. I didn't think it was any problem, given we have plenty of room. She'll be gone in a day or two." Titus avoided her gaze, focusing on moving a few strands of hay about with his foot.

Faith sighed. "It's not a problem. I just wondered why he didn't take her home. His stable is far larger than ours."

The big man shrugged. "Master Ezra didn't say."

She would have to ask him. Turning out of the stable she heard the sounds of hooves in the street. Startled, she looked up to see a wagon master hurrying his goods into town. The clattering of hooves brought back memories of the ball. If not for Will, she would likely be dead. But what was he doing out so late and why did he disappear? Indentured servants had very little freedom. He should have been over at the printers doing whatever tasks the widow Clements assigned him. Nor had he been conjured from imaginings drawn from drinking too much syllabub. Will had saved her from terrible injury or death before disappearing. Thanks, needed to be given. She also needed to know what he saw. Someone had shoved her into the street. For all her nosiness, Faith had turned up nothing, no evidence; nothing to indicate who had killed Phineas Bullard. Yet someone had felt threatened enough to silence her. But who?

Restlessly, Faith went to her desk for a quill and foolscap. It took a few minutes to find them. Frowning, she looked at the surface. Something was odd. Although outwardly tidy, it looked different. Everything seemed slightly askew. Her letters lay flat instead of propped against the inkwell. The letter she had begun for Olivia and Titus now had a faint smudge.

"Now I know I was careful not to do that," she muttered. That missive had to be perfect, immaculate, well thought out, persuasive, and undeniable in its reasoning. Had Titus or Olivia decided to read it? But Titus could not read and Olivia did not come in these rooms often. If she had, there would have been no evidence. Someone else had been at her desk. Faith was puzzled as to why anyone would be concerned with her affairs. Her business was neither influential nor powerful. Realization sliced through her like a cold wind. The letter! Despite frantically rifling through the papers on her desk, nothing surfaced. Nothing emerged from the cubby holes and drawers. The letter to Bullard was gone. She last remembered seeing it the morning of the ball. It had been hidden from sight under her ledgers where no one should have seen, unless someone was searching for it. The thought made her shiver. The words had been full of rage, a message from a mad man. Her intention had been to compare the writing to the signatures in her ledger; an opportunity now lost. But how would anyone know she had it?

The laundress stepped in as Faith was lost in thought. "Excuse me, mistress." She held up a child-size gown. "This came out of your wash. I tried everything I knew, but those stains are not coming out completely."

Faith shook her head. "We have no small children here."

"It was tucked in one of your apron pockets," the laundress insisted. "I remember."

Faith frowned then remembered. "I found it in the yard a few weeks ago." Taking the small item, she thanked the woman and dismissed her. Laying the gown out on the desk, she studied it. The child who had worn it had been young enough to still wear skirts, but not yet old enough for breeches or a dress. Faded rusty stains marred the fine stitchery along the border and along one sleeve. Could it be blood? The idea chilled her. Faith lifted the muslin off the bed to examine it more closely. Such embroidery took exceptional skill. Her fingers traced the silhouette of a tiny bird amidst a profusion of once brightly colored blooms. "Who did you belong to?" she murmured. More importantly, how did something so carefully made come to be discarded in her yard?

Tomorrow was the Sabbath. It was important that all but the most necessary labors be completed by tonight. There would be baths and clothes to be laid out. But for now, she had a few minutes and she desired to speak to a printer.

After letting Olivia know of her plans, Faith headed south toward the market and the house where Georgia Clements lived and operated her press. The house lay on the northern side of Duke of Gloucester Street which made it a long walk from Faith's tavern. Although it was not quite summer, the day was already uncomfortably warm. Humidity made the heat more intense. Faith's hair dampened with sweat. She was huffing by the time she reached the sturdy brick building where Mistress Clements lived. She didn't know what she was going to say or how she would approach him.

Gathering up her courage, Faith entered the print shop. It hummed with activity. White painted walls made the room seem bigger, amplifying the light of the afternoon sun that drifted in through the windows at the front of the shop. Her feet made little noise as she walked across the wooden floorboards inside. Every available surface had been put to use. Pages of the gazette were strung on lines across the room like laundry, their ink drying in the warm air. The press stood on one side of the room. Books stacked on a table had spilled over on the floor. There was a huge case of type, as high as a dresser and as wide as a shipping trunk. Ink balls inhabited another table. Only the fireplace remained open and clear of papers or books. Mistress Clements spoke with a gentleman Faith vaguely recognized from one of the shops. Was he an apothecary, a milliner? She could not place him. Will leaned over the press placing type, assisted by a younger boy that Faith was guessing was Mistress Clements' son. He had her sturdy nose and square jaw. Will was wearing a white cloth shirt with his sleeves rolled up past his elbows revealing strong muscles. He was no stranger to hard work. Crisp dark hair curled lightly on his forearms as he leaned over the press setting each letter and symbol of type in place. He worked swiftly and rose, letting the boy take over and place some type on his own. There was sweetness in his smile as he looked down at the child that made Faith's breath catch. His expression changed swiftly when he saw her. Will leaned down to the boy and whispered in his ear.

"Finish up setting the type for the advertisement for Master Pulliam's horse. I will be back in a moment to check your work." He touched the child's shoulder and walked over to Faith.

"Mistress Clarke, what business brings you to the *Virginia Gazette?*" Although his tone was proper, his eyes strayed to her face which was faintly bruised, and to her hand which was neatly wrapped. His hand began to reach out to hers before he stopped it and dropped it to his side. There was tightness in his expression that she did not understand.

"I wanted to thank you for saving my life."

One dark eyebrow rose. "Mistress, I know not what you mean. I may have offered you tea and comfort when you were distressed but it was not life-threatening." His eyes slid away and did not meet hers.

"Last night," she insisted, "at the governor's ball. You stopped the horses from trampling me."

"I don't attend balls, Mistress Clarke. Perhaps amidst all the dancing and drinking you became confused?" Will's left eye had a slight tick. His voice was cool and emotionless as if nothing she said had any meaning. Looking away from her, he began sorting loose pieces of type back into their place in the case. His back was to her.

"I am not confused. Why are you acting this way?" Frustration made her voice go up. He was acting strange. Faith could not understand his behavior. Surely saving a life was a noble act?

Why was he lying? She had not been drunk! She would not be carelessly brushed aside. Tired of being ignored, Faith stepped toward him, wearing what her mother would have called a mulish expression. She laid a hand on his arm, determined to make him answer her.

"Keep yer voice down," Will hissed.

"Then quit lying to me," she hissed in return. Their eyes met, both glaring like angry cats.

The door shut noisily making them both jump. Faith was startled to see Captain Grant enter the shop. Will stiffened. Mistress Clements looked uneasy as she strode up to greet him. Faith wondered why so much tension permeated the shop. Half hidden by the press Grant did not notice her. The captain focused his attention on Mistress Clements who waited upon him as he purchased a book, paper, and some quills. Remaining in the shadows, Faith watched him. There was something feral and deadly in the smile he flashed at the older woman.

"I have taken to reading your paper, Mistress Clements. I find fascinating the information you provide to so many here in Williamsburg." His voice was a virtual purr, but there were claws beneath the velvet. "It would seem that many use your paper as a means of sending messages."

"Newspapers provide information to all who care to read," Mistress Clements said. Her hands were hidden under her apron. Her dark eyes met Grant's calmly. Her stiff carriage and pallor were the only indications of fear. "Or has Parliament ruled against that as well?"

"Parliament has always been intolerant of sedition and those individuals who would disrupt the society that England has developed over the centuries. You would be wise to have a care about what causes you support. The day is coming when the crown will separate the wheat from the chaff. And any who try to emulate those fools in Boston will assuredly face punishment. The price for treason is hanging and our king has little patience for rebellious and ungrateful colonials."

"We have asked naught but to be treated as citizens of England and to be treated the same under the law as any Englishman. Is demanding justice treason? Then England runs rampant with it."

"The English have better sense than to thumb their noses at their own rulers, dear lady. You would do well to remember that associating with rebels can leave a stain that cannot be hidden or removed. It might be better if you focus your talents on the business and events within your fair city. Or better yet raising your sons to be proper citizens of the crown. Your older boy Amos studies theology at William and Mary, and what does your younger son, Samuel, do? He is nearly a good age to become a drummer for my men."

The older woman's face went ghost white. "He is a child."

"All children grow up sooner or later. In these times, innocence is a luxury." Grant left, turning on his heel and striding out with a swiftness that was jolting. Out the window, they all could see him striding toward a group of his men, their red coats distinguishing them from the local populace. After speaking to them, one separated and went to stand within sight of the print shop.

Will muttered something ugly under his breath.

"Will," Mistress Clements reproved. "I'll have no such language spoken here."

He growled an apology, and then glanced over at Faith.

"Ma, I don't want to be a drummer."

The boy who Will had been helping spoke to Mistress Clements, who walked over to him and took him into her arms.

"God willing, you won't have to be. Even if I have to send you somewhere safer."

Faith realized this must be Samuel. He looked not much older than Andrew.

Will's expression was grim. "Given the current state of affairs, it is not safe for you to associate with us, Mistress Clarke."

Faith caught her breath. She was certain she had remained unseen. The captain had been focused on other prey. He had never treated her that way, but he could, she realized. Grant would turn on her the moment he considered her a threat. Given his rumored involvement with the Bullard's niece, her fate might not matter to him, not as much as she had once thought. What could he possibly want from Georgia Clements? Her paper was no more seditious than any of the others in Williamsburg.

She turned towards Will and his mistress. The older woman sagged against the wall. "He suspects. The next time he may return with troops to tear down the press and occupy my home."

Will MacKay cast a warning glance at Faith. His mistress shook her head. "Mistress Clarke is not the enemy, Will. If she were, she would not have come here to talk to you privately; she would have reported your presence to Captain Grant. As for yon lobster back, he will have to work harder to find willing spies."

Faith's brain was whirling. What had Grant meant and why was he so angry? She thought about the paper and what it printed. "You've been printing letters,stories about the incidents in Boston, but how?"

"There are no laws against letters, as yet," The printer replied defiantly, her eyes flashing. "Virginia has had correspondence societies since the incident with the *Gaspee* a few years ago."

Faith vaguely recalled the incident. "It was a British ship, run aground."

"Run aground by Americans unwilling to pay British taxes!"

"Surely the men responsible have long been punished for that." Faith said.

Mistress Clements explained, "If they had they would have been shipped to England for trial, not tried here."

Faith froze. "That makes no sense. Americans should be tried and sentenced in the American Colonies. That is the law to be tried by one's peers."

"That is what the law is supposed to be," Will corrected. "But the British use their law to their own ends. They do not wish for justice but order and will do what they believe necessary to achieve their ends. Look at what is happening in Boston. Do you believe they will stop there?"

Faith looked at him. He had begun to fill out in the flurry of weeks since their abrupt meeting. Muscle was filling in what had been skin and bones. There was darkness in his eyes that made him look older than he probably was. Looking at him, she realized they were probably close in age. What, she wondered, had driven him away from his home and to the colonies to be another's servant for seven years?

"What does Grant hope to find here?" Faith asked quietly.

"A trail that will lead to the Sons of Liberty," Mistress Clements replied. "He's come to a goat's house for wool in that regard."

Faith was not too sure about that. Will had remained out of sight when Grant had entered and he had denied rescuing her. There was no reason for that unless he had something important to hide and she was certain he did. The Sons of Liberty were considered heroes by some and rebels by others. Any association with them was dangerous. He could be risking the gallows if he were not careful. As Faith watched, he went over to rearrange the books in the front of the shop, avoiding her as if she were a bug. Exasperated, Faith strode over and blocked his path.

"I'm not leaving until we talk," she said bluntly. "I never asked what you were doing and I won't, but don't treat me like I'm feeble-minded or foolish."

Will sighed and ran his ink-stained fingers through his hair which already had stray curls escaping their club. "It would be far safer for you if you forgot what you saw, Mistress Clarke. These are dangerous times and I'll not put a lone woman with a child in harm's way."

Faith was puzzled. "You saved my life. How is that putting me in danger?"

Will took her hand and pulled her to the back of the store away from the windows and prying eyes. "Someone pushed you in front of that carriage. Whether it was because you were in the wrong place at the wrong time or someone wants you dead, I am not sure. Royalists and rebels do many things they would wish unseen by night, even by notably tipsy women. You would be far safer serving the fine people of Williamsburg in your tavern than watching what happens in the streets and alleys around the capitol."

As Faith drew in her breath to answer, he laid a finger across her lips. She looked up at him, they were close in height. Their heads were mere inches apart, close enough that his breath caressed her cheek. He smelled of ink and the outdoors and faintly of sweat. A curl of hair tumbled over his left eye giving him a faintly roguish look. Will's expression turned serious, "It was too dark to see much, but I believe you. Everyone knew Bullard reported to the crown when it profited him. I'm sure there are quite a few relieved that he's gone and don't want you stirring the waters. Let the crown find Bullard's killer before someone decides to silence you as well."

"What if the crown thinks I may have had a part in it?" Faith whispered. "My tavern's reputation is tarnished by his death. I have no choice but to continue. I have to know what happened." Frustration roughened her voice. She was scared and hated showing it. He reached out and grasped her hand, gently because of the wrappings. It was a comforting gesture, surprising because she had not expected it.

Will shook his head. "The crown is dealing with far more serious issues than the death of one of their supporters. Soon these colonies will free themselves from the burdensome yoke of King George. When that happens, they will be focused on hunting more valuable heads than yours."

Faith shuddered. Many had labeled the latest round of Parliamentary acts intolerable. She had heard the outcry in the tavern and throughout the town and it frightened her. "Surely it will not come to blows."

"Shhh! There are ears everywhere." The printer's face was grim. "Is not the fate of Boston enough to convince you? They will not stop until the entirety of the colonies is under their thumb unless brave men and women are willing to mtake a stand."

Faith looked over at Georgia Clements. She had said nothing but her hands were tightly clenched together. She had not ceased looking out the window since Captain Grant had left. Her fear was palpable. "The crown will destroy any they consider traitors," Mistress Clements whispered. "But if we let King George roll over us, we will be little more than chattels and all this country stands for will be destroyed."

Faith stared at the other woman. Afternoon sunlight drifted through the windows casting shadows over her face. Despite the grimness of her features, her eyes were clear. The older woman looked at her. "My husband is dead. What I choose to do affects the future of my sons. The time is rapidly coming when we all will have to decide whether these colonies should seek independence or remain under the yoke of England." Her eyes took on a sly twinkle. "Besides, most men tend to underestimate the fairer sex."

"Pray I will never make that mistake," Will said ruefully. Turning he looked at Faith. In truth, he was like no servant she had ever known. Even now she could see he was far more than a simple journeyman.

"So, are we traitors or patriots?"

Faith did not know what to believe or who. "Can't we all live in peace?" She had a child to raise and an inn to run. Angering the crown could only lead to ruin. Suddenly she was tired, tired of being afraid, and alone; tired of being told what to do and what to believe. No one had the right to order her about anymore. Faith was an adult and no one's wife. "I believe that no one should tell another what they must believe. That is between them and God. My heart weeps for Boston. They have been treated savagely by Parliament. But surely there is a way for us to reconcile with our mother country." Rebellion was unthinkable. England would never let them go without a fight. She had seen the British soldiers drilling on the green. They were arguably the best fighting force in the world. Who could stand against them?

"Have you not seen the way the road goes? They do not desire for us to grow and prosper. They wish to subjugate us in order to profit." He drew in a breath. "You don't know what it is to be under the boot of Mother England, but I do."

Faith had no answer. Her heart pounded as if she had been racing. "I need to think."

"What do you intend to tell Captain Grant?" Mistress Clements asked.

"Nothing. This has naught to do with Phineas Bullard's death." Faith refused to think about Stephen Grant. He had not stopped by since the ball although she had seen him once in a carriage with Prudence Wright. Seeing them together had stung although she knew her circumstances were not that to tempt any man, much less one with ambition. She wanted to forget that evening. Forget that Grant had chosen to pursue wealth and influence in the person of an insipid girl. The ball had been a fantasy dressed up in a borrowed gown. Now reality permeated her life and she was stronger for having faced it, or so she told herself.

Will had saved her life; if he needed her silence, he would have it. Faith was not ready for rebellion. People she loved were on either side of the divide. She would not take sides. Her energy needed to be devoted to finding out the truth about Bullard.

Will MacKay once again escorted her home. Neither spoke as they traveled down Duke of Gloucester Street toward the Capitol, past the heart of the town and onto the outskirts where Clarke Tavern lay. Soon it would be time for supper. The white sign advertising her tavern was a welcome beacon of calm. Within those walls were the ones she loved. It housed all that was precious to her and she would do anything to protect it.

Faith turned to thank him, but he brushed it aside.

"Tis nothing, Mistress Clarke," he said softly. "I would no more let you walk home unprotected than I would my own sisters."

"How many sisters do you have?"

Will's face darkened. "I have four sisters. I used to have five. Morag died in the custody of the British while awaiting trial for something she did not do. She was seventeen."

She stared at him in shock. "I'm so sorry."

"You had naught to do with it. But when the weak and fragile have no protection then they will be destroyed. No one should be held indefinitely without cause." Pain roughened his voice. "I couldn't save her. They never even let any of us see her until she was dead. They said it was a fever. No one told us she was sick. Then they hauled her out in a cart like a dead animal. No one should die like that, alone and afraid."

Images of Stella ran through her mind, her lost, desperate face as she had left her, the still dead body discovered the next day. It always seems to be the vulnerable that suffered most. The pain of losing someone so close seemed unimaginable. "Is that why you joined the Sons of Liberty?"

"I am the servant of Mistress Clements. Whatever I do is at my lady's behest or at the dictates of my conscience." Will stopped at the gate to Clarke Tavern. Bowing, he watched her walk past him and towards the entrance. There was nothing left to say. He waited until she was safely within before turning back toward home.

Faith walked quietly down the hallway. To the left there were men sitting in her main room, talking in soft tones, expounding on whatever personal or public business that concerned them. Titus served drinks and kept an eye on the liquor cabinet. His large presence provided Faith with a sense of security she would have never had alone. What would she do if he and Olivia decided to seek their fortunes elsewhere once they were free? Faith swallowed a sudden lump. It would be their decision, not hers. A few flies buzzed lazily around the room. If they became much worse, the boys would need to fan them away from their guests during mealtimes. Andrew hated that. He did not always understand the necessity of small tasks that made eating and meeting at Clarke Tavern more amenable. Faith frowned. Maybe she should consider apprenticing him to a lawyer or physician. Andrew had a clever mind. Eugenia would be pleased at the notion, but what mattered most to Faith was what dreams her son had for his own destiny. He deserved the right to choose.

Chapter Sixteen

The sun rose, coloring the world with its clear-eyed gaze. The Sabbath provided a brief respite from the workweek. A few guests remained at Clarke Tavern, gentlemen preparing to return home after the dissolution of the House of Burgesses. Although the representatives no longer formally met, Faith knew many of them continued to gather in taverns and homes. Already the Raleigh Tavern was gaining a reputation as a stronghold for those unhappy with England. Despite the governor's intent, the delegates had no intention of quietly dissolving. Tension hummed through the air, as prevalent as the honeybees that traveled from plant to plant, pollinating each one and inspiring it to grow.

Although Quaker, Faith had not attended a Meeting since her marriage. Jon had insisted they attend his family's church, where the Clarkes kept a pew on the main floor. Taxes paid for its upkeep. She continued to attend after his passing because of the music and also because it had become familiar to both Andrew and her.

Ezra had once told her that this church was older than the town of Williamsburg. Faith found this hard to believe. Yet whenever she entered the sturdy brick building, there was a sense of timelessness that could convince her that this church could have been here since nearly the beginning of time. She was being fanciful, but that was not unusual. Jon had frequently teased her about the places her imagination would go. These days there was little time for such idle pleasures.

Entering the church brought back memories of her marriage, a relationship that had provided great joy and pain. But for him she would likely still be in Pennsylvania, attending meetings with her family. She missed them but that loss was diluted by the wealth of experiences that had come from leaving and starting a life far removed from the one she'd had.

They had met by accident. Faith had sneaked away from the mindless boredom of beating rugs to go to town with her brothers. It had been a crisp fall day, one of the last before cold and snow engulfed their farm, confining them for the winter. Restlessness had made home unbearable. Whenever her mother wasn't finding more chores for her to do, she was suggesting potential suitors all of whom bored Faith to tears. Spotting a widower her mother had been encouraging; she ducked into a local dry goods store to avoid him. Faith collided headlong into Jon Clarke, who was like no one she knew. He had been spending his summer with his uncle, helping out at the store and studying the business of being a merchant. His smile was kind and he always had time for her many questions about his life which seemed exotically different from hers. Seeing how she liked pretty things, he would save leftover spools of ribbon for her, the brightness of which horrified her mother.

"It's not plain," she said, glaring at Faith.

"Why does everything have to be so dull?"

"We are Quaker. We avoid the garish things of this world."

"Didn't God create color, like in the rainbow? What's wrong with ribbon the color of the sky or the trees?"

"It's not what we do. That boy is not one of us and you should not encourage him. It would be better to spend your time with someone more appropriate like Hezekiah Stills."

Faith was horrified. "He's old and he has five children." He'd smiled at her once and she'd realized that he was missing most of his teeth. The thought of getting to know him better made her nauseous.

Patience Payne narrowed her eyes at her daughter. "It is not for you to decide. Master Stills has a good size farm next to ours. He is amenable to the arrangement and would even allow you to use one of his small wagons to go into town when your skills are not required at home."

Faith stared at her mother as if she were a monster. "I won't do it."

"You will marry whomever your father and I choose. Children should respect that their elders know what is best for them."

Faith ran from the house as if fleeing Hell. Her father found her hours later underneath the abundant branches of the willow that flourished near a stream that meandered along the eastern side of their property, well away from the border shared with Stills.

When her father located her, Faith's skirts were stained with grass and dirt. Her braid had tumbled out of her cap enough that strands stuck out like a porcupine's quills from her head and neck.

Isaiah Payne looked at his second oldest daughter. The afternoon sun touched his face, highlighting the creases around his eyes and the odd crescent-shaped scar on his cheek he'd acquired fighting the natives in the last war. His lips tightened. "You don't have to marry Stills."

"Mother said…"

"I've spoken to her." He stared up at the setting sun. "Potatoes could use tending before the sun sets." He slapped the straw hat he'd been carrying onto his head and walked back across the fields.

Faith stared after him. Her father spoke little, but always seemed to understand her heart. The subject of marriage was not brought up again that summer. He knew she continued to see Jon Clarke whenever there was an opportunity. Her father never voiced an opinion, but Jon told her later that Isaiah Payne had let him know his daughter was to be treated honorably.

Fighting in the French and Indian War had left its marks on her father. His limp came from a musket ball; Faith had seen other scars he didn't discuss. Sometimes by the fire at night, he told stories about long marches in the wilds of New York hunting for hostile Indians as well as the French. Other times Isaiah Payne would disappear from the farm and into the nearby woods without explanation, not returning for hours. When asked, Faith's mother would tell her. "He needs to clear old ghosts from his head, don't fret." Yet her mother stopped from her own tasks from time to time to watch for his return.

Whatever had been said made an indelible impression on Jon. Before the leaves had completely changed color, Jon had asked for her hand, agreeing to farm a rich parcel of land that her father had recently acquired. They wed over the Christmas holidays and Andrew was born a little over a year later. There had been a few sweet years before Jon tired of the hard work of farming and sold their home for an easier life in Williamsburg. Now her future lay in Virginia dependent on her decisions and her own work.

Summer had yet to fully bare its teeth and the morning's dew kept the walk from being dusty. Faith liked the relative peace the Sabbath brought. The only people she saw were those headed to worship in various churches scattered throughout the town. She had always felt that it was up to each man's conscience to decide how best to worship God. Inside the wooden gates that enclosed Bruton Parish, Faith stared up at the elegant brick structure with its large arched windows. To the west lay the octagonal tower where the steeple rose against the skyline. Within these doors many of the residents of Williamsburg worshiped. Shoes whispered over the floor as worshipers found their pew whether in the resident section in the central nave or where students of the College of William and Mary sat in the rear. Galleries in the wings and south side of the west end housed other worshipers. Usually women sat in south section while men occupied the north, but Ezra had paid handsomely for a family pew so they sat together amidst the rabbit warren of seats within the sanctuary.

The Clarkes were residents so it was down the main aisle that Faith and Andrew went to join them. As they progressed, she noted that the church was quite full. Over the high back of the pew, she could easily see the top of Eugenia's bonnet. If Faith were any judge, it had enough space to also house a fair-sized melon in addition to her coif. She grinned ruefully, if she voiced that thought, there would be no end of trouble. Andrew looked up at her inquisitively and Faith shook her head. Adopting a look of suitable gravity, she paused before the small door on the side of the pew and waited to be invited in.

Ezra Moore rose immediately and welcomed them. He was followed more slowly by Louis, Jon's younger brother, and Ezra's son, Daniel rose from his seat beside Martha who smiled gently as she encouraged her children to welcome their step-aunt. Eugenia was last, but no one could accuse her of poor manners in public. Faith moved to the seat behind them within the pew. Andrew wanted to sit with his younger cousins, even if one was a girl. She nodded her permission and settled herself just as the swell of the organ began.

If she were to be honest, it had been the music that had captured her from the beginning. Quaker meetings did not have music so it had been a bit of a shock to hear voices raised in praise accompanied by instruments. By the time they had moved to Williamsburg, Faith had settled into Jon's Anglican faith. The organ had been a revelation, such a deep majestic sound, played with strong feeling and delicacy.

Looking in front of her, Faith could see Mr. Pelham, the organist, at the keys. He had brought a prisoner from the gaol to pump the bellows as he played. The joyous sound resonated through the building. As the music swelled then ebbed, Faith felt the tension within the building ease as if by turning towards God the burden of earthly existence lightened. It was what she preferred to think. She composed her expression and thoughts and prepared to listen to the sermon.

After worship, Faith was surprised and pleased to be invited to dinner by her father-in-law. Seeing the happiness on Andrew's face, she agreed, contenting herself to watching him race his cousins down the street towards the Moore's Williamsburg residence.

Eugenia always had set a remarkable table and today was no exception. Looking at the sparkling crystal and elegant salt-glazed dishes, Faith felt a faint stab of envy. She had never aspired to wealth but she had always appreciated the works of skilled craftsmen. Looking at the Moore house, it was plain they were a comfortable family. The ceilings had elaborate plasterwork and the wallpapers had to have come from Europe. Even the rugs on the floor were richly colored and designed and obviously made of fine wool.

Faith appreciated the generosity of the table. There were biscuits and a fine terrapin soup that had been seasoned with cloves and allspice. These were followed by delicate fish cakes made with parsley and onions as well as a fricassee of chicken with white sauce and potatoes and green peas. They finished with a lovely custard flavored with coffee.

Remembering the governor's ball ruefully, Faith sipped her wine delicately. It was a mild and fruity variety, probably imported from France or Italy. She sniffed it appreciatively. The bouquet was slightly floral, but with fruity overtones.

Ezra noticed her approval, "It comes from Saxony. I managed to acquire a few bottles to enjoy with family and special friends."

Faith nodded at the implied compliment. After expressing her genuine appreciation for a fine meal, she had planned to return home, but instead found herself in the parlor with the Moores. Ezra was an engaging speaker with a melodic baritone that would serve him well should he be elected to serve in the House of Burgesses. She had not realized how strongly he felt about Lord Dunmore's dismissal of the body.

"Dismissing the members will not silence them," he said, staring into the empty fireplace. "It will fan the fire of discontent even higher than it already is."

"What could they possibly do?" Eugenia inquired. "The Lord Governor is His Majesty's representative in Virginia. He controls the courts and the military. There is nothing they can do no matter how unjust his actions."

"Men in Boston did not believe that," he noted quietly. "They stood by their beliefs and got King George's attention."

"His wrath," Eugenia noted dryly. "There is not much joy in Boston these days."

"Men should have the right to express their opinions freely without condemnation." Ezra pounded his fist on the chair's arm. "While we sit here and muddle, Parliament plots more taxes and more laws to enslave these colonies."

"What would you have us do?" Faith asked. She had never dreamed her stepfather-in-law had such feelings but his normally bland features were flushed and his eyes burned with a fervor that she had never before seen. Those penetrating eyes turned on her, examining her features as if he were weighing her character. She shivered and his glance broke, shifting seamlessly into the genial blandness with which she was familiar.

"Forgive an old man his ramblings. Perhaps I have been spending too much time in taverns listening to men brood."

Remembering Will MacKay's words, Faith said carefully. "There are those who believe the only course left is to break away from England and the tyranny of King George."

"Indeed, there are those who say that, but it can be a dangerous sentiment to have."

Faith nodded bleakly. "So Boston has discovered. I cannot imagine how difficult it must be to be closed in by His Majesty's troops, cut off from the outside world."

Ezra eyed her thoughtfully. "Come, daughter. Let's take a turn in the garden before duty calls you back home." Eugenia said nothing either in expression or action as they passed. But Faith was sure she missed nothing.

The afternoon sun cast a gilded light across Eugenia's herbs and flowers. Already, Faith could smell the sweet scent of basil and dill. An apothecary rose was preparing to bloom in one corner of the yard. And she could see the broad green leaves of peas as well as the sharp blades of onions poking up from the reddish soil. There would soon be carrots and potatoes as well as the various squashes. Looking at the well-turned earth gave her a sense of peace.

"This life we have is a rare and precious gift," Ezra said behind her. "It could all be taken away by the selfish greed of men who will never come to these colonies, never smell the scent of freshly cut hay or listen to the hoot of owls at night. They will never smell the river or hear the sweet cries of frogs in the warm evenings of a Virginia summer."

"Is there no hope of reconciliation?"

"It is not the colonists who acted against England, but the lords of Parliament who seek to take away our rights as Englishmen and human beings. They forget that we have rights under English Common Law as well. But that is not why I speak with you now. I have something for you."

Faith turned as she heard the rustling of paper. Her father-in-law handed her a small piece of parchment. It was a receipt, signed by Charlotte Bullard. "What is this?"

"I bought your note. Jon was in the most debt to Bullard, but I found others as well. You need not worry about losing your home."

Speechless, Faith stared at her father-in-law as the meaning of his words sunk in. It was as if someone had presented her with the severed head of the dragon personifying all her nightmares. It took a few moments to find her voice, "You paid all of them?"

Ezra nodded, taking off his spectacles and wiping them with a handkerchief.

"I am in your debt." She could not imagine being out of debt. Why would he do that? Did it matter? The wolf no longer waited outside the door to ruin them. Faith realized she had a fresh start, one without all the encumbrances Jon had left them. Tears gathered in her eyes. She sniffed trying to hold in the tumult of emotions inside.

Ezra looked vaguely alarmed. "There, there child. It's no great matter. Dry those tears. This is happy news. Now I won't worry so much about you and Andrew being at the mercy of creditors."

Faith hadn't realized he'd been so concerned. Now, she owed him a great debt. The thought chilled her as she made use of his beautifully embroidered handkerchief.

"I must pay you back."

Ezra Moore shook his head, "No, you are not in my debt nor anyones. But I would ask a favor of you." He stared at her intently. "Let me rebuild your private meeting room. It would be useful to me to have such a place to conduct business without disturbing Eugenia and it would provide some extra coin for you and Andrew."

Faith nodded. It was little to ask in return. The sense of relief was overwhelming. She had not realized how deeply she had feared losing the inn. Feeling dizzy, she took a breath. It was then she realized she had quit breathing. His lovely piece of linen lay crumpled in her hands. Embarrassed she smoothed it out and saw the delicately embroidered birds and blossoms on the edges. It looked familiar, but Faith could not recall where she had seen it previously. She tried to return it but he pressed it into her hand.

"Keep it. I have plenty more. Do I have your permission to start work?"

Faith nodded. After such a generous gift who was she to say no to anything he might ask?

Tension eased out of his shoulders at her assent. "Good, I will send one of my men out tomorrow to see what needs to be done. I have kept you too long from home. Forgive an old man; I'd see all of my family more often these days."

Impulsively, Faith hugged him then released him blushing when it dawned on her that she was being too familiar. Ezra didn't seem offended at all, but then he had always treated her as a daughter, not a mere connection through marriage. It had been his acceptance that had warmed her to the plump, bookish man. It was just like him to quietly offer a hand where needed.

"I will repay that debt one day," she told him, holding his gaze with hers.

"Tis not a loan, but a gift." Ezra waived aside her protests. "My mind is set upon this course. I would have you and Andrew as secure as possible in these troublesome times. I confess I have lain awake some nights wondering if I could have been more supportive to Jon. I had thought he needed to pull himself up and learn from his mistakes as I did, but not all men are the same. He died too young. Perhaps his many worries sapped his strength."

"No one expected Jon to succumb," Faith said quietly. "You and Eugenia were always supportive of us. He considered Williamsburg home. It was where he felt secure. He needed to make the tavern a success by his own labor."

Neither spoke after that but remained in the serene beauty of Eugenia's garden. The flowers and herbs were neatly planted in between trimmed hedges that formed an intricate pattern of green. A simple dirt path led visitors down the center of the garden so each design could be admired in turn. The vegetable garden lay close to the separate kitchen, where the cooks could easily go and gather what was needed.

Daniel walked them home, despite Faith's protests. Daniel looked at her in faint exasperation. "You know his knees trouble him too much to do it himself. At least let him feel he is doing his duty. It does not trouble me a whit to escort you safely home."

Faith surrendered and let her stepbrother walk them back to the tavern.

It looked quiet in the light of the late afternoon sun. In the grass, she could hear the chirp of crickets as well as the rustling of birds in the trees. It felt good to be home and have a moment's quiet before the bustle of the week began on the morrow. Andrew ran ahead through the gate and up the steps into the house. Daniel waited until she was safely inside the gate, whistling a jaunty tune before returning to his wife and family.

Faith changed out of her Sunday best and into a less elaborate gown. There was still planning to do for the next day. Despite what others might think, she could not let the matter of Phineas Bullard's death rest. Her inn remained the site of a murder. Even the fire had not changed that, although now no one could go into the room and peer about looking for signs of the crime. Perhaps that was a blessing of sorts but not enough to make her appreciate the near destruction of her home and business.

Faith sharpened a quill as she thought about what to do next. She knew very little of Bullard personally. They lived in different circles of society, only meeting when Faith delivered payment for Jon's loan. Distrustful instincts had always made her insist on a receipt of payment. But who else had dealings with Bullard and who hated him enough to kill him? All she really had was the information in the letter, now missing. The writer had been very angry and perhaps frightened as well. He or she had been very upset about the disappearance of two people. Dipping her quill in ink, she wrote,

"Who are David and Felicia Verity?" She had never heard those names, but Williamsburg was a growing town, a center for trade as well as the colonial capital. She frowned, considering the best sources of information. Running a tavern provided a certain amount of knowledge about goings-on in town.

She could ask Captain Grant if he was familiar with the names. He would answer but he would insist on knowing why. Given his familiar behavior at the ball, Faith felt leery of approaching him. He had not entered the tavern since the announcement of his engagement to Prudence Wright. Faith hated feeling foolish. Her face still burned when she recalled how giddy she had been. Faith frowned, forcing her mind to return to the current problem. She could also ask Ezra. He might know the family through his business contacts.

Her head was still reeling from his much too generous gift. Yet she still didn't understand why he would do such a thing. Faith couldn't help wondering why he wanted to rebuild her meeting room. They had not discussed the horse he had placed there, although the next day she'd discovered it was gone and an exhausted-looking black gelding there instead.

Faith had frowned as she stroked the delicate nose of the animal that nickered at her. She fished out the apple she had planned on eating and presented it to the grateful beast who quickly took it between his teeth.

"I wonder where you came from." There was no one about to answer that although she could see he had been well cared for. Ezra had explaining to do.

Tiredness enveloped her like a blanket. There were too many unanswered questions burning in her head.

Chapter Seventeen

A light breeze teased hair out from under Faith's straw hat. This early the market was crowded with both buyers and sellers of goods. It was also a place to learn about anything and anybody in town. She hoped to discover who the Verity's were. If her suspicions were correct, they held the key to Phineas Bullard's death.

Standing still for a moment, she paused to gain her bearings. Seeing a profusion of red and smelling the sweet smell of ripe fruit, Faith procured strawberries from a farmer eager to trade them before they spoiled. She had promised Olivia she would check for fresh crab. It was while hunting for the crab man that she began asking questions. Amidst questions about freshness and cost, Faith slipped in a casual question or comment. Although familiar with many of the people hawking goods and they her, no one seemed to know the Verity's.

Nearby a woman sold bunches of herbs. "Do you know the Verity's?" Faith asked casually while examining a small bunch of dill. Its smell filled the air and had she not had a ready supply at home, she would have considered bargaining for it. The woman stared at her. "If ye want to do business with freed slaves, you'd be better off going where they are." She gestured with a plump arm to a section of stalls Faith had not explored. It took a moment for the words to penetrate. Felicia and David Verity were freed slaves. Emboldened by new information, she walked to where the woman had indicated. She passed coopers hawking their barrels, pounding wooden staves into metal rings that would hold them in place. The scent of fresh bread assailed her nose as she strode past a stand of bread and cakes. Further down were the animals brought in from local farms. A fine flock of chickens and geese honked noisily as she passed. Loud squeals revealed that hogs were near as well, their earthy scent drifting in on the breeze.

Her first inquiries netted nothing. No one admitted knowing the Veritys. Spotting a basket maker nearby, Faith strode over to inspect her work. Baskets of sturdy white oak splits lined the table. The seller was a woman with dark coppery skin who stood nearby. She was shorter and more generously curved than Faith, with dark hair covered in a kerchief that had faded to the color of the sky. Her clothes were clean but worn and faded to an indeterminate shade of light brown. She kept an eye both on Faith and another woman examining her wares. The baskets were excellent; tightly woven with sturdy wood handles and flat bottoms. Nodding with satisfaction, Faith picked up a medium-sized one with moderately high sides. After they decided on a price, Faith smiled at her as she handed over her coins. "By the way, do you know where I would find Felicia Verity? A mutual acquaintance wished me to extend my regards."

The woman stared at Faith for a long moment. Pain crossed the woman's face before she smoothed it out to polite blankness. "No ma'am, I don't know where they are."

"You know them. I can see that you do."

The woman shrugged, "I can't help you." She turned her back to Faith and headed back to where a bucket of oak splits soaked, waiting to be worked.

"I mean them no harm; I just need to speak with them." Faith put a hand on her arm. "Please, help me."

She removed Faith's hand. "There is nothing you can do. They are dead."

"How?" It was a foolish question, regretted the moment Faith uttered it. Everywhere she turned, people kept turning up dead.

The basket seller motioned for a teenage boy to take over the booth. She gestured and Faith followed her blindly to the shadows of a large tree where they would not be easily seen. The woman looked at her thoughtfully as if making a difficult decision.

Faith met her glance. "Please."

"Slavers took them." She waved a hand to hush Faith when she would have interrupted. "Doesn't matter if you are free if someone thinks they can make a profit off you. Some folks just disappear. Usually, they take and trade them down the coast where no one will find out."

Faith felt sick. That someone could be snatched from their home and sold was an evil she had not considered. It explained the panic and rage in the letter. "How do you know they are dead?"

The woman sighed, "There was a camp down near the river, waiting for a ship to take them poor souls to Savannah. Fever swept through. People talked. They don't mind guarding them, but men don't like to stay where there's sickness. Too afraid they'll catch it. Some left and went into town. Once word got out, some of us folks went to tend them, but it was too late. Most had died; some of fever, others from lack of care." The woman shuddered. "It was awful."

Shock kept Faith from speaking. To be left dying uncared for and alone was unimaginable. Yet she had seen the silent misery of those slaves sold at the market and looked away, unable to take in such pain. And too much a coward to make a difference she reminded herself with a shot of anger. This was what came of silence and ignoring the obvious. Good people died. Silently Faith said a prayer for all those lost to slavery. If Bullard had been responsible for this, Faith could comprehend why someone would want him dead.

Faith's voice shook. "God rest their souls. Do they have family who need to be informed?" Perhaps they had written the letter, but few freed slaves were literate and the letter had been written by someone fluent in language and letters.

"They that need to know have been told. I need to get back to work." Composing herself, the woman edged away and walked back to her baskets. Faith considered following but forbore. She had learned all she could here. The facts were sickening. Why Phineas Bullard died was no longer a mystery, but she still did not know who.

On her arm, she still carried the strawberries gotten earlier. The cool of the morning was rapidly evaporating, leaving the growing steaminess of a Virginia summer. Picking up her steps, she turned to go home. She had not gone far when inspiration struck. Looking into her basket, she realized there were more than enough to share with the Stauntons. It was a good enough reason to call and if she were fortunate, Martin would be home. Although he didn't speak of it much, he had let it slip that he attended the needs of freed slaves in the area. She hoped he knew something.

It took only a few turns before she was on their stoop. Faith frowned. Temperance probably was unaware of the gently rundown look of the entry, but Martin should. The lack of care was not obvious, but taken as a whole, the dusty windows, sagging step, and faded door spoke of neglect. Thankfully, the cobwebs were swept away. The maid had apparently tended to that. At her knock, the door was opened swiftly by the maid, a young lady of perhaps sixteen.

Faith smiled. The girl smiled back hesitantly, she recognized Faith but was unsure how to proceed. "Please tell your mistress that Mistress Clarke is here to call upon her."

The maid nodded and closed the door. Faith was surprised when Martin opened the door a few moments later. "Please come in," he said gently. "I don't leave my guests standing out on the stoop."

Faith smiled. "I'm sure she meant no harm. It is yet early to call, but I was at the market and realized I have too many strawberries. I thought perhaps that Temperance might enjoy some?"

The doctor looked tired, but his eyes did light up briefly. "She might indeed. If you will allow a few moments for her to complete her toilet, she will join you in the parlor."

The parlor was a familiar room. It boasted hand-painted wallpaper on all four walls with an elaborate woven rug in shades of blue covering the floorboards and a marble mantle imported from Italy. An ebony and ivory chess set lay on a nearby table, poised to be used. On another chair was a copy of *Pilgrim's Progress*. There was an aura of comfort and peace in this room. Everything was well made and had obviously been cared for and used. It was not a place to impress but to welcome.

"Can I offer you hot cocoa or coffee? I am afraid we no longer serve tea. Its presence can prove upsetting to some." He strode off before she could respond, presumably toward the kitchen.

Female voices drifted down from upstairs, undoubtedly Temperance and her maid. Faith sat quietly pondering if, in her impulsiveness, she had been rude. Yet she had known the Stauntons for a while and they had never been strict adherents to social form.

Faith looked up to see Martin lending an arm to steady his wife. Temperance looked pale and thin, even more fragile than Faith remembered. Her gown hung on a skeletal frame while a snowy kerchief wrapped around her shoulders and framed her prominent collar bones. Guilt stabbed when Faith realized how long it had been.

The doctor settled her in a chair before sitting down himself. "Would you care for breakfast? I am sure our cook could provide something shortly. I believe she has recently returned from the market as well."

Faith demurred. She had hastily eaten before leaving the tavern and had also availed herself of some of the strawberries she carried. A maid brought in a silver tray with a steaming pot of coffee along with a pitcher of cream. A few moments were taken up with the pouring of cups and the passing of the sugar cone.

Faith quietly sipped and looked at them. It did not take great powers of deduction to see that Temperance was growing weaker. Although never told directly, she suspected that Temperance's heart had become weak from the fever that had taken her child. She had not been pregnant in some time. Even though Martin was faultlessly gentle and tender, there was no sense of intimacy. Temperance said nothing although her hand stroked his wrist as he handed her coffee. The doctor did not react. Her face flushed as her hand dropped back into her lap. Faith pretended not to see. Some pains were best kept private.

Threads of silver were visible in the darkness of Martin's close-cropped hair. Lines of weariness underscored his eyes creasing his face from nose to lips. Although gracious, he seemed distant and somewhat sad. Faith wondered if caring for Temperance was becoming too much of a burden. After finishing his cup, he excused himself, saying there were patients he needed to tend.

Temperance smiled hesitantly as he took his leave. "He never ceases his work these days. There was never a more dedicated physician than Martin. I worry he pushes himself too hard."

"Martin's patients are fortunate that he is so steadfast." Faith remembered well how often he had called during Jon's illness. After his death, the doctor continued to drop in to check on Andrew and her. That he came by to offer encouragement and good cheer had meant a great deal in those first grim weeks of widowhood.

When the maid cleared the tray, Faith realized that there were no slaves in the house. She frowned thoughtfully. "You have new staff."

"Yes," Temperance said. "A few years ago, Martin decided he would have no more slaves—that it was immoral. I had no objection to that. But I would have liked to have kept Felicia as a paid servant. She had been with us a long time and she knew my needs better than anyone. But he would not have it. He arranged for her to work at a millinery shop down near the palace. She was exceptionally skilled with a needle. I still have a few items she embroidered for me. I dare say she was beyond comparison in these colonies. Many of the men in town carried handkerchiefs edged with her work. Now my maid is an indentured servant from England who can barely read, much less create fine lace and embellishments." Temperance looked tired, "At least Caroline can brew cocoa for me and she is of a pleasing disposition."

Faith leaned over and set her cup down to hide her face. Her heart raced. It was not a common name but she had to be sure. "Felicia? I don't remember her."

"I doubt you saw her much. She was my personal maid. My father sent her to us as a child when I first became ill. She was very gentle and intelligent. Martin taught her all the herbs and treatments that I might need. I did not even have to tell her what to do. She knew." Temperance sighed, "I did not feel so helpless when she was here. But Martin felt a moral conviction about owning people. He helped her and the others start new lives, occupations where they could make their own living. Felicia was an excellent maid. I had heard she had a child, but I don't know who her husband is. There were plenty of freedmen who would have gladly courted her, she was a pretty thing."

Faith nodded sympathetically, "Did Felicia have any friends among the staff?"

Temperance shrugged, "Not that I noticed. The servants pretty much keep to themselves. Why are you interested?"

"Eugenia would like me to improve my wardrobe." That was no lie. Eugenia always had something to criticize.

Temperance laughed, "Still trying to appease Jon's mother? You should know that no woman is ever good enough for any mother's son. Martin's mother died not long after our wedding and there was no pleasing her. Felicia is probably still at the milliner's. Martin may be able to tell you for sure."

"And the other slaves?"

"Martin took care that all of them had opportunities for work." She frowned and set down her cup. "I do remember one young man. He drove the carriage. Aaron, his name was. I believe he works in the stables at a tavern, Anderson's I think it is called now. Why are you interested in freed slaves?"

Faith answered, "I can no longer support the notion of owning people. Olivia and Titus have been faithful and honorable servants to me. They deserve to be free."

"I am glad to hear that, Faith," Martin spoke from the shadows of the room. Faith had not seen him enter. "No one deserves to be treated with less honor and care than a horse or cow." He walked into the room and tucked a rug around Temperance's lap. "Don't tire yourself, dear. I wouldn't want you to become ill."

"I am as well as I ever am." Although her eyes were shadowed, they still looked at him longingly. "I am well enough. It is good to see Faith again. It has been some time since last we called on one another."

"Not as often as we once did," Faith agreed. They continued talking but of gentler things such as fashion and the activities of Lady Dunmore who was well-liked even if her husband was not. Before long, animation faded from

Temperance's features and her skin took on a waxy pallor. Faith started to say something but Martin caught her gaze and shook his head. She fumbled for an excuse, "Andrew will need me to check his sums. He is probably wondering where I am," she said, rising. It was not her best sally, but it was all that she could produce.

Temperance nodded her head graciously. Her normally sweet smile looked forced and tight. "Perhaps you can call another time. Martin, if you could call Caroline to attend me?"

Martin walked Faith to the door. Behind them, they could hear the bustling of the maid in the parlor. "She prefers not to discuss it." .

"Is there nothing…" Faith began then stopped when he shook his head.

"Her heart is weakening. It is only a matter of time," he said. "Some mornings she has not the strength to rise from bed. The best thing you can do is come and talk of fashion and flowers and share the local gossip. The distraction will do her good."

"What about you?"

"I am well enough. I have done all that I can to protect and care for my family. There is naught much to do but continue as best I can." Pain etched his features briefly before he hid the expression. "Go home and focus your attention on that fine son of yours. In that child, you are well blessed."

She nodded and walked thoughtfully home. Dr. Staunton was correct. She was blessed. Even though she did not turn back to look, she knew he watched her walk down the street for a time. It was a common grief they shared to watch one's beloved die and be helpless to stop it.

Chapter Eighteen

Faith filled yet another tankard of ale, pausing briefly to wipe the sweat from her face. Her main room was busy, filled with the sounds of men grabbing an evening meal or meeting with friends. Despite the outward courtesy of most, she couldn't avoid noticing the rising tensions within the taverns in town. Nor could she miss the increased presence of British troops as they drilled and marched. Captain Grant or his men patrolled the city or perhaps she was simply more aware of them and him. Keeping busy kept her mind off the captain and the continuing mystery she could not seem to unravel.

Her head buzzed with too many questions. The Veritys rarely left her thoughts. Their tragic end filled her with both sadness and anger. Someone had avenged them. The question was who? She had to find someone who knew Felicia.

Talking to Martin was out of the question. Already burdened with his wife's care, he did not need her to add to his concerns. He had seemed odd at their last encounter, exhausted and sad as if he were already grieving. If Faith were to discover who the Veritys, were, it would have to be through someone else. Temperance had told her how to find their former groomsman, Aaron. Surely, he knew something.

A party of traders came in from the western mountains, filling her tavern and leaving little time for investigating. Their raucous behavior and ravenous appetites kept her running from kitchen to main room while Titus kept the men in line. Although she was grateful for their coins, a mixture of English, French and Spanish pieces, her mind longed to discover more about Felicia Verity. When they finally left en masse to head up the coast, she wasted little time taking off for Wetherburn's Tavern. Given the oppressive summer heat, she was fortunate that her destination was not far.

Sweat ran between her breasts and made her shift stick. They would be serving cool drinks within. Not that she would be entering. Even though she operated a small tavern, coming in the front door would not be proper. Ladies did not frequent taverns. Faith followed the earthy scent of horse easily, locating the stable behind the main building. Not surprising, given the enormous size of the tavern, there were many men working in the backyard, who could be either slaves or freedmen.

Biding her time, she watched the men in the yard, narrowing her search down to likely candidates for the Stauntons' former slave. In her mind was a vague memory of a young man with reddish hair and a wiry build. Faith was not good at names but she hoped it was Aaron. Her wait was soon rewarded when she spotted a likely candidate in the yard. The afternoon sun turned his hair the deep red of the dying sunset. He walked slowly, sweet-talking a dappled gray back to the stable. Gently, he stroked the animal's nose, leading the nervous animal into the dark of the barn. Under the shade of a young tree, she waited by the barn for him to appear.

"Aaron," Faith called.

"Ma'am?" he asked with surprise. Ladies normally did not go into the backyards of taverns to speak with servants. He stood uneasily, his eyes downcast, a foot making patterns in the dusty earth. Dressed simply in a blue shirt and brown breeches, he looked not much older than Joshua, except for the stubble on his chin.

"You used to work for Dr. Staunton," Faith said. "I remember how well you cared for our horses when my husband and I called upon him and his wife."

"Yes, ma'am. I had been his slave since I was a boy. He freed me about six months ago. Now I work here for Master Anderson as a free man."

"Congratulations," Faith said, smiling to show her approval. "I was hoping you could tell me about someone else who worked for Dr. Staunton. Felicia. Someone said she used the last name Verity."

Aaron stiffened. "I haven't seen Felicia since I left the doctor, ma'am. I don't know anything about her." He looked around nervously in the quiet yard. "I need to get back to work. Master Anderson expects hard work for his pay."

"You know she's dead, don't you?" Faith hated being so blunt. The young man's agitation made his knowledge obvious. "What happened to her was a tragedy."

Aaron continued backing away. He would escape into the stable in moments. "I mean no harm. I need to know who the father of her baby was. Was it you?"

The stable hand shook his head vigorously. "No, ma'am. I handled the horses and yard for Master Staunton. Felicia was a house servant. She took care of Mistress Temperance. I hardly saw her."

"You knew she had a baby?"

"There was no missing that ma'am." Aaron looked at her. "Felicia was pretty, real pretty but she didn't associate with the other slaves. She was tight with white folks: The Stauntons, the Smythes. Master Smythe thought she was real pretty. He used to bring her things behind Master Martin's back, lace, ribbons from his store. Didn't want his wife to know why he was at the doc's all the time so he claimed to have stomach pains. It stayed that way until Doc Staunton threw him out and told him to find another doctor. I thought that was the end of it until she started throwing up all the time. She was already showing by the time Dr. Staunton freed her. He made sure she had a job, a place to stay. He took care of all of us."

Faith felt sick. "Smythe was the father of Felicia's baby."

Aaron looked her in the eye for the first time. "Yes, ma'am. I think so. Doc didn't want anyone to think badly of her. He paid a family to take her in until David was born. He delivered the baby then helped her find work with a milliner. I would see her in town once in a while. Then she disappeared. No one knew where she was until it was too late." He shrugged but there was sadness in his eyes. "Felicia was the first one he freed but she didn't stay free. Even here in Williamsburg, sometimes it's not safe. David wasn't my boy, but I would have protected her and him here. No slave traders bother us at the tavern. It's too public."

Faith nodded. He was right. The dirty business Phineas Bullard engaged in required secrecy. That Josiah Smythe had been involved with Felicia was news. She had not seen Bullard's brother-in-law since Stella's death, perhaps it was time for another conversation.

Aaron left while she paused to gather her thoughts. Felicia's baby had been half white. Had Bullard known that? Did it matter? How had he managed to take them without anyone finding out?

Faith walked down the street not sure if her feet dragged from heat or sadness. Eugenia had taken her to a milliner's just off of Duke of Gloucester Street once a few years ago. She wondered if it could be where Felicia had worked. Within a space of minutes, Faith found the establishment and purchased a length of ribbon she really did not need. In the course of conversation, she found that the freedwoman had worked there until her disappearance, living with her small son in a few rooms above the shop.

On her way home, Faith paused by Raleigh's Tavern. The door stood open to catch the afternoon breeze. She did not expect to see her father-in-law cozied up to Josiah Smythe inside. There was nothing wrong with either man catching a drink in a tavern but the sight of them together jarred her, especially in light of what she had just learned. Faith's hands clenched her skirt then someone bumped her, making her recall her surroundings. A busy street was nowhere to be standing still gaping like an idiot.

Down the street, an auctioneer called for bids for a new shipment of slaves. Sadness swept through her as she saw a small group of women in chains. Men clustered about them some gaping openly at the nearly naked creatures, others stepped boldly forward to examine limbs and pull aside lips to assess teeth. Nausea coiled in her belly as she contemplated how frightening it must be to have one's fate in another's hands. She thought of Felicity Verity who thought herself free only to find freedom has value when it is supported by others.

The next day Faith was startled to see Will MacKay, stripped to the waist, working alongside the other men framing the walls of her new private room. Catching her glance, he grinned and clambered to the ground with an easy grace. Turning to face her, Will nodded appreciatively when he saw she carried a bucket and gourd with her.

Will grabbed his shirt from where it lay across the woodpile and tossed it on before trotting over. Filling the gourd, he tilted it to his mouth and emptied it. Tiny droplets of liquid sprinkled down his neck and chest where they glittered like diamonds against his bare skin. The muscles in his throat contracted as he continued to swallow. He did not notice Faith's attention. Finishing the gourd, he handed it back with a short bow and a roguish grin.

"Good Day to you, Mistress Clarke. Work progresses swiftly on your tavern. Even a poor Scotsman can pick up a day's worth of labor."

Sweat caused the tendrils of hair that had escaped from their tie to stick to his face while the sun flushed his skin. He had gained weight and muscle in the weeks since their first meeting. Will's clothes no longer hung on him like bags.

"It's good to see you, Master MacKay," Faith replied.

He took the heavy bucket from her and left her to follow him with the gourd to the rest of the men Ezra had hired. Faith marveled at how different everything looked. With the exception of the smoke scars on the side of the tavern facing the Private room, all evidence of the fire was disappearing. The timber framing looked pale against the fire-darkened wall where it joined the tavern.

Mindful that full stomachs made happy workers, Faith told them that dinner would be served in another hour. Already the scents of meat and bread wafted out of the kitchen. Once the bucket emptied, she carried it back to the house, pausing to watch the men work.

When one of the men broke into song, she was surprised to hear the others join in forming a chorus of male voices that filled the air. Hammers provided a tempo fitting with the tune. Andrew and Joshua came out on the back porch to watch. Faith brushed by them on her way inside. "Don't forget your chores." Both nodded, only half paying attention.

The warm summer air was filled with the scents of fresh-cut lumber, honeysuckle, and the rich, musky scent of hard work. Faith had plenty to be grateful for. Her greatest debt had been settled. Her private room was being repaired and the tavern was full of paying guests. She should be content yet Faith knew there would be no rest until she found answers.

She went to the kitchen to help Olivia serve the main meal. Olivia had somewhere found young potatoes which she had boiled and seasoned with salt, butter, and parsley. There were still plenty of green peas, mixed with onions as well as fish Faith had procured in the market that morning. Faith turned to grab a platter to take to the main room. A spark shot out from the fire burying itself in the folds of her skirt. Flame shot out from the muslin fabric.

Olivia screamed.

Faith dropped the platter as she whirled about beating flames that would not die. Olivia grabbed a bowl of broth waiting to be warmed and doused her. Her hem smoked, the lower edges blackened but the fire had died.

"Mistress, are you burnt?" Olivia asked urgently.

Faith shook her head. "I don't think so." In truth, she was dazed. If not for Olivia's quick actions she could have burned alive.

Olivia checked to make sure the fire was out. "You are fortunate, mistress, it could have been far worse. Your outer apron is ruined. I can try to get the stains out of your skirt."

"Tis only fabric, Olivia," Faith said. "And you are busy enough in the kitchen without worrying about that. I can use the skirt for gardening. If not for you…" Faith could not finish her thought. Rising smoke from her clothes caused her eyes to tear. Her legs felt numb, whether from shock or injury she did not know. Breath came hard in her throat as she coughed; unable to breathe.

"Let's get you outside." Olivia put an arm around her and guided her to the bench outside the door.

Faith fell onto the bench trembling. Her legs were beginning to sting; lifting her skirts she examined them. Olivia knelt to look.

"I don't think it's too bad. There aren't any blisters but I bet you'll be red in places shortly. I have some salve that will help."

Faith nodded as her breathing slowed. Tears rose in her eyes that she brushed away.

The women's eyes met. "Thank you."

Her voice cracked as she continued, "I cannot imagine how Andrew and I would survive without you and your family helping us."

Olivia flushed. "It's my job."

"You are more than a slave. You, Titus, and Joshua are family in all but name."

"The law don't see it that way."

"My hope is one day it shall. I have submitted a request to the governor for your and Titus's manumission. I pray it will be granted."

Olivia's mouth opened but no words came out.

Faith hurried on, "I cannot promise what the governor will do, but from now on, you are not a slave to me, but an employee with rights and wages. I cannot afford much, but what I have, I will give." She started to rise, using the wall to steady herself. "I need to get that food inside."

"I'll do it." Olivia pushed her back down. "You look ready to faint. Take a moment. I'll put the boys to work and get you that salve." She left returning a few moments later with both boys and a jar that she pushed into Faith's hands.

"Mistress, your skirt is a mess. Go tend to yourself."

"Faith stumbled back to her room, hoping no one saw her. Dropping her skirts, she eyed her legs. Red splotches dotted them. As she rubbed in the ointment, the pain lessened. Faith found another skirt and apron to put on before heading into the main room.

No one would let her haul a tray. Andrew handed her a pitcher. "Olivia says you need to fill tankards, we'll handle the food."

Given her shakiness, it was probably a good idea. As she made rounds to her guests, she spotted Ezra eating near the fire. He had three other gentlemen with him, two she recognized as previous guests, one by his reddish hair and fine clothes. The second, a fair-haired man, looked familiar but she wasn't sure why. The other man was a stranger. His well-cut coat and breeches indicated a person of means. The man was unusually tall with a serious demeanor. His keen glance looked directly at Faith. Ezra gestured for her to come over. She stopped to fill another drink, when she turned, the pale-haired man had vanished. Ezra smiled at her as his foot pushed the spare chair away against the wall.

"May I introduce my daughter-in-law, Faith Clarke, mistress of this fine establishment?"

Both men rose and bowed to her. She dipped a brief curtsy in return. It was neither the time nor place to ask about his drink with Smythe. Conversation had ceased with her appearance. Ezra Moore smiled at her gently as the men introduced themselves. She recognized two from when the House of Burgesses was in session. Since Clarke Tavern was so close to the capitol building, many men from distant areas of Virginia would come to dine and gossip between sessions. Mr. Jefferson, she had seen before. Mr. Washington had never been in her establishment that she could recall, although she had seen him and his wife in town. His manners were formal and somewhat stiff, but it was his eyes that caught her attention. They looked as if they carried the weight of the world. "Your pea soup was most excellent," he said.

Faith smiled, "I will convey your compliments to my cook, Olivia. She will be most pleased." She filled their tankards and took her leave, noting that the table's conversation did not resume until she was out of earshot. What sort of business were they engaged in? Ezra Moore had many contacts in town and was a skilled merchant as well as owning over 600 acres just outside of Williamsburg. He owned slaves as well. Faith had many questions for him, but now was not the time. Her father-in-law remained occupied for some time with his acquaintances.

They spoke in hushed tones so that she could not hear. Washington sat where he could see everyone who entered and left the tavern. Although discreet, Faith realized those shrewd eyes missed nothing. He seemed a grim man for her mild-mannered father-in-law to converse with. Once they had left, she refilled his tankard one more time.

Ezra laughed, "This is quite hospitable of you, dear child, but if I indulge in much more of your fine spirits I fear that Titus will have to tote me home in a wheelbarrow!"

Faith grinned. "I don't believe that will happen. I've never seen you worse for drinking."

"Faith, you tend to see the best in me."

She paused briefly. "May I have a private word, if you have the time?"

Those guileless eyes looked at her. "I believe, dear daughter, that I have time to examine the progress on your new private room."

Faith nodded. "Titus, if you could watch over our remaining guests for a few minutes, I need to speak to Master Moore." The man nodded as she handed over the keys to the liquor. There were still a handful of men in the room. A couple of merchants were at a corner table playing chess. A few others played cards. Most were eating and talking amongst themselves. The sheer ordinariness of it was comforting far more than the conversation she intended to have with her father-in-law.

Outside in the backyard of the tavern, it was quiet except for the buzz of a few insects. The workingmen were inside eating. The sun was blazing as it baked through Faith's cap to her head. They walked together until they found shelter from the sun in the shade of a maple tree. The shadows of the leaves made the air only slightly cooler, enough that Faith felt less smothered.

Ezra studied the framing of her new private room quietly, waiting for her to speak. He was good at waiting, she realized. While many people rushed to fill silence with words, he felt no need. Faith, however, did not have the luxury of time.

"What can you tell me about the slave trade here?"

"It's a dirty and brutal business," he responded bluntly. "It is no place for a gentlewoman to involve herself."

"Was Phineas Bullard involved?"

His gaze sharpened. "Bullard? That was no secret. Yes, he engaged in the buying and selling of slaves without thought or care of those poor souls." Ezra Moore kicked the dirt, smudging the shine on his shoes. "He did nothing illegal that I have heard."

"Even if he captured and sold freed slaves?"

The anger that whipped out of her father-in-law's eyes frightened her. The genial gaze was gone. In its place was the dangerous gaze of a predatory serpent, ready to strike.

"Who told you this?" Moore said. His voice rose barely above a whisper. "What proof do you have?"

"None," Faith said. Straightening her back, she returned his gaze. She had to know the truth. "What do you know?"

Moore's gaze was hard and dark. She had never considered him dangerous before. Belatedly, she recalled hearing that his wealth had come from trade, not from birth. Faith had never stopped to wonder how he had become so wealthy.

"Leave Bullard alone. The man is dead and can do no more harm to anyone."

"He died here," Faith reminded him. "There are those who think I am responsible."

Moore's smile was grim. "Folk may whisper, but nothing will come of it, I promise you. Digging into the life of another person is a dangerous thing, child. You may learn things you never wished to know." He gestured at her tavern and the skeleton of her new private room. "You have a business clear of debt near the capitol. If you work hard at it, you will have a fine legacy to leave your son. Don't delve into matters for which you are not suited. It is best to let Bullard's secrets die with him."

"How well did you know him?"

Ezra's voice was cool. "He was a fellow businessman with a nasty reputation. I avoided him whenever possible. He was rumored to be ears for the British but I never saw any proof of it." He grasped her arm. "Faith, listen to me. You need to quit asking questions and prying into others' business. War is coming and neither side will tolerate a busybody. Leave Bullard's death alone. If you anger the wrong people, even I cannot protect you."

"I don't understand."

"Good. Knowledge is dangerous. Focus on the inn Jon left you, and on that precious boy. I don't want to bury you next."

Faith stared at him in shock. She opened her mouth but he shook his head.

"Enough, Faith. Let it go. I must leave. There are pressing matters to which I must attend."

Faith watched him walk out her back gate. His jacket hung oddly bulging slightly on the left side. With a chill, she realized he carried a sword. It was not uncommon among gentlemen and soldiers. As the tensions with England increased, it seemed to become more common than not. Bullard had probably been killed by such a weapon.

Faith had known Ezra Moore ever since Jon had relocated their family to Williamsburg a few years ago. He was a finely dressed, somewhat plump man she had always thought harmless. She didn't think that anymore.

Walking restlessly back inside, she stopped by her desk but her mind could not settle enough to do accounts. Her stomach rumbled. Faith realized she had not eaten since dawn. The main room was quiet except for a few men playing chess. There was time to grab something to eat. Slipping out quietly, she walked back to the kitchen which was deserted. Despite the banking of the fire, it remained incredibly hot. "No wonder Olivia stepped out," Faith murmured as she found spoon bread and greedily dug in. A wedge of cheese and some apples sat on the table. It made for a fine meal. Stepping outside to find a breeze, she soon realized flies also liked to eat. Diving like devils, they harried her all through her impromptu meal. Brushing off crumbs, Faith looked about for Olivia. She could see the two boys weeding the beans. Titus was inside minding the great room.

Growing concerned, Faith started to go ask Titus where his wife was. Just as she put a foot on the bottom step, the cook came in through the back gate. Soft muffled sobs made Faith turn and go to her. Olivia's face was swollen with grief.

Faith whispered. "What's wrong?"

"Mary Martha's in a bad way," Olivia rasped. She fought for control but gave up as Faith wrapped her arms around her. Her body shook as she fought to control waves of grief.

Faith thought for a moment recalling. "Mary Martha is upstairs maid for the Bullard's. She is ill?" There was more to this, much more. Olivia's body was rigid. Her breath came in harsh gasps. There was too much pain for simple answers.

Anger sparked in Olivia's eyes and she jerked out of Faith's embrace.

"Mistress Bullard said she fell. But then she would, wouldn't she? Mary Martha has never fallen in all her years there. Now down the stairs, she's all busted up, just when Ms. Lottie was going to sell her daughter? Louise just turned thirteen."

Faith shuddered. Masters could do anything to their slaves, and did. Anger steamed through her. "Take me there, let me see what I can do," she said quietly so Olivia could not hear the rage sizzling up her spine.

"Dr. Staunton says her back is broken. Nothing he can do."

"He will do what he can," Faith said. "I will talk to Mistress Bullard about Mary Martha and her daughter. Wash your face while I get my hat and we will see about this." Faith hurried before her anger cooled and she had time to consider the rashness of her actions. As she returned through the back door of the inn, she saw Joshua with his mother. Olivia was composed although she was still shaky.

"Tell your father that Olivia and I will be back before supper," Faith said crisply. "We have some business at the Bullard residence. She felt Joshua staring after them as they rapidly walked away.

Duke of Gloucester Street was hot and dusty. It had not rained for a few days although the humidity hung heavily in the air. Large clouds drifted overhead in the pale cerulean sky. Few people were about. Most had conducted their business in the morning before the sun-baked the air. She could hear children in the distance playing, probably underneath the shade of trees under the watchful eyes of their mother or a servant.

Faith was huffing by the time she reached the gate of the Bullard residence. Olivia's face was flushed. Dust clung to them both sticking to exposed sweaty skin. The house was silent—too silent for comfort.

Faith knocked on the door. It took a few minutes for someone to answer. A liveried manservant answered. His expression told Faith that he was not pleased to see them on the front doorstep.

"The trade entrance is in the back," he said as he started to close the door.

"You mistake us," Faith said coolly, pressing the door open. "I am Faith Clarke and I need to see your mistress immediately."

The man curled his nose then staggered as Olivia shoved the door unexpectedly, making him slip and stumble. The two women pushed him aside and swept in like a storm.

"Check on Mary Martha," Faith called. "I will find Mistress Bullard." Then they were going to have a talk about the value of people and their children. Faith was too angry to abide by niceties and civilities and rules. Dodging around a maid, Faith launched herself up the stairs. The layout of the Bullard house was not dissimilar to the Moores' home. She figured the master bedroom would likely be in a similar location. If not, she would try another. So far no one had come to stop her. Faith flung open an ornate inlaid wood door. Inside the walls were covered in an elaborate floral and vine design on wine-colored paper. The bed curtains were drawn enclosing the bed and blocking out the light of the afternoon sun.

"Mistress Bullard, we need to talk." Grasping the near curtain, she pulled it back, spilling light onto the bed. The first thing she saw was the light hitting the highly polished buckles of shoes, then silk stockings embroidered with flowers and vines that climbed delicately up delicate ankles. Charlotte Bullard's petticoats and skirts were neat and unwrinkled, rising neatly into her bodice. A kerchief covered her breasts and shoulders, pure white except for a few faint damp spots. Despite lying in bed, her clothes were smooth and unwrinkled. No one slept this perfectly, Faith thought, shaking her head. The woman looked like a doll. Her skin was as delicate as a pearl and unblemished. Her hair with its elaborate coiffure had nary a strand out of place. A few curls drifted across the embroidery of the pillow. The only flaw was the excessive pallor of her face, her lips looked faintly blue. Something felt wrong. Faith realized Charlotte Bullard's chest was not rising and falling. Reaching out, she took the woman's hand hoping for warmth but their coldness made her shiver. The fingers curled stiffly into the palm. Faith felt lightheaded for a moment the realization dawned that she looked down on a corpse, not a living being.

A maid burst in. "Mistress, you do not belong in here!" she cried, "Mistress Lottie is resting."

"She's dead." Faith dropped the hand and backed away, the curtain dropped in place hiding the body of Lottie Bullard. Her fingernails dug into her palms.

The pain helped steady her as the maid came closer, looked closely at her mistress, shrieked, and ran from the room. Faith wanted to shriek too, but knew it would not help. Outside the room, Faith heard the hysterical cries of the maid. Another servant ran in, undoubtedly one in higher authority than the previous one.

The large black woman eyed Faith quietly. "Is what Sara says true?" She didn't wait for Faith to answer but checked for herself. Faith heard prayers murmured under the woman's breath as she backed up and away. The servant's feet clattered on the stairs as she went to summon help.

As the shock wore off, Faith looked around. Charlotte Bullard's room was tidy and expensive. A goblet of wine rested on the table, its rosiness a sharp contrast to the rich blue of the papered walls and delicately turned furniture. The Bullards had spared no expense for their comfort. Faith walked over and picked up the goblet. A faint white residue powdered the rim. Dusting it with a finger, she sniffed but detected no odor. It looked like sugar. As she put it back down, a small amount blew off forming a tiny translucent cloud that tickled her nose. A violent sneeze consumed her, making her nose burn as she inhaled. Puzzled Faith stared back at the bed. Lottie Bullard had looked perfectly well at Lady Dunmore's ball. Why was she now dead?

A fly buzzed. Feeling ill Faith left the room. She met Dr. Staunton at the head of the steps.

"Faith!" he exclaimed. "Why are you here?" He grasped her arm, looking concerned.

Gray fogged her vision. Holding onto the rail, Faith took a breath hoping to clear her head but it did no good. The room looked warped as if the walls breathed in and out. Cold sweat broke out on her forehead. Staunton stared at her oddly.

"I came to see Mistress Bullard concerning one of her slaves." Faith paused to gather her thoughts. Why was it so hard to focus? "But she's dead. I walked into her room and she was so cold." Cold crept down her limbs as well, making her shiver. Another wave of dizziness washed over her. Could she be ill? "I feel odd," she said as darkness swirled over and engulfed her.

The setting sun streamed in a window and across Faith's face. She opened her eyes in a strange room. Her head throbbed, "Where am I?" The room whirled as she sat up. "Charlotte Bullard is dead."

"Yes, mistress," Olivia sat by the bed. "Dr. Staunton said her heart gave out. Mary Martha is dead, too." Her flat tone contrasted with her tear-streaked face.

"Shock apparently caused you to faint, Faith," Dr. Staunton said calmly. He stood at the foot of the bed and ran fingers through his wig, dislodging a few strands from the dark ribbon that tied it back. His dark eyes bored into hers, "I regret that you discovered Mistress Bullard. I had meant to check on her after I tended to Mary Martha."

"She's dead," Faith said quietly.

"Her fall broke her back," Staunton said. "There was no hope for recovery. At least she did not suffer long."

"Did Mary Martha serve here long?"

An older woman answered, "Mary Martha came to Williamsburg as a child. She started downstairs as a maid. She became Mistress Bullard's maid a few years ago. She took good care of her when she was feeling poorly."

"How often did that happen?" Faith asked.

Dr. Staunton answered, "Charlotte Bullard was no invalid. She liked to play the part, but there was really nothing wrong with her other than the desire for attention. Most of my visits here had little to do with actual illness. However," He paused, "I had become concerned with her of late. Her behavior had become more erratic. Phineas' death upset her greatly."

"I guess no one knows when death comes," Faith said at last. Her thoughts scattered before she could gather them. It was as if she were floating. It frightened her to feel so strange. "It would be best if Olivia and I returned home so these people can deal with their loss." Faith dearly wanted to be home where she felt safe, where she could lay her head down until it stopped spinning.

Dr. Staunton's eyes missed nothing. "Mistress Clarke, you are unwell. Let me help you." Strong hands grasped her wrist. "Your heart is beating strangely. I would hate for anything to happen to you."

Faith shivered as she sat up. "Too much death." There has been too much death lately. She could not understand why.

"Yes, you have seen a lot of death," he agreed. "It has distressed you greatly. You have seen too much."

"Faith is my responsibility, Martin." Eugenia stood in the doorway. "I will tend whatever ails her."

The sight of her mother-in-law shocked Faith. "How did you get here?" She locked her elbows to help herself stay erect. She was not prepared to handle Eugenia. "I'm fine."

Eugenia ignored her. "Faith is coming home with me until she recovers. There is no need for your attention. Come, Faith, my servant will help you."

Faith stood and wobbled to the doorway. Stubbornly she ignored the servant's outstretched hand. Eyeing the stairs carefully, she gripped the rail and edged down mindful of the maid's fate. She felt odd. Olivia stayed close to her, putting a hand under her elbow when she paused to catch her breath.

A light breeze blew through the window providing welcome relief. Olivia watched as Faith drew in a breath. Eugenia's manservant drew closer. He didn't touch her but his intent was clear. He would catch her if she fell. Faith felt somewhat relieved at the thought. Slowly they made their way to the Moore house. At the steps up the porch, Faith wobbled. At Eugenia's instruction, the servant scooped Faith up and carried her into the parlor, setting her down awkwardly.

Faith put her head in her hands. "I don't know what's wrong with me."

"Did you eat or drink anything while you were there?" Eugenia asked. She took in Faith's sweat-drenched face and shaking hands. For once, her coolness did not bother Faith. She could accept being treated like a bug if it meant her head would quit spinning.

Faith shook her head and quickly regretted the motion. "There was some kind of powder in Mistress Bullard's room, I think I inhaled some by accident."

"I would say you have been drugged," Eugenia said. "Charlotte has mentioned using a tincture to calm her sick nerves. I suspect it was laudanum and you are acting like you have had some."

Faith felt sick. "Where would she get it?"

Eugenia smiled unpleasantly. "Anywhere she wanted. Physicians dispense it for virtually every malady." She paused. "It has its uses. But one can develop a craving for it. I won't have it in my house for that reason. I had an aunt who took too much and never woke up. Right now, you need a purgative to make sure the same doesn't happen to you."

Olivia winced. Faith wanted to object, but if Eugenia was right, then she was in danger and she was dreadfully tired.

Eugenia handed her a goblet. "It's Madeira with a little antimony. It provides a gentle vomit that will clean out your insides from whatever poison ails you."

Faith took it without comment. Despite Eugenia's angelic look, Faith thought she probably enjoyed the treatment's effects more than she should, but that could be pettiness on her part. The treatment kept her from working until the next day and left her wondering if the treatment was worse than the ailment.

Sleep came readily although hazy images peppered her dreams leaving her feeling frightened. When she awoke blind terror gripped her for a moment although she couldn't remember why. Troubled, Faith rose feeling exhausted and anxious.

The sun rose over a steamy landscape. Mist rose off the road and trees like a warm fog, making clothes and skin damp. Olivia was baking, God help her. If it was warm out in the yard, the kitchen would be hellish. Feeling guilty, Faith decided to take a turn in the kitchen. No one needed to stay in such constant heat. Perhaps when evening came, she could call on Martin and ask him about Charlotte Bullard. He would know if she took laudanum. Temperance would enjoy hearing stories from the tavern as well. Faith could not imagine the life of an invalid. She had always been able to move about and do what she needed. She had never considered how terrible it would be to be dependent on others.

The heat hit Faith like a wall. Upstairs where Olivia, Titus, and Joshua lived must be even more intense. Joshua was in the kitchen fanning the air; cooling it slightly and keeping the flies away from the meats and vegetables that Olivia was already preparing for later in the day. Even with his efforts,

Faith felt sweat dampening her hair and palms. Olivia's skirts were tied up revealing her ankles and undoubtedly keeping her cooler.

"Tis miserable hot," Faith said. "Would you like me to watch the food for a while so you can cool off?"

Olivia's eyes met hers. Despite the heat, the cook looked regal. Her ivory kerchief looked impossibly clean. Her face was calm and composed despite being dewy with sweat. This was Olivia's domain, Faith realized. It was the one place where her word was law and she gave the orders. "I'm fine Missus," Olivia said. "Joshua helps keep the air moving and I have everything I need." Looking outside, Faith saw Titus cutting more wood for the fire. Seeing the York family together, she realized that Olivia really did have all she needed, except to be free. Faith stepped back outside; silently praying her petition for them would be granted.

Work on the private room was almost complete. Will climbed back up on the roof joining the other men. He spotted her and waved. Faith flushed, but lifted a hand in acknowledgment before turning to enter the tavern to do the work she needed to be doing.

"Not a bad-looking man there," Titus commented from the porch.

"I wouldn't know," Faith muttered, her face still burning.

Titus raised an eyebrow. He didn't have to say anything. They both knew she had been staring where she shouldn't.

"They would probably appreciate a drink," Faith said at last.

"No doubt they're trying not to get overheated. You look like you're a bit heated up yourself."

Faith glared and sighed ruefully. "Perhaps I am. Please take them something to drink with my thanks for their hard work."

"I'll take drinks out there," Titus agreed. Under his breath, he said, "Though I don't think that's all you're thankful for."

Faith knew her face was burning and not from the heat. She needed to focus on her work. Entering her tavern, she helped Titus pour tankards of short beer and then helped him take it outside. Will and the others had donned their shirts when Faith called out that they were bringing refreshment.

No one had discovered who had killed Phineas Bullard. Stella's death barely created a ripple in the community. Charlotte Bullard was now gone as well. Somehow it was tied to the terrible end of Felicia and David Verity. Faith just didn't know how.

"You look troubled," Ezra Moore said. He must have come through the tavern to have come up behind her.

Faith forced a smile on her face. "Just wool-gathering, I'm afraid." She pointed to the private room. "It has gone up quickly, has it not?"

"Indeed."

"Yet," Faith paused, "no one really knows who killed Bullard."

Ezra Moore frowned. "The crown seems satisfied that his slave did the deed but you don't seem satisfied with that answer."

"No," she admitted, "It seems too convenient."

"But not unlikely," Moore said. "By all accounts, Bullard was not an easy man either to his business associates or his servants. Stella may have been abused one too many times."

"Did you ever see Stella?" Faith exclaimed with exasperation. "She was a frail-looking thing. Do you truly believe she could take a saber from Bullard, slash his throat, then gut him? He was over twice her size!"

"Desperation can make one capable of many things," Ezra murmured. "And you would do well to lower your voice if you are going to talk of such things."

Faith dropped to a whisper, "What about the weapon? Captain Grant and his men searched this tavern thoroughly, not a rock was left undisturbed yet it was never found."

"Why would she throw away something of value?" Moore retorted. "She would need money to get away. A side piece like Bullard wore would be worth some coin."

"I cannot think of any place where a slave selling a sword would not attract attention," Faith argued.

Moore smiled, "There are places in any town where one can buy or sell most anything, Faith. Dark corners of town where members of a less than gentle society reside.

"Then inquiries need to be made," she said determinedly.

"Not by you," Ezra said firmly. "It would not be safe and it would ruin your reputation. I know you wish to clear the name of your tavern. Being seen there would only make things worse." He met her eyes and the power of that direct gaze was formidable. "I have people I can use to make inquiries. You will have to content yourself with that."

Faith wanted to protest but she knew he was right. If someone was trying to silence her, it would be best not to go to places where her death was easier to accomplish.

Chapter Nineteen

As the sun began its journey towards the western horizon, the shadows within Clarke Tavern deepened, casting rooms into shadow. The summer's heat smothered Faith as she squinted at her accounts. No cooling breeze came through the open window. She gazed longingly outside at the nearby trees, where cooling shade beckoned. Sweat beaded at her brow running down her face as she bent over her work once again. The quill stuck to her fingers refusing to let them escape. Across the page, her accounts barely maintained control within their columns. Nothing added up. She rubbed her head and realized that she had probably smeared ink on her face. "Now I'm marked like Cain," she muttered.

Determined not to surrender, Faith sharpened the quill. The blade slipped in her sweaty fingers, cutting into unwary flesh. Stifling a cry, she stuffed the injured digit into her mouth. Staring down, she realized that bright red drops of blood stained the page beneath her, smearing the line of accounts. Her breath caught as the unwilling memory of previously spilled blood assaulted her memory.

Blood pooled on the polished wood of the floor, coagulated into reddish-black stains. The blood had not been content to remain around the body but had left splatters on the table and chair before trailing out to the door. Startled, Faith sat up. Where had that picture come from? Closing her eyes, she pictured the old private room as it had looked that awful morning. The sultriness of her room faded away as did the faint noises of the few men still drinking across the hall.

When she had entered, the room had been dark and still. The dying fire had left the room smelling faintly smoky, enough that she had not immediately noticed the metallic scent of blood. Bullard had lain on the floor, a bottle of wine on its side next to him. Enough of it had spilled on the floor to anger her. She had hoped he was unconscious from too much drink despite Olivia's warning. But wine hadn't been the only thing spilled. Her shoes had become sticky with blood, which had been in more places than just around the body. But why? It struck her like a lightning bolt. It had been splattered during the attack. Could the killer have been injured in the fight? Bullard was a large man, he would have endeavored to fend off the attack. Faith wracked her memory. Had there been anything else? She clenched her fists in frustration as nothing else came to mind. Setting her accounts aside, she put her mind to the night Phineas Bullard died.

It had been busy. Both Titus and she had kept filling tankards and feeding guests. They had taken turns going back and forth to the kitchen for food. Andrew and Joshua had been caring for the animals before retiring for the night. Faith shuddered. The boys had been out there at the same time as the killer. But then so had she. Her arms and feet had ached by the time she had fallen into bed. As she thought of Joshua and Andrew, she wondered where they were. It would be dark soon and they should be home.

Rising, she went to find them. The weather had taken a mild turn. A breeze cleared the humidity and lowered the temperature. Faith thought about where two young boys would go on a mild sunny day. Pondering the favorite pastimes of childhood, her thoughts took her northwest where a favorite fishing hole lay. Trees covered the banks of most of the streams, sending thirsty roots into the soil to capture the swift running water. It did not take her long to spot two figures under the shade of a maple overlooking a quiet stream. Two poles dangled lazily in the water creating circles that spread out and disappeared into the water. The stream was shallow this time of year; its path littered with medium-sized stones. Light sparkled on the water as it coursed down on its way to the nearest river.

"Any bites?" Faith asked leaning down to see the faces underneath the wide brims of their straw hats.

Joshua shook his head. "No ma'am. Nothing's been biting in this stream."

He stared down into the quiet water. It was quiet except for the ceaseless buzzing of flies hovering about, biting at sweaty necks and arms. A distant plunk indicated that somewhere the fish were lazing about. Looking into the mirror-like depths, Faith saw plenty of tadpoles but no fish. Given all the infant frogs, mosquitos should be little trouble or so she hoped.

The dappled shade cast shadows on the water coloring it greenish-brown. Faith watched both boys, full of the curiosity and innocence of childhood, and felt a fierce protectiveness rise up. There was nothing she would not do to keep these boys safe. Her thoughts went to David Verity who had died so young. At this moment she could understand what could motivate someone to kill.

"Do you remember when Master Bullard died?" she asked quietly. "I need you to remember what you were doing that night. Think about what you saw or heard. Anything you remember could be helpful."

Andrew looked puzzled. "I thought his slave killed him," he said. "Why does it matter what we were doing?"

"I doubt Stella killed anyone," Faith said bluntly. "That poor child would have been no match for a man as big as Bullard."

"Then why did she run?"

"She wanted to be free," Joshua answered with a sadness that tore at the heart..

Faith drew in her breath. "I imagine she did," she said at last. "Did you see her that night?"

Joshua nodded, "She ate with us that evening. Ma was put out that I was late finishing my chores, but she didn't say so in front of her." He looked at Faith apologetically. "I got delayed feeding the animals because of Master Moore's horse."

Faith nodded although she had no idea what he was talking about. "His horse?" she repeated.

Joshua nodded. "He brought a lame horse into the back yard. Pa wasn't there so he asked me to take it into the barn and care for it. He came and got it a day or two later. Pa usually takes care of the horses he leaves here."

"How long has this been going on?" Faith's voice was sharp.

"I don't know, maybe a couple months." Joshua looked uncomfortable.

Faith realized it was unfair to be angry with the boy for what adults had done. She took a breath to calm herself. This was a discussion to be had with Titus and Ezra.

"Hey, I got something!" Andrew cried as his line pulled taut. Its weight began to bend the pole into a straining arc.

Joshua dropped his line on the ground to help his friend. "Don't let it get away!" The larger boy put his hands below Andrew's as the weight began to drag at his arms. Together they hauled at their catch. It was dark and slimy, yet when the sun hit it, something reflected light that was almost blinding. Long and slender, yet deadly looking even as they stared at it on the ground.

Faith knew without any doubt that she was staring at Phineas Bullard's saber. It could belong to no one else. No one would throw away such an expensive weapon. "Don't touch it."

Joshua took out a small knife and cut the line. Both boys stared at it in fascination. Despite the weeks spent in the water, it still bore vestiges of the elegant weapon it had once been. The hilt was tarnished to the point of blackness and weeds clung to the blade like a shroud.

"Get Captain Grant. Don't talk to anyone else. Tell him you've found Bullard's weapon." The boys took off, wasting no time to ask questions, leaving her with the weapon at her feet.

Faith felt the sun on her back as she stared at the ostentatious piece. She hated weapons. Quakers abhorred violence. Despite the fact she had been cast out for marrying outside the faith, years of teaching were still embedded in her heart. Thinking of how the piece had been employed sickened her.

Hearing hoofbeats, she turned. It was Grant. He was leading the animal to keep pace with the boys. "Mistress Clarke," he said without surprise. He handed the older boy the reins and told them to find it a place to graze. When they were out of earshot, he looked at her without expression although his eyes glittered. "Well?"

Faith gestured to where the saber lay on the grass, drying in the sun.

"Are you certain it is his?"

"Pretty sure," Faith admitted. "I've seen it once or twice, but weapons are not an interest of mine. But who would throw such an ornate piece into a stream? Whoever did must have hoped the current would carry it away."

"Perhaps, but it would be too heavy to be carried away in this little brook" Grant knelt down and using a stick, lifted and turned it. "The armory may have knowledge of this piece. I will take it to Master Geddy to examine." His cool gaze met hers. "You know that it is very unlikely that a slave would have disposed of a saber here."

Faith nodded. A frightened girl, fleeing slavery was unlikely to have headed to a popular fishing hole to dispose of a weapon. The risk of being seen was too great.

"I never believed Stella murdered Bullard," Faith commented.

Grant looked up at her. "Neither did I. She could not have bested Bullard in a struggle. He outweighed her by a good hundred pounds." His pale blue eyes caught hers. "But if she did not, then who?"

"I believe I have an answer for that," she said quietly. The time for secrets was over. As the sun sank lower in the sky, she told the captain about her discoveries and her suspicions.

Grant was quiet for a moment. "I would have liked to have seen the letter myself." He stood up, dusting his perfectly cut breeches. "If Bullard was responsible for the death of Felicia and David Verity, it would provide a powerful motive to someone. Do you have any idea who?"

"Possibly," Faith said. "I've spoken to a former slave who knew Felicia. He said that Josiah Smythe was most interested in her." She chose not to mention her own misgivings about her father-in-law. That he could have a hand in this was more than Faith could bear contemplating. There were too many secrets swirling about and she was not sure she was prepared to know them all.

Grant eyed her quietly. A small tic was detectable at the corner of his eye. "Why didn't you inform me of your suspicions earlier? Did it not occur to you that this could be dangerous?"

Faith met his gaze realizing as she did that it didn't hurt as badly as she had once thought it would. "I have no proof and no way to get it. All I can do is ask questions and hope it leads to the truth."

"That won't matter if the killer decides that you are causing too much trouble." Grant's voice turned icy. "You were nearly trampled to death at the Governor's Ball. Someone pushed you deliberately into harm's way. You should be more careful, both for your reputation and your life."

Faith shuddered. He could be right, but she had to clear her name too much was at stake. Some risks she had to take.

Grant picked up the weapon, wrapping it in a broadsheet he had brought with him. "Go back to your tavern, Mistress Clarke. I will talk to Smythe and whomever else my inquiries will lead me to. You are far better off keeping your mind on your own affairs."

Faith did not reply. She wanted to ask if he were happy with Mistress Wright, but lacked the courage. Grant motioned and the boys brought his horse over to him. The captain mounted and headed back into town. The boys surrounded her. "Let's go home," Faith said firmly. "There is much to do before supper." They darted ahead once they realized she would answer none of their questions. Hopefully, they would forget what they had seen. Faith had other business to attend to such as finding out what Ezra Moore was involved in.

Her mind whirled. She had always assumed the few horses in the barn belonged to guests and Titus had never told her differently. But then he had been Ezra Moore's slave for many years before becoming hers. He would not hesitate to do what her father-in-law asked. The secrecy troubled her.

Titus sensed her disquiet. "Master Jon didn't mind if he left a few horses here once in a while. Master Ezra said it helped in case he had to get a message out quick." The big black man looked uncomfortable. "It's not any extra trouble, ma'am."

"It's all right, Titus," Faith said. "My father-in-law has always supported us. It does no harm if he wants to keep a horse here." What she did not say was that Ezra Moore had a palatial residence in town. Why did he need to keep horses sequestered secretly on the other side of Williamsburg? More importantly, why had no one told her? She had been mistress of Clarke Tavern for a year now. It was her inn. Yet apparently, she did not know everything that went on in her own place of business.

All answers lay with her father-in-law, to whom she owed so much. Faith would have to corner him upon his next visit and discover his plans. For now, as Grant noted, she had plenty to occupy her at her tavern.

Moore did not appear for dinner at the tavern for the next span of days. It was frustrating. She wondered if he was aware that his secret had been discovered and was purposefully avoiding her. It was an uneasy thought compounded by the guilt she felt in having suspicions about a man who had saved her from penury. Finally, after supper had been attended to and the next day's meals decided, Faith decided to act. Whispering thanks to the almighty for long summer days, Faith put a pot of strawberry jam in a basket, tied on her summer straw hat, and set off on the long walk to the Moore's Williamsburg residence. She hoped that by the time she arrived, she'd have the right words to say. How did one discover if their father-in-law was a murderer?

Avoiding the busyness of Duke of Gloucester Street, Faith skirted the Presbyterian Church and headed down James Street towards her in-laws'. Few folks were out this time of evening. They were at home or settled into their tavern of choice to dance, play cards or discuss things better not discussed at home. Although expressing personal neutrality, Faith was well aware that discontented people gathered in taverns to discuss the increasing enmity with England. Governor Dunmore's high-handed governorship had not softened people's minds.

Walking down the street toward the fashionable neighborhood where her in-laws lived, Faith wondered about Ezra. He was one of the most easy-going people she knew, but could lose his temper if tested too sorely. Faith had never forgotten his reaction when he had discovered a horse that Jon's brother, Louis had left for a servant to attend. Unfortunately, he had not told anyone. Ezra had found the exhausted and dehydrated animal standing tied outside the barn. After seeing to its care, he had come into the house.

Faith and Jon had been living with them until the inn was made more habitable. She knew something was wrong when she saw his face. His expression frightened her.

"Who left the bay tied up in the sun?"

All sound stopped as everyone looked at him. Outwardly, Ezra Moore's face was composed, but a tic made his left eye twitch. There were touches of white to his lips where they were tightly compressed. His eyes glittered strangely. Faith realized he was enraged.

Jon looked at his stepfather and backed away, "I haven't been out all day." Standing behind Faith and baby Andrew, he made his case.

Ezra Moore's eyes flickered over his elder stepson without stopping and then went on to Louis who was seventeen. Louis was in the midst of a game of cards and had not bothered to turn around when his stepfather entered the room. A plump, indolent creature, Louis had at various times studied law, medicine, and the ministry. According to Eugenia, he was currently learning about trade.

Faith could not think of anyone less likely to succeed at business, but then he had his mother to support whatever trade he was currently dabbling in. Even though he was at home with family, Louis was dressed in tight-fitting breeches obviously tailored in a London style. These were paired with highly polished Hessian boots of ebony. His vest was brocade and the embroidery was thick enough to make one dizzy. His ensemble was completed by a white shirt of linen. The effect of such expensive tailoring was muted by his soft double chin and the faint pout of his mouth. Only the tension radiating from his back and neck indicated he had heard the voice of his stepfather. Eugenia laid down her cards. Her petticoats rustled as she rose to make her escape from the parlor.

"Louis." Ezra's voice cracked like thunder from an impending storm.

Louis shrugged which was a stupid thing to do. His dark eyes flicked upwards at his stepfather. "It hasn't been that long. Surely Titus can take care of it."

Ezra smiled grimly. "Titus takes excellent care of all the horses, but he isn't here. He's at the farm working with the colts. It is your responsibility to see to the care of your mount especially after a hot ride. Come with me and see what your carelessness has done." With that, he hauled Louis off the chair.

"Unhand me," he shrieked. Ezra grasped him by the scruff and dragged him out of the parlor, down the hall, and out back. Faith watched in shock. Further back in the house, she could hear Eugenia shriek.

"Ezra, he's just a boy!"

"If he's man enough to ride a horse, he is man enough to care for it properly!" A door slammed.

Faith stared up at Jon who was busy studying a volume of Latin which she knew he did not read. Dizziness struck her. Realizing she was holding her breath, she inhaled and tried not to imagine what was happening outside. Unfortunately, the open windows left little to the imagination. Louis wailed as he was being dragged to the barn. Eugenia was crying. Faith wanted to leave but she could not without Jon who was pretending nothing was happening.

"We should go," she whispered.

"Not yet," Jon said. "Let's see what little Louis looks like now." Her husband's face held a look of smug satisfaction.

"You're enjoying this," Faith accused.

Jon shrugged. "All through our childhood years, he could do no wrong. Mother always protected him from me, from Pa and he lorded it over everyone. It's time he was held accountable."

It was not long before Louis staggered back in, reeking of the barn. His face was red with exertion and tears. He looked about wildly and stumbled up the steps where Eugenia cried for servants to bring bathwater and fresh linen. It was only then that Jon was willing to leave.

The memory was still fresh in her mind as she stood in front of her father-in-law's home. At this time of day, he would have completed his business and returned for supper and a snifter of French cognac. Before her courage left, Faith knocked on the door. The servant did not comment on her late visit but led her to the parlor.

"Faith, my dear," Ezra said as he rose from his chair. "What brings you here?" He indicated the chair across from him which she took. A manservant poured her a glass of wine.

Faith sipped the wine to provide time to catch her breath. Unfortunately, wine was not made for inhaling. She coughed until Ezra leaned forward and pounded her back. Recovering, she stood. Her face was flushed as her breath gradually returned. "I want to know why you keep horses at Clarke Tavern."

"I see. This is not a social call." Ezra smiled benignly but his dark eyes studied her. His features made Faith think of an owl, outwardly benevolent-looking but inside always a predator. The thought almost made her shiver but she refused to be cowed.

"If your stable is crowded," Ezra began.

Faith shook her head. "It's not that, and I am grateful for all you have done for me. You have done more than my own father and I do not forget that, but I want to know your reasons, sir."

"It would be safer if you did not. Eugenia is at a ball with my son and his wife. They will not be home until late. We will not share this conversation with them or anyone else."

"I have no desire for idle chatter," Faith said quietly as she adjusted her skirts on the chair where she sat opposite him. "As long as no laws are broken, our words need never leave this room."

Ezra laughed. "What do you think I am doing, child?" His face was guileless. It was like playing chess with a master and she had not played chess in a long time.

She met his gaze. "I don't know. What I do know is a man was murdered in my inn and no one has found his killer. He was involved in capturing and selling freed slaves and God knows what else. Now I find that you billet horses for unknown reasons and men come and take them out without explanation."

"How do you know this?" His unflappability unnerved her. Faith was shocked to realize that she was frightened. There was too much going on around her that she did not understand and ignorance was dangerous, perhaps deadly. Ezra Moore watched her, sipping his brandy. Despite his genial features, there was a faint sheen of sweat on his brow. He was waiting for her response. She could either be a pawn or a queen in this game. The move was hers to make. She could either trust him or not but she had to decide now.

Haltingly, Faith told him about the letter, her conversation with the basket lady, and the stable hand. She told him about her observations of Josiah Smythe's visits to where the freed slaves lived. Lastly, she mentioned the incident at the Governor's ball although she doubted he realized that someone had pushed her.

Not once did he interrupt her or silence her with a glance. His eyes when he met hers were sharp and bright. "I had no idea you were investigating Bullard's murder." He shook his head. "I thought you quiet and meek; a little Quaker mouse that Jon took a fancy to, but plainly there is more to you than meets the eye. Listen carefully. I do not trade in slaves, free or otherwise. I own slaves. They are part of our family and have always been treated with dignity." Ezra drew in a breath. "I did business on occasion with Bullard. I knew him for an ostentatious bully with expensive tastes. He was also a spy for King George, which would have made him many enemies if he had been revealed.

"I keep horses at the ready for my convenience. I have men who travel throughout the colony gathering news of various types and bringing it back to me. In these times, information is a precious commodity and I would know what the British are doing before they are beating down my door. These are not the times to cower or look away if we are to survive. I have broken no true law of this colony, nor will I."

Realization sent a chill down her spine. "You favor revolution."

"I favor having the same rights as other Englishmen. Rights the king has denied us. Neither he nor Parliament seem open to reason or truth of late."

"If you are found out…," Faith breathed.

"Do you intend to betray me to your friend, Captain Grant?"

Faith shook her head. "No. I may not wish for revolution but I will not betray my family. A man or woman should be able to freely express an opinion without legal repercussions."

"Well said. Now let us turn our thoughts to whoever ended the life of Phineas Bullard. Given the attempt on your life, it was not a random stranger but someone here in Williamsburg. That sort of death takes a great deal of hate so it was not over something minor. I fear your letter holds the key.

Tell me everything you remember of its contents."

Faith repeated what she recalled, also that it had disappeared before the Governor's Ball.

"Interesting," Moore said. "But I doubt you lost it. I believe someone realized it was in your possession. Who had access to your writing desk?"

Faith looked at him.

He returned her gaze ruefully. "That was a rather foolish question to ask the mistress of a local tavern. I apologize. But someone must have realized you had it and that is why you were pushed in front of a carriage." He looked at her over his glasses. "You cannot continue to take such risks, Faith. You are all Andrew has."

"Phineas Bullard was insufferable, but that does not give anyone the right to cut him to pieces in my tavern," Faith protested. She wasn't being ladylike, but she could not let this pass.

Widowhood and the owning of a business forced her to face the less delicate truths of life.

"Agreed," Moore said. "Being a businessman of long-standing in Virginia, I have more resources at my disposal. Let me find out what there is to know about Bullard's dirty little business dealings. That may allow us to flush the killer out. And you, my dear, need to stay home surrounded by people you trust. Keep Titus nearby. He's protected me from harm on many a trip when he traveled with me. Had Eugenia not been insistent on making him and Olivia a wedding present, I would have arranged his manumission long ago." A shadow crossed his face. "I regret that. The only salve for my conscience is that his son lives as a free man and has an education as well. I will pay for his apprenticeship, once it is decided upon." He smiled at her.

"I admire your desire for peace, Faith, but keep in mind that lasting peace is most often bought at a great price. Right now, the men, women, and children in Boston are suffering terrible deprivations at the hand of King George."

"Because of the tea," Faith said. "That was the work of a crowd of ruffians, surely anyone can see that."

Ezra ruffled his hair, showering them both with powder. "King George sees the colonies as disobedient children to be punished and therein lies the problem. He does not seek to punish the guilty few so much as to punish the entire colony. I am a merchant and have traded with England for many years, but I cannot stand by and watch innocent women and children suffer needlessly, dependent on the temper of one man, even if he holds the title of king." His gaze hardened, "Having horses allows me to send news and supplies to our beleaguered sister city north. My sister lives there and the shortages are appalling. I will not abandon her when she needs me most. Her husband has traded with Samuel Addams. Now he must remain in hiding to stay alive. My men carry food, medicine, and news to Helen and her children." His eyes reflected pain and helplessness. "I cannot change what is happening in Boston. Would you have me abandon her?"

"I would not ask you to," Faith replied. "I did not know. I mean," She fumbled. "I knew that Boston harbor was closed but I did not know that conditions were so terrible."

Ezra smiled grimly, "That is why it is important that information is spread throughout the colonies so that people are aware of what the British are capable of." He looked at her, "Until tonight you could have proclaimed your innocence to what I was doing. It would have been safer to keep you ignorant, dear."

"No, it wouldn't," Faith replied, "No one would believe I did not know. At least now, I know that your horses and men go to help my fellow countrymen." Her stomach was a bit queasy with the realization she could be accused of treason, but her heart refused to abandon her family.

"What will you tell Captain Grant?"

"I shall not tell him anything," Faith answered wryly. "I have no desire to stir up a hornet's nest." With any luck, Grant would never realize that the horses did not belong to borders. He had ceased coming around as frequently. Apparently, the captain had other fish to fry.

Her father-in-law looked thoughtful, "I am grateful for that." He sighed quietly. "There is not a delicate way to put this. At the ball, he seemed to show some interest in you. Has he spoken to you? Given any indication of his intentions?"

Startled, Faith looked up. "No. He has not."

"Good. Then he is not a complete cad."

Faith was startled. "Why do you ask this?"

"Grant is a busy man even when he is not tracking down patriots. He has been visiting the home of Peyton Randolph. He has cut quite a figure among the ladies. Young Grant has also spent a good deal of time visiting Bullard's niece. A young man like that will be looking to marry a woman of means with connections that will enable him to rise."

It still stung but Faith knew she was far from the classes where Grant was a familiar face. Nonetheless, she had enjoyed his attention. It had been a while since she had felt treasured in that way. She smiled when she saw her father-in-law's concern. "Fear not. 'Tis nothing but my pride that is pricked. It is an injury that I will soon recover from. Martha told me of his engagement to Mistress Wright." She sighed ruefully. "It is past time I returned home. There are responsibilities that will not wait."

Her father-in-law insisted on providing an escort despite her protests. "The day is late and you do not need to be out and about unprotected. I do not want you caught unawares should your attacker find another opportunity." His words unnerved her enough to submit. Titus was at the front window looking out when she arrived. Although there was still light in the sky, the shadows had grown deep.

"Mistress, did you send Joshua on an errand?"

"No," Faith responded. "Why do you ask?'

"Olivia and I haven't seen him since he helped serve dinner. We thought he and Andrew had gone off fishing but then Andrew came in without him. We don't know where he might be."

A chill went down Faith's spine. Joshua was dependable. He would have never left the younger boy alone. "Andrew," she called.

Her son had apparently been listening. He looked worried. "He went after a ball out on the green and he never came back. Some of the other boys had been teasing him so I thought he got mad and went home."

"How long has he been gone?" Faith asked, her voice sharp with worry.

"Hours." Olivia's voice was hoarse. "I checked all through the house and barn. He's not been here. His dinner is still sitting in the kitchen." Her voice trembled. "Joshua never misses a meal."

"We need to look for him," Faith said.

Titus said, "I already checked where they were playing. Nobody has seen him. I've been through the market and down through the green."

"What about the Bray school?" Faith asked. "Did he have any reason to go there? Maybe he wanted to speak to his teacher?"

Titus looked up, desperate hope gleaming in his eyes. "I'll run down and see. Maybe he lost track of time."

Faith didn't want to frighten them anymore than they already were. An ugly thought formed in her mind, one she didn't want to contemplate but dared not ignore. "Let me send a message to the Moores. They will help." If someone had snatched the boy to sell, she would need Ezra's help to get him back. She wanted to be wrong. She wanted Joshua to come walking down the street with an excuse but Faith already knew something terrible had to have happened.

Titus ran down the street toward the school, while Faith paid a boy to take a message to Ezra's house. There was little more she could do. Olivia said little but her eyes tracked every movement from the street. Finally, she moved from the window.

"I need to go to the kitchen when he comes back. Joshua will want a hot meal."

Faith nodded. It made sense to keep busy. She poured drinks and sent Andrew back and forth to the kitchen to feed a small number of guests. The sun rode low in the sky before one of Ezra's servants came by with a message. Her father-in-law promised to send men to look for the boy and contact the sheriff. His words made her uneasy. He knew that a young boy like Joshua was valuable. It was also possible that the boy had seen something the night Bullard died but did not realize the significance. She did not believe his disappearance was an accident but another assault on her family. Instead of frightening her, it made her very angry. No one had the right to threaten her life or those around her.

Phineas Bullard had died a brutal death in her tavern. He had eaten a meal, drunk at a table in her private room with someone just as he had on other occasions. What changed? Faith thought back to that night. It had been cold and Titus had gone back and forth for wood to feed the fires. There had been a fire lit in the private room as well along with a generous supply of wood to keep it going. Bullard had dismissed his servant in order to be alone. That meant he didn't want to be seen with whomever he was meeting or that the business itself could have been unsavory or illegal.

Once again, her thoughts turned to Felicia and David Verity. Their end horrified her. She had no doubt Bullard had been responsible even if indirectly. But who had avenged them? It was too soon to know what Grant had discovered about the saber. He had not dropped by nor had she sought him out. His engagement had built a wall between them, one she was unwilling to breach. Night fell with no news about Joshua. Faith went to bed but sleep proved elusive. In restless dreams, she heard the cries of a child begging for help but no one ever came.

The next day brought no resolution. It was as if Joshua had disappeared into thin air. Titus left at first light to continue searching. Faith watched his back disappear in the light fog of the morning before turning to care for their few guests. The morning dragged with no news of the boy. Her father-in-law dropped by for a drink. He shook his head at her frantic glance.

"I've heard nothing about the child. My groomsman and all the staff I can spare are out looking for him. He'll turn up soon."

Faith doubted that. Joshua would never worry his parents like this. He was cautious around strangers. His parents had taught him from an early age to be careful.

Ezra consented to minding the liquor while she took a load of dishes back to the kitchen. "Olivia?" she asked before stepping in. She dropped the dishes into a tub to wash later.

Olivia stirred a kettle over the fire before slowly turning about. Shadows lined her face making lines around her nose and eyes prominent. "Is there any word?" Her tone was flat, having lost all the musical cadence of her native Jamaica.

Faith shook her head. "Everyone is still looking. We won't give up."

"Do you think he's dead?"

Faith shook her head in violent denial. "No, I do not. We will find him alive." She had to believe that. Her mind could not accept another death. Spinning on her heel she went back inside the tavern hoping for news that never came. The tavern felt like a ball and chain keeping her from doing what she wished. Faith snapped at a guest, then apologized. "It's been a difficult day."

The man nodded, mollified by a free tankard of ale although as she walked away, he muttered to another man who laughed and made a bawdy joke about women. Faith lacked the energy to take them to task. Staring out the door did nothing to bring word about Joshua. Waiting for answers chafed at her. The summer heat made her restless and unable to focus on the simplest task. By dinner, most guests had left, leaving the heat of the tavern for the comfort of shady trees or cooler buildings. Still no word came. Faith wanted to badger Captain Grant for information but he was nowhere to be seen. She wondered if he had gone calling on his affluent fiancé. Picturing the feather-headed Prudence presiding over tea made her ill.

Titus came home late. The droop of his shoulders and the despair on his face told her of the futility of his efforts. Tears burned her eyes as she silently prayed for a miracle.

As the sun started down in the sky, Faith escaped outside to tend the summer garden. Andrew had forgotten to tend to it. Taking a break, she stood beneath a tree where it was only slightly cooler. The rustle and slap of branches made her look about for the source. Josiah Smythe stood outside the tenement nearest to her, but rather than head to the tavern for supper or to the street, he chose to use the trees and bushes to blend into the shadows. Immediately, she came to attention. Everything about his movements suggested a desire for secrecy. Since the discovery of Bullard's body, she had become increasingly aware of strange behavior. Smythe had no reason to be here that she knew of and his actions suggested nothing good. Faith watched from the shadows of her tree and slowly moved to follow him. It was time for some answers.

She kept a good distance behind him, watching as he stayed close to the hedges that separated yards and made for Nicholson Street. The only place Faith knew about here was the goal and she could not imagine what someone would want there. When he emerged from the yard, Smythe looked around. Fortunately, trees hid her. From there he turned west away from the goal and toward town. Faith continued to follow. Nicholson Street was a long venue that would eventually take one to the Governor's palace although she was certain that this was not his destination. He acted too secretive for this to be regular business. It was not long before he turned off the larger road to a smaller one and yet another. Faith was unfamiliar with this area of town. The houses were smaller and more roughly built. This was a working-class neighborhood, not a place for a well-to-do merchant to skulk. Smythe did not waver but continued down the street, passing yards with sheep and horses with their small gardens visible from the street. Faith caught the scent of roasting meat nearby. Someone was fixing supper. Her stomach growled. It had been a while since her last meal. People on horses and traveling in carts continued down the road into town where the taverns and businesses lay. Faith pulled her hat down and continued even though her nerves were jumping. Her quarry continued on foot through the neighborhood. Slowly but deliberately he paused at a house. A woman hung laundry on a line in the yard. Faith guessed that laundress was her occupation from the large number of items, many of them uniforms that covered her line.

Faith slowed down and hid behind a tall scraggly bush. Peeking out, she noticed that Smythe was talking to the woman. Moments later he was joined by a shorter man with pale hair. He was familiar. Frowning she tried to recall why. Then it hit her, he had been with Ezra at the tavern, but left before he could be introduced. Although she had thought it strange, other matters had consumed her thoughts at the time. Now he was having a secret meeting with Josiah Smythe. Although she could hear their voices, Faith could not make out their words. They shook hands.

"Tonight, then," Smythe called out as he left. He strode away briskly from Faith's hiding place, undoubtedly cutting through the side streets on this side of town. If she didn't act soon, he would be lost in the warren of alleys and cut throughs. Focused on her quarry, Faith didn't immediately notice the sudden silence until she was whipped around.

"What are you doing?"

Faith gasped. The woman towering over her had to be at least six feet tall and a good two hundred pounds, all muscle. Her skin was copper brown and her dark hair was tucked up under a fiery orange cloth. Her age could have been anywhere from thirty to fifty.

Faith was struck dumb. Her mouth opened and closed like a landed fish. As her scrambled wits stumbled for a reply, the other woman clamped an iron grip to her arm and dragged her over to where the blonde stranger still stood. She yelped and tried to get away but the other woman was easily twice her size.

Her captor spoke. "She's been spying on you. I saw her in the bushes, trying to blend in." She eyed Faith scornfully. "You don't belong on this side of town."

"Is that true?" He was slight with fair freckled skin and ash blonde hair tied back. At first, she thought him a boy because he was short and slender, then she looked into his eyes and realized he was a man. Faint lines crinkled the corners of his eyes. There were a few faint pockmarks near his hairline, but not enough to mar his features. His was a face marked by experience and there was no mercy in his gaze. She was deep in trouble.

Faith didn't answer. The other woman shook her until Faith was certain her teeth would fall out. "Answer him." She started to shake her again until the man held up a hand.

"Easy, Athena. Let Mistress Clarke catch her breath." He looked at her grimly. "This is no place for a casual journey. You will not leave until you answer me truthfully. I need to know who you report to as well as why you are here. I have no interest in underlings."

Faith looked at him indignantly. "I came of my own accord, sir. I spy for no one."

"Very well, then, why do you spy on me?" His expression made it clear he did not believe her.

Fear and anger battled for control. Anger won. "I don't know who you are. I have the same right as anyone to walk through town."

"Propelled by simple curiosity?" Sarcasm marred his voice.

"What business is it of yours, how I choose to conduct my business?"

The stranger's eyes were a cool green "I doubt you were out for a stroll, Mistress. My sources tell me you've been asking questions all over town. You possess all the subtlety of a ship's cannon. It's a method guaranteed to make enemies. He gave her an assessing look, "You are Ezra Moore's daughter-in-law which is enough for me to keep you alive. You own that little inn near the capital since your husband's death last summer."

"And who are you?" she retorted. Faith tried to free her arm from Athena. Already it was getting numb. She had no doubt that she would be wearing a monumental bruise tomorrow, provided she was still alive. Somehow, she had stumbled into something more than she had anticipated. The green-eyed man watched her. Faith glared back.

"Jeremy Butler," he replied. The lack of recognition on her face seemed to please him. "While I doubt you are a Tory spy, I can't risk any idle chatter. I have no choice but to keep you until my work is done. Then your fate will be decided." Butler's irritation was apparent. "You should have stayed home, Faith Clarke. These are dangerous times." He shook his head, "I do not willingly hurt women, Mistress Clarke and I have friends too fond of your chicken pie to eliminate you. Tonight, you will have to suffer my hospitality."

Faith stared at him shocked. The suggestion was unseemly at best. She felt Athena's grip on her arm. Escaping her would be difficult. He took one look at her expression and laughed, "Fear not, your reputation will remain intact. You will remain in the care of Athena. Not even I would brave her wrath. She will release you in a respectable place when what you have seen and heard will not matter."

His face looked intense in the shadowed light. Faith wondered what was so important that he would hold a gentlewoman against her will until he was done. Such a man might have the answers she needed. "Do you know who killed Phineas Bullard?"

Butler looked surprised. "No, I don't. His death caused me a great deal of inconvenience, probably almost as much as you. Bullard ran many profitable businesses. He was a source of information even if he was unaware of providing it. He was quite useful alive."

Realization hit her. "You did business with him," she said quietly, then with rising anger. "I bet you know all the businesses he was involved with, legal or not. That's why you met with Smythe."

Butler didn't deny the accusation. His face was unreadable as he waited for her to continue.

He infuriated her. "You had to know about his secret business in capturing and selling freed slaves and yet you did nothing about it. You're despicable."

Athena pinched her. Faith bit back a cry as Butler frowned at Athena. "That's not necessary. I like a woman who speaks her mind." He looked faintly amused. "You have a high and mighty opinion for a slave owner or perhaps you salve your conscience by saying they are like family. They're not, you know. Slaves are a commodity and you cannot tell me if it comes down to selling that big buck of yours or keeping a roof over your head that you won't value the coin over the man."

She did slap him that time. Or she would have if he hadn't blocked her with a lightning-fast reflex of his own arm. "That's beyond low," she hissed. "I would never sell Titus. I am trying to free him and Olivia. But then I am sure you are completely unaware of how challenging it is to manumit a slave." The last was delivered in a sarcastic tone Faith had not realized she was capable of. She rubbed her arm. It felt like it was on fire. Faith stared at Butler refusing to run or act frightened. If he was going to kill her at least she wasn't dying a coward.

"Bravo. I had not thought there was so much fire underneath the quiet exterior. Bullard completely underestimated you. Now I have to wonder if you did kill him."

Faith glared at him. "I would never kill anyone in my own tavern."

Butler grinned. "No, I guess not. I imagine it's been bad for business."

"What do you intend to do with me?"

"Good question," Butler replied. All the humor left his face. "Your nosiness has inconvenienced me beyond measure. Yet your disappearance would cause more trouble than it would be worth in the short run. You need to keep your mouth shut. If you need motivation remember that you only have one son."

Faith started to speak but his look stopped her. "I'm a reasonable man, Mistress Clarke, but these are not times to be foolish. I have urgent business to attend. You are going nowhere until I return. I leave you in the care of my trusted Athena."

"Master Jeremy—" Athena began.

Butler shook his head. "I can manage on my own. Don't worry yourself over me."

"I raised you. Never was there a boy to take so many chances," Athena shook her head. "Come back, elsewise I won't know what to do with this." She indicated Faith distastefully.

"I will always come home to you, dear lady." . "Until you find someone worthy of you."

Athena snorted. "Been married once, I'm not doing it again. I work for you."

"You are my family." His gaze on the older woman was gentle and affectionate. "You were mother to me when I had none. Watch this one for me." He inclined his head toward Faith. "Do what you must short of murder to keep her here until I return." Butler stood at the door, gazing at both women. He stared at Faith. "Don't give her any trouble, she packs a mean wallop."

Chapter Twenty

Faith shivered, although the air was warm and humid. Shadowed by the indomitable Athena, she paced the floor of her temporary prison. Butler had left before night had fallen headed undoubtedly for whatever sordid business he had. Shadows deepened in the room as the sun sank in the sky, but her guard lit no candles. Perhaps she did not feel the need. Having little else to do, Faith sat and pondered what mess she had stumbled upon.

Josiah Smythe had come to meet Butler, undoubtedly about some joint business. With both Phineas and Charlotte Bullard dead, he would be in charge of Bullard's interests. Faith frowned. She knew little of Bullard. He had been a powerful merchant, a shipper of goods, and member of the House of Burgesses but none of this required secrecy. Only one did.

Smythe and Butler were trading in freed slaves. The urgency meant that they were acting tonight. If they had Joshua, he would disappear forever. Faith looked over at Athena. The woman might as well be made of stone so impassive was her face as she sat in a chair by the only door. Surely, she could not approve of marketing in freed slaves?

"How can you possibly approve of what he is doing?" Faith demanded.

"You don't know anything."

"I know Smythe deals in slaves, selling free people as well. Your master," she emphasized, "is out doing business with him."

"Jeremy doesn't trade slaves," Athena snarled. "He helped free my daughter and her children. He gave them money to go west to Ohio. That's the kind of man he is."

"Then why is he meeting with Master Smythe?" Faith demanded. "What possible reason could he have to meet with him?"

Athena's face took a shuttered look and she ceased speaking.

"Information," Faith said slowly. "He said Bullard was a source of information, now that Smythe has taken over, he serves the same purpose. But what does Smythe know that Butler needs to know?"

Athena ignored her, busying herself with lighting candles to chase away the increasing shadows in the room. She then picked up a shirt and began sewing a button on it.

Faith's mind continued to churn. She was missing too many pieces. She needed to escape and find Smythe and Butler. She was convinced one or both of them held the key to finding Joshua.

Faith dropped her gaze and kept her expression meek. "It grows dark, will he be long returning from his journey?"

"It's not that far." Athena spun around but Faith kept her gaze on the floor. She looked at Faith. "Jeremy was right, you are nosy."

Faith shrugged. "I run a tavern. People talk. I try to take care of their needs."

"I just bet you do and there you sit looking like butter wouldn't melt in your mouth. I bet you don't miss a thing." Athena rose to stand before her. "Were it not for you getting your shift in a knot, I would be with him watching his back, not babysitting the likes of you."

"I wasn't planning on spending my evening with you, either. I have an inn to run. I could care less what your master does as long as it does not impede the exchange of coin in my business."

Athena looked at her scornfully, "I'm no slave. I've been free since I was twenty. I stayed to raise that boy when his momma died of a fever. You say you run a business and you have a boy but you've been all over this town asking fool questions. You're about as subtle as a lovesick tomcat. It's no wonder Smythe tried to kill you."

"What?" Faith felt like all the air had left her lungs.

"Don't faint on me," Athena ordered, pushing Faith's head down between her knees. "I am not playing nursemaid to you. You keel over; I will leave you in a pile on the floor."

As the dizziness passed, Faith's mind whirred. "I feel ill," she gasped, putting her hand to her mouth. "A bucket, please." With any luck, her warden would think the hoarseness in her voice was illness, not terror at what she was about to do.

"You are not vomiting on my clean floor!" While Faith moaned, she ran across the room and grabbed a sturdy bucket, and shoved it under Faith's face. Faith grasped the sides and began making as horrible a noise as she could. As she hoped, the other woman backed away in disgust. Swaying as she bent over, she tightened her grip whilst continuing to heave and moan. The bucket was heavy, possibly oak which made it a substantial weapon. But Faith would only have one shot. There was no way she could overcome Athena in a fair fight, but then she had no intention of fighting fair. She drooped over feeling grateful for having forgone stays in the summer heat. Her mob cap flopped over concealing her face but also her line of sight. Only the creaking of the floorboards let her know that her goaler was creeping closer to check on her.

"Hey!" Athena called, "you all right?" She was close enough that Faith could hear the rustling of her petticoats. Faith feigned limpness hoping the large woman would assume she had fainted. Athena edged closer.

Faith waited. Soon two huge feet appeared, followed by the sweep of a cornflower blue skirt. She tightened the grip on the bucket, hidden by her own skirts and apron. Just as Athena leaned over to check on her prisoner, Faith swung the bucket up and slammed it into Athena's head. The woman cried out and fell back onto the floor. Faith didn't hesitate. She dropped the bucket and ran out the door as if the devil were chasing her. Not trusting the street, she cut through the woods on one edge of the property. Vestiges of twilight clung to the western rim of the sky. The moon was beginning its rise in the sky and provided a dim beacon of hope. Faith kept running hoping she would eventually end up on Nicholson Street. She dared not stop and ask for direction. There was no telling who was friend or foe and she was certain Athena would be right behind her. She hated to think what the brawny woman might do to her if caught.

"God, help me," Faith whispered between labored breaths. She had never been so frightened in her life. Already pain stabbed her sides with every breath but she dared not stop running. If her suspicions were correct, Butler intended to do something involving Josiah Smythe. If he was moving slaves tonight, she had very little time to find Joshua, assuming she could find him. The faint glow of a street's lanthorns led her out of the trees.

Faith couldn't breathe. She paused to catch her breath. As her eyes cast about the darkened streets, nothing looked familiar. It was too dark even with the lamps lit, everything was shadowed and gray. With a rising sense of panic, Faith knew she was lost. Off in the distance, she could hear voices, male but indistinguishable. She could also hear singing. The wind shifted and the earthy scents it carried told her there was a barn nearby. north, south, east, or west, she did not know. It was hopeless.

A branch broke behind her, causing her to jump with a frightened cry.

"Faith? What in God's name are ye doing here?" Will MacKay moved out of the shadows. He was dressed in dark clothes and riding boots, but she really didn't care. Here was someone who made her feel safe.

"Will." Faith's voice wobbled. "I need your help." She stumbled as she moved to him. He caught her before she fell.

"You're hurt!" He pulled out a handkerchief and dabbed her lip. She had bit it during her panicked run. "Faith," he whispered urgently, "talk to me. What's happened?" He grasped her shoulders and stared into her eyes.

Faith felt an overwhelming sense of relief. She looked at that good, honest face. Here was someone to trust. Still gasping for breath, Faith told him about her escape and her suspicions.

His eyes were dark and angry. "Butler held you against your will? He had no cause to do that!" He let go of her shoulders and looked about, pulling a side piece out of his belt. Belatedly, Faith realized that Will had no reason to be out at night either. Indentured servants normally didn't go about town armed. "Where was he headed?"

"He was meeting with Josiah Smythe," Faith said urgently. "We need to find them. Smythe may have Joshua."

Will looked at her. She had lost her mob cap somewhere in her wild run.

Hair straggled down her back and one of her sleeves was torn. She was scratched and bruised and undoubtedly dirty. "You're not going anywhere but home," he said bluntly. "I'll go find Smythe once I know you're safe."

"There's no time," Faith protested. "Butler's been gone for a while. God only knows what has happened."

"I don't care," Will said roughly. "I will not put you in danger although you seem determined to place yourself there."

"That's not fair," she protested, "I never…"

Will grasped her arm, making her yelp as he reached where Athena had grabbed. Her arm was probably purple. He loosened his grip immediately and slid it down to her hand. "You are hurt. We aren't far from Dr. Staunton. Let's get you there."

Faith rubbed her arm. Her head throbbed and she was starting to feel sick and dizzy. Martin might be willing to help. She looked down at her hand in Will MacKay's. He held it lightly as they moved through the night. Will obviously knew where he was going. They moved past darkened houses and yards with barely a glimmer of light to be seen beyond the small halos of lanthorns and the pale moon now high in the sky.

Night deepened as they walked to Martin Staunton's home. The moon had been joined by stars spread out like snowflakes in the midst of a storm. Were it not for the urgency of her journey, she would have stopped to marvel at the sight. Faith wanted to hurry but as fear left her body so did her strength. Her feed dragged behind Will despite her best efforts.

Lamplight shone dimly through the window as they approached. Someone was still up and about. Botetourt Street was quiet, too quiet for Faith's liking. Will banged on the door.

"Staunton, need your help!" Will called.

"I'm not badly hurt." There was nothing wrong with her that she couldn't attend to herself later after they had found Smythe. He ignored her, holding firmly to her hand as they waited for someone to answer Staunton's door.

Martin Staunton opened the door himself. He was fully dressed despite the hour. He looked surprised to see Faith. "McKay, Mistress Clarke. What is it that brings you out so late in the evening?"

Will pulled Faith across the threshold where the doctor could see her in the light of the fat candle he held.

"You're bleeding." Staunton's eyes narrowed as he looked her over. "Hold the candle for me, Will. Let me get a look at her injuries."

"They're minor, really," Faith repeated. Both men ignored her as Staunton took in the bruises, scrapes, and cuts that covered her face, neck, and arms.

"They still need cleaning," Staunton said. "Are there other injuries?"

Faith shook her head. "No, I'm fine."

"No, you are not fine," Will bit out. "You have bruises on your arm, rope burns on your wrist, and blood on your face. I found you running through the streets as if the devil pursued you. You're telling me wild tales about Josiah Smythe having Joshua and trading in freed slaves. You are definitely not fine."

Staunton went and got a basin of water, clean cloths, and ointment. "Let's clean these up. These cuts aren't deep, but they need care to prevent infection."

Will stood close by, his face grim. "Who hit you?" he asked bluntly. His face was pale as Staunton washed the blood from Faith and gently applied ointment to the cut.

Faith winced. "A freedwoman who works for Butler. He wanted her to keep me there until he returned. She was watching me."

"Apparently not well enough," Will said with a half-smile. "I thought Quakers were pacifists."

"I abhor violence," Faith said. "But I will not ignore what happens around me. Not anymore." Her head throbbed. Her body stung from various abrasions but there was no time to hide. Somewhere in the night were Jeremy Butler and Josiah Smythe and possibly a frightened young boy. "We need to find them now." Why couldn't he understand the urgency? Faith stood up. There was no time to lose. "This may be our last chance to rescue Joshua."

Will nodded. "I'll go tend to that business. No need for you to concern yourself." His jaw was clenched. Faith was certain he was about to do something stupid.

"Getting into the slave camp will not be easy," Staunton noted. "They will have guards to prevent any escapes."

Faith eyed him. Something bothered her about the way he said the words. He was too calm. He finished cleaning her scrapes and turned to set the basin aside. "You need help to rescue the boy."

Faith stared at him. "What about Temperance?"

A shudder went through Martin Staunton's frame. Suddenly she realized how tired he looked. "Temperance died in her sleep just hours ago."

Faith inhaled and the breath felt like a knife. "Martin, I didn't know." Words failed. She had meant to see Temperance but had been too busy or distracted to go. Now it was too late. Martin and Temperance were friends and she should have come. Tears burned in her throat. "I'm so sorry."

His face was bleak. "She doesn't suffer anymore and I have no one left who matters. Fate took my wife and Bullard my son. I thought this evil stopped with him, but Smythe has picked it up. He needs to be stopped."

"David Verity was your son."

Martin's face was bleak. "I had given up the idea of children. Temperance was so frail. Felicity became a friend, then more. We both loved Temperance. Both knew she was dying. We comforted each other. When she told me about the child, I couldn't believe it. I delivered David myself. He was perfect. I didn't realize when I freed her that she would be in danger.

We had planned to go west once Temperance passed. There no one would know she was once a slave, but Bullard only saw her as property. I could not find her. He laughed when I accused him of taking them, then he named his price. I went to the camp to buy them back, but they were already dead from the fever. I buried them."

Faith's eyes burned with unshed tears. It all made sense. Staunton talked in a calm voice although his hands shook. "You killed him."

"Yes, I did and I told Stella to run as far away as she could, but she didn't want to leave her sister. Her death was regrettable."

Staunton looked at Will. "You're in league with the rebels. I've seen you up and down these streets at night. Butler pays you. You know where to find him. Smythe has that boy. You know it."

Will remained still. "The rebels have naught to do with this business," he said at last. "Butler trades information, not slaves. I have not seen the boy."

Faith stared at him in horror. It felt as if the earth had moved out from underneath her feet. "You work for that man?"

Will looked miserable. "It's not what you think. We only want to be treated like other Englishmen. Butler works to keep us from suffering the same fate as Boston.

Staunton smiled sadly. "There is nothing you or your friend can do about that. British authority is absolute. Sometimes a man must seek his own justice." He raised a hand to silence her. "We can argue all night or we can save this boy while there is still time."

Will hesitated. "It's no place for a lady."

Faith rolled her eyes. "I can take care of myself and Joshua is not going to trust a stranger, not after what he's been through."

"Enough," Staunton said. "I know where the camp used to be. We can start there."

Realization lit Faith's mind like a torch illuminating it. "They must be at Bullard's store! Smythe keeps all his books there. He would have to gather his coin in order to pay the traders to take the slaves out of Virginia."

The doctor's eyes were unreadable but his breathing was rough and unsteady. "You are certain of this?"

"It makes sense. I just hope we can catch them before they head out to wherever they are keeping the slaves."

Faith could not process what she knew, nor was there time. It was as if she were in a dream as they exited the doctor's home and turned toward the heart of Williamsburg.

"This way." The doctor turned down Duke of Gloucester Street toward Bullard's store. Faith struggled to keep up with him. Will offered his arm but she waved him off. He stubbornly refused to leave her side. They both watched as Staunton ran to the house of his enemy.

Faith picked up her skirts and ran. The street lamps provided barely enough light to navigate the road. Only the taverns remained open. Laughter came from Raleigh's Tavern. Faith realized they must be hosting a ball. The muffled merriment struck an odd note as they rushed past. Will glanced about sharply but it looked deserted. Then they heard the faint murmuring of voices.

"In back," Will whispered. "Stay here." He ducked around the house without waiting for a response.

Faith followed stumbling in the darkness over tree roots on the ground. Gravel scraped her palms. She pushed up and hurried after Will. As she entered the backyard, she paused listening. Her eyes swept the dark shadows that covered the yard. At first, the only thing she could hear was her breath and the hard hammering of her heart. Faith tried to steady her breathing but her oxygen-deprived lungs demanded air. Moments passed before she could hear anything else. The backyard was ghostly still. Then she heard the soft nicker of horses.

There were two tied up across the yard. A faint breeze stirred her hair bringing with it the song of crickets. A murmur of voices caught her attention. The back door of Bullard's store opened revealing Butler and Smythe. In the silence, their voices carried across the yard.

"The shipment is ready?" Butler inquired.

"Ready to load aboard ship as soon as I pay the captain. The guns are hidden among barrels of molasses and corn. I can deliver them easily among my other goods"

"What about the British?" Butler enquired.

Smythe chortled. "Bullard had them in his pocket. He knew who to pay to look the other way. A lot of them don't care as long as their pockets are lined. Slaves, rum, powder, I can move whatever you want, provided I am reimbursed for my trouble."

"Really?" Butler said.

"You'd be amazed what a few coins will buy." Smythe seemed almost jovial.

Faith found the exchange sickening. It was as if they were talking about barrels of rum, not human lives. Inexorably her mind turned to Olivia and Titus. Butler was right that they were vulnerable. Even freed they could face monsters such as these. She would have to find a way to protect them. The weight settled on her shoulders. She would not ignore it. They meant too much to her. Already her plea for their freedom had been submitted although when it would be reviewed only God knew.

Faith realized that once they reached the horses there would be no stopping them. Their business would conclude and some poor wretch would be sent forever from friends, family, and freedom. She couldn't permit it.

The horses were tied firmly to a tree limb. Butler passed a flask to Smythe. Faith smiled grimly. He'd gotten him drunk in order to make him easier to handle. That worked for her as well. Watching out for potentially slapping limbs, Faith slipped around to where the horses were, using the trees and smokehouse as cover. The horses didn't seem terribly disturbed by her presence so she reached up a hand to where the reins were tied. Her nerves were as tight as the knot she struggled to untie. It took her a few moments to figure out how to unloose it, and then came the next one. The men were getting closer, too close for comfort. Time was running out.

"Who's there?" Butler, ever sharp-eyed had spotted her.

Thinking quickly, Faith slapped the freed horse's rump sending him off into the night. Spinning, she turned to run.

A shot rang out into the night. Faith dropped to the ground, praying it would miss. A nearby groan told her it had not. Raising her head, she took in the situation.

Staunton held a gun over Smythe. "Roll over, dog, before I put you out of your misery."

Smythe whimpered, "You gut shot me."

Staunton's voice was raw. "A more merciful end than those you send to a living hell in Savannah. Or did you not think them worthy of your compassion? Men like you have none. You trade in living souls as if they were sheaves of wheat."

Butler had vanished. She had no idea where Will was. Faith was alone.

"What are you doing, Martin?" Her heart beat in her chest like a snared bird, trying desperately to escape..

"What needs to be done." Staunton's face was bleak. "Your business in selling freed slaves ends now."

Faith pushed herself up off the ground. "Killing him will not end slavery,

Martin, as noble as the notion would be." She kept her tone gentle. "There is no point destroying your own life and reputation for a dog such as this. You are better than this."

"Am I?" Martin's voice was low. "You mistake my actions for nobility when in fact they are deeds of retribution."

"Retribution?"

"They killed my son and his mother, whom I loved." Martin drew in a pain-filled breath. "Felicia made the prospect of losing Temperance bearable. She was beautiful and kind. David was a gift. He was the child I thought I would never have. I freed them and then they vanished." He closed his eyes for a second. "I have no life left, Faith. They were my hope." His dark eyes were haunted. "You should go. There is no need for you to see this." He pulled a second pistol from his belt and raised it to his head.

"No," Faith cried and jumped at him. The pistol fired as they both fell to the ground. Staunton leapt up.

"You shouldn't have done that. I wish to rejoin my family."

"It's not for you to say when that will happen, Martin. Only God decides when it is time for us to die." Her breath was heavy. Nearby, she could hear Smythe whimpering. "You are a healer. You are supposed to save lives."

"I am a man, Faith Clarke. They depended on me. I failed. I should have protected them. So, I avenged them."

"You killed Bullard." . His expression confirmed her suspicion.

"Does it matter?" Staunton asked wearily. "Not one of them will return my son to me. My wife and my lover are long gone."

Faith's sharp ears picked up the sound of men on the road. It was probably a patrol or a party leaving a tavern late. She didn't care. "Help!" she screamed. "Help me!"

A shout told her someone had heard. Running feet approached the back of the house. Staunton shoved her aside and ran toward the remaining horse. Mounting it, he rode into the darkness. Faith stumbled to her knees unsure whether to pursue or wait for help.

"Let him go," Butler said, stepping out of the darkness. He offered her a hand up. "God knows he's living in his own Hell."

"Why do you care?" Faith rounded on him.

Butler stepped out of her way. "Are you hurt?"

Faith shook her head.

"Good. MacKay is coming shortly with some of his majesty's troops. Tell them what you saw. They will take care of this. I have other business to attend."

"Selling slaves," Faith said bitterly.

"Freeing those who do not belong in bondage," he said shortly. "Since you are determined to pry where you are not welcome, I will give you an answer in hopes of keeping your mouth shut. Bullard and Smythe were despicable men, but they were a means to an end. My job was to engage them in order to discover how they were smuggling goods into Virginia. I had no more knowledge of this business than you until after Bullard's death. My loyalties demanded I continue."

Faith was speechless.

"Satisfied? Good. I must be off. There is no time to waste if you want that boy of yours returned." With that Butler whistled which drew in the loose horse. Clucking softly, he took the reins and rode off into the night leaving Faith with a dead body and more questions than answers.

Chapter Twenty-One

Faith piled coals onto the Dutch oven so the bread would bake evenly. In the weeks following the death of Josiah Smythe, her life had been a whirlwind. Martin Staunton had disappeared that night leaving his dead wife and his practice behind. Troops had searched diligently for the first week or two before abandoning the chase.

"Let the savages deal with him," Grant had said over a pint of ale within her tavern. That had been the last time he had visited although she had heard enough to know he remained busy with unrest within the town and his upcoming nuptials.

Will had brought Joshua home, thin and scared. He had never explained to her about Butler. When asked he shook his head and said, "Best ye not know, Faith. He's a good man. He got Joshua and arranged for the others to go home. That's enough."

Sleep continued to be a struggle. Images of violence haunted her dreams; blood, screams, and Martin Staunton's face filled with grief. Remembering his losses made her pause in her mending. Setting down the breeches she was patching, Faith stepped outside to look for her son.

Andrew and Joshua played with a hoop in the yard. The light picked up the copper strands in her son's hair and turned them to gold. He stayed close to his friend. Joshua refused to leave the yard without his father. It would take a long time for Joshua to recover. At night sometimes she heard him cry out and Olivia or Titus sang to comfort him. Right now the boys' laughter floated across the air. She could not imagine life without them.

The heat of the kitchen made her face shiny with sweat as she leaned to the fire to check on dinner. Oddly enough, working in the kitchen helped her nerves. Helping Olivia bake the bread and prepare the many meals her tavern served kept her from dwelling on what had happened.

Her tavern kept her busy with men coming in to talk and drink. There was no way to avoid overhearing the debates. Her father had sent her a letter telling her of the disquiet in Pennsylvania. Isaiah Payne had never written his daughter before so it had been a shock to see his broad scrawl. He feared for her and the coming conflict.

Do not doubt, daughter, but that war is coming. The outpouring of grievances against England continues to swell into an outcry that cannot be ignored. While I would prefer you not to be involved in this matter, I fear it may not be possible to remain neutral. Pray for peace and I will continue to pray for your safety and that of Andrew.

War was coming. Faith hoped not. She had seen enough bloodshed.

"Miss Faith, you better come out here," called Titus.

Frowning, she stepped out of the kitchen and then hurried to the front of the house as she heard the drum and fife amidst the sound of marching feet. Faith watched in amazement as the British troops marched out of town. Captain Grant rode by without even a glance in her direction. She wondered if he was happy with his fiancée. It was hard to imagine him wed to a sixteen-year-old girl, even one with a well-connected family and wealth. It still stung a little although she knew she was a working-class woman, not a person someone with ambition would wish to tie themselves to.

Her reverie was interrupted by a familiar face. Will MacKay joined her in the yard puffing a little with exertion. She realized he had utilized the back roads to avoid the congestion of troops marching down Waller Street undoubtedly heading to a ship on the York River.

"Mistress Clarke," he said bowing. As usual, his apron was ink-stained as were his fingers. Something about him made her smile. His eyes brightened.

"Master MacKay," Faith murmured. She wiped her hands on her apron. She had been making biscuits and flour dusted her hands. "What is that?" she asked, seeing a pamphlet in his hands.

"A document, written by Master Jefferson, of the House of Burgesses," replied Will. "I thought you might enjoy a copy. It is circulating the town."

Faith looked down. "*A Summary View of the Rights of British America,*" she read. A chill went down her spine. Jefferson spent time with Peyton Randolph, Patrick Henry and others considered radical. Whatever this pamphlet contained, it was bound to inflame the British. Faith intended to read every word. "Do you know what it says?"

Will nodded. "I set the type. I agree with him. It's time for the British to recognize that the colonies have rights and are not their vassals."

Faith did not respond. She had spotted another document in Will's hand. It was heavy paper and bore the governor's seal. "What is that?"

Will's face was still. "Butler gave it to me before he left. He left instructions to bring it to you the following week."

Faith took the document. Folded within was a note written in a graceful copperplate hand. *Mistress Clarke, although you have been no end of trouble for me, I respect your intentions. Keep these documents safe, I made use of a few friends to acquire them for you. I think should you allow yourself the right to think freely, you would make a fine patriot. Jeremy Butler.*

Unfolding the document carefully, Faith's eyes widened. These were documents of manumission granted for Titus and Olivia York. Wordlessly, she showed them to Will.

He whistled. "That's quite an accomplishment. Do they know?"

Faith turned and looked over at her former slaves. "They will. They are my family. It's long past time I treated them as such."

Faith gave the documents to Olivia to share with Titus. As she headed back to her biscuits, she heard the cries of hallelujah. A weight eased from her soul. Pausing in between the two buildings, she watched the troops disappear in the distance becoming indistinct in the dust of the road. Seeing the faint flash of a red-jacketed man on horseback, she wondered about Stephen Grant and the choices he had made. Once she had thought he had some regard for her, but he had chosen another path. Her life lay here. She kneaded dough on the table, rolling it into a loaf to rise. Faith stopped when a shadow fell over it. Looking up, she saw light from the sun illuminated fiery highlights in dark auburn hair. Will stood in the doorway to the kitchen watching her. Faith smiled as she covered the bread to rise and wiped her hands on her apron.

"Would you like a drink?"

He joined her in a heartbeat, his steps matching hers as they entered the back of the tavern. As he held the door, she smiled. Already she could hear voices of men entering the front both boisterous and reserved.

War was coming. She had no doubt and all that mattered to her lay within these walls. Faith prayed they all would endure whatever lay ahead.

A Note from the Author

Writing about history is not for the faint of heart. There are an astounding number of details to be reckoned with as well as the need to reconcile one's heartfelt beliefs with the abiding attitudes of the time period. Slavery is an ugly truth that existed during the time frame of this story, and determining how it would be covered in this novel was difficult. I opted to let it be seen, not because it is acceptable in any way, but because to deny it marginalizes the lives of those who suffered under its yoke.

Acknowledgements

I remain forever grateful for the input of my fellow writers at the Piedmont Author Network, especially Lynn, Karen, Sayword, and Micki. My husband Bill, who spent many nights reading drafts, and to the gracious staff at the Rockefeller Library in Williamsburg, VA, who patiently answered so many questions. Any historical errors are mine alone.

About the Author

Julie Bates grew up reading a little bit of everything, but when she discovered Agatha Christie, she knew what she wanted to write. Along the way, she has written a weekly column for the Asheboro *Courier-Tribune* (her local newspaper) for two years and published a few articles in magazines such as *Spin Off* and *Carolina Country*. She has blogged for Killer Nashville and the educational website Read.Learn.Write. She currently works as a public school teacher for special needs students. Julie is a member of Mystery Writers of America, Southeastern Writers of America (SEMWA), and her local writing group, Piedmont Authors Network (PAN). When not busy plotting her next story, she enjoys doing crafts and spending time with her husband and son, as well as a number of dogs and cats who have shown up on her doorstep and never left.